D1475236

The Betrayed
Book Two of the Painted Maidens Trilogy

By Terra Harmony

A Patchwork Press Title
www.patchwork-press.com

Editing team: Jessica Dall, Cathy Wathen, and Kara Baird
www.sparklepressediting.weebly.com

Cover design by Keary Taylor
www.indiecoverdesigns.com

For Aiden and Kiera

- here is to puttering around the lake, dancing in the rain, and tadpoles

For all at last return to the sea...

Chapter One

Calming her fins, Serena's natural buoyancy carries her to the surface until her head rises just above the water. The glassy coating protecting her eyes when she is under retracts, and The Dry comes into focus. The plump moon behind her illuminates the shimmering bronze sand, beckoning Serena to come ashore and bury her toes there. It is the shadows creeping out from the forest beyond the beach that warn her to stay away.

Serena scans the beach and the Ungainly footprints pockmarking the otherwise pristine surface. The footprints disappear as the tide inches higher. The wind moves in to decimate what the waves do not reach, blowing granules of sand and blurring the outline of sandaled feet. Her eyes come to rest on a different set of prints—three of them in total. These are not Ungainly, these have claws—and they are fresh.

The werewolves have already begun their patrols, barely after the last of the Ungainlies have left the beach. Each night since the King's Massacre, one less wolf is spared for the patrols. Serena can't decide if they are growing tired of waiting or are doing it to entice the Undine out.

They can't be that smart, Serena thinks. But the predictability itself gives cause for concern. Werewolves are anything but predictable.

Like Liam—the one person I thought could lead us on a path of peace alongside the wolves. Instead, he turned out to be one giant roadblock. *And my twin brother.*

Liam sustained injuries during the King's Massacre, but they weren't life threatening. He must be with his pack now, but the question remains—is he persona non-grata? Is he being punished for the secret meetings he had with Serena? Or did they go just as he planned, leading the Undine to a war ultimately resulting in the death of their king?

Serena bites her lip, and she can hear Nerin's voice echoing in her head. *A queen does not bite her lip.* The Queen's Second is relentless when it comes to etiquette. Serena releases her lip, instead gritting her teeth. There has been a lot of that as of late.

She considers her options, but the truth of it is, the Undine are running out of choices. In three short months, Cordelia will give birth to the only calfling blessed to Society since Serena herself. Cordelia needs a place to do it, and she needs to feel safe while doing so. Poseidon-forbid the child enter the world weak and dying. It would not be a good foretelling of Serena's reign to come. Kelp reaches up to tickle Serena's fins. She flicks it away.

A queen does not play with her food.

Serena grits her teeth again.

Back on the beach, an aged skunk lumbers out of the tree line and makes its way toward food wrappers left by beach picnickers. It noses through them, unconcerned with the shadows at its back.

Would it be out if wolves are still in the area? She trusts the skunk's nose better than her own; it has survived the forest this long.

Serena's fins go stagnant once again, until her neck and shoulders rise above the water. The skunk pauses, looking up, but it cannot distinguish her form amongst the waves. He goes back to pawing through Ungainly trash.

Serena moves forward, already eyeing the breaker that will bring her to shore. Bubbles float up in front of her, popping open along the surface. Serena has only a split-second to lean back when a golden trident shoots up, piercing the air in front of her. Three sharp barbs come into focus, inches from her nose. In between them, the blurred form of the skunk scurries back into the tree line.

The trident lowers as another Undine head breaches the surface. Serena allows herself to breath and a small, one-sided smile creeps onto her face at the sight of sea-green eyes. "You again?"

In front of her, Kai smiles back. "You aren't very good at sneaking out."

"I made it to the surface this time, didn't I?"

Kai moves his trident to his side. "Only because you had outside help. You knew Morven couldn't resist Rayne's noodled kelp."

Serena briefly thinks of the guard on watch; his rumbling stomach made her getaway all too easy.

Kai sighs, briefly looking up at the moon. It will be full by the end of the week. "I suppose I'll just have to trade my rounds out for more watches with the queen."

Serena bites her lip.

Kai looks back at her and frowns. "A queen doesn't—"

Serena splashes water at his face with both hands, effectively cutting off his reprimand. The smile is gone from her lips.

He runs his palm down his face and shakes the water from his sandy hair. It has grown longer since the Queen's Guard increased their duties; there has barely been time for them to eat, much less for personal grooming.

Serena moves around him, eyes locked on the shore. In one swift movement, his hand shoots out, grabbing her arm above the elbow.

His grip is tight, painful almost. Serena doesn't twist away. His touch, however uncomfortable, is a welcome sensation. No one ever touches the queen.

Kai loosens his fingers, one by one, then lets go all together. He reaches down and yanks up, dragging a freshly plucked kelp stem with him. Serena moves back, watching as he winds the brown seaweed into a tight ball around his fist. His eyes don't leave her face.

Once done, Kai grips the ball with his other hand, turns toward the shore and takes aim. The wet ball of seaweed arcs in the air. The tail becomes loose and hisses as it vibrates back and forth. The whole thing lands with a splat on the sand, just in front of the tree line.

Not seconds later, the furry muzzle of a werewolf emerges, sniffing at the kelp.

Serena's breath catches in her throat.

That damn skunk would've been the death of me.

The wolves have been there all along. Another muzzle shoots out, baring his teeth and forcing the other one back into the shadows. This muzzle is black, indiscernible from the dark forest other than the shiny nose and gleaming, white teeth.

Serena remembers those teeth well, tearing into the kings neck, then ripping away pieces of his beautiful, rainbow tail—the last of its kind. Alaric, the first of the wolves, is out tonight. It could be that he is there every night, patrolling the shores and keeping the Undine at bay.

Serena and Kai exchange a glance as the wolves slip back into shrouded shadows. Serena nods at Kai; it is all the thanks she will give, and even that much is wholly unnecessary according to the Queen's Guard. Kai returns the nod anyway.

"Summon Cordelia to the Great Hall," Serena says. "We need to talk." She turns away, preparing to dive.

Kai's hand on her arm stops her once again. "After I escort her majesty safely back to the kingdom, of course."

Serena glances at his hand, then back to his wild green eyes. "Of course."

Chapter Two

Kai dives first, leading the way with strong, sure flicks of his tail. Serena follows, only able to match his speed by pulsing her fins twice as much. When he turns to skirt around the northern edge of Vancouver Island, following the currents of the strait, Serena trails behind.

She opens her mouth, clicking and whistling under the water to catch Kai's attention. He pauses, looking back. Gesturing with her head, Serena signals to take the long way around. Though it has mostly to do with delaying her inevitable entrance to court, she also doesn't ever miss an opportunity to survey the corals.

Relenting, Kai now keeps his pace slow, letting Serena take the lead. She moves to the seafloor where the strength of the current lessens, though it still has an effect. Here the water is crisp and clear, washing the corals in constant fresh seawater. The coral forests are a living, breathing ecosystem, moving in sync with the pulse of the ocean and displaying a kaleidoscope of colors. Schools of fish travel in and out of the spiny grottos seeking food and refuge.

Dipping lower, Serena is careful not to touch any of the delicate structures, and she keeps the movement of her fins smooth and slow. Cabbage coral in varying shades of green, beige, and pink grow in an expansive field on the slope of a seamount. Layer upon layer of stiff leaves surrounding each other in endless circles of protection. Up close they remind Serena of the roses she sees Ungainlies sometimes carrying on the beach;

a romantic gesture given from one mate to another. She glances at Kai, cheeks heating. Exchanging freshly plucked plants would be more like an insult to the Undine.

As she moves forward, tiny crustaceans and bright-colored fish dart down, taking shelter amidst the dark crevices in between the layers of cabbage coral. Serena can almost detect a subtle glow of life emanating from the reefs. Gliding around a spindly, bright purple sea fan coral, Serena imagines it looks much like the complicated network of her own veins, delivering essential nutrients and blood to the region around them.

A small lingcod peeking out tentatively from a clump of rocks catches Serena's eye before he disappears. When it comes out again, the blue-gray fish swims down to a small cove in between rocks. She follows it, stunned to find hundreds of white eggs, snuggled together. The lingcod is their father. He tends to the eggs, nudging them with his lips and nose, cleaning and aerating them.

Despite his attentive care, their survival rate will be extremely low; especially as food becomes more and more scarce. It reminds Serena of Cordelia and the new life growing inside of her. Despite everything Society might do for the calfling, the prospect of survival isn't good. Serena sighs, then swims on.

Right up against the edge of the current, Serena braces herself for what is to come. She pauses, waiting for Kai to join her. Without looking at him, or even thinking about it, she holds out her hand. He takes it, squeezing tight, and they cross out of the current together.

The change is night and day. Coral fields spread out before them are nothing but crumbling skeletons—mere twigs from what once was a thriving forest. There are but a few dots of color, brain corals struggling to survive. Algae dominates these corals, choking the life out of them. The temporary regrowth will soon die. The stench of rot and death surrounding the algae isn't as frightening as the white-washed nothingness crawling across the rest of the fields. There are no fish here. No sea stars, mollusks, or sponges. Just a few snails—bottom feeders wandering aimlessly over the skeletal coral remains.

Serena floats toward one, ushering it to a particularly nasty section of algae. A lump forms in her throat as she looks up at Kai. These coral fields are hundreds of years old, alive and thriving even before her father was born. Now only gray and white remain of the once vibrant colors. They look beat up and gnarled, like an old man's fingers.

In just the past year, the Undine have come to realize the perishing condition of the ocean is the reason they can't give birth to healthy male calflings, and now the females are showing signs as well. Almost eighteen years ago, a desperate attempt to save the male calflings actually transformed them into the pack of wolves they are today. For a while, the two species bred from the same lineage lived peacefully, the wolves even serving as Undine protectors. But the night Serena was born, the wolves revolted, ending her mother's life, separating Serena from her twin brother, and turning each species against each other.

If only the ocean could stay healthy, Serena thinks, brushing the pad of her finger against one of the hardened, bare corals. *None of it would have happened.*

Kai takes Serena by the hand, urging her away from the destruction. Corals grow so slowly, only a centimeter every year, recovery would take a few hundred years. Kai and Serena will never witness these fields come back to life.

They move toward Society slowly, as if the surrounding dead ecosystem sucks the energy right out of them. Once they cross the borders to Society, they pick up speed. The chain of life is apparent—the corals they pass begin to show color, then freshly grown polyps. As more and more of them crowd the area, so does other plant life and the water itself turns greener rather than dull gray. A school of salmon bustles around Serena and Kai, silvery-gray scales shining out on their hunt for food. The moonlight above them darkens. They glance up as the beams are blotted out by a fever of stingrays.

Finally, the first Undine come into view. Yellow, bright pink, and deep purple—they manage to shine out from the colorful underwater world like flowers on a cliff. Undine gardeners pick at the terrain, salvaging food for Society, but careful not to damage what is left of their ecosystem.

Serena follows Kai, who has moved in front of her to assume an escort position, as if he has been there all along. She does her best to avoid the stares of her kinsmen as she passes, keeping her eyes ahead—always ahead. They angle down, enter the first caves, and then ascend to make the transition from water to air.

Kai's transformation into Ungainly form is fast. His light brown scales sink into the skin of his legs, revealing strong, thick thighs and calves. He uncrosses his legs, keeping enough scales down his thighs to stay decent in front of Serena.

Serena follows suit, only slightly behind him, and they both kick the rest of the way to the surface. When Serena and Kai enter the Great Hall, they call forth more scales, covering themselves down to the ankles in the traditional dress of the Great Hall.

"Nerin and Murphy wear the same frown," whispers Kai.

Serena looks up at Nerin standing next to the throne and Murphy, the Head of the Guard, next to her. "And it probably has nothing to do with the fact that they are mother and son," says Serena.

"Next time, maybe you'll think twice before trying to go to The Dry unescorted," Kai lifts a chiding eyebrow, then falls in step slightly behind her, matching her stride. It is Serena's turn to lead.

Serena steels herself, taking a deep breath in and straightening her back. Murphy descends the stairs to meet the queen. Stepping through the rigid wall of the Queen's Guard who are lined up in front of the throne, Murphy motions for Kai to take his place at one end. Serena watches, looking for some sign of his mood after their swim, but his face has gone blank—the impenetrable façade indicative of the Queen's Guard. Nerin clears her throat and Serena whips her head back around. The Second's eyes are wide, silently chastising Serena for her wandering gaze.

Murphy spares Serena any more taciturn rebukes by bringing the guard to attention. There is a sharp clang of feet and scales snapping together.

"Morven Redwood, step forward," Murphy says.

Without hesitation, the largest guard member marches forward and comes to attention by Murphy's side, directly in front of Serena. Morven's shoulders span so wide, even he often underestimates their range. He bumps into his commanding officer. Murphy has to break his rigid stance in order to catch his balance.

"You stand in front of the queen, Morven," Murphy says, frowning at him.

Morven's eyes go wide. He steps forward and bends in a bow. "Your majesty."

Serena leans back so the large Undine does not knock heads with her. As he straightens, Serena catches a whiff of Rayne's noodled kelp on his breath—evidence of his misdeed.

Morven steps back. He is the tallest guard member by far, standing a full head taller than Murphy, even. Serena has to crane her neck back to look at him.

"Failure to carry out orders. Abandoning post. Subjecting the queen to unnecessary danger." Murphy barks out accusations like he has been practicing for days. Morven winces at each one.

"Since I've stood post as Head of the Guard, never have I seen such incompetence. And never, *never* has a guard member shown their queen or king such disrespect—"

"Disrespect?" Serena interrupts Murphy. "I'm sorry but I fail to see how following my orders can be interpreted as disrespect."

The Head of the Guard presses his lips together. He tries to take a deep breath at the same time, which results in a high-pitched buzz as air is sucked in between his teeth. "While I realize your majesty released Morven of his watch, he must still abide to a specific set of orders."

The room goes quiet. Anyone can follow the argument through to the basic problem. Whose orders supersede all others? Those of the queen or the Head of the Guard?

It is a problem best left alone—Nerin has told Serena as much. The two heads of Society should never contradict each other. The fact that Serena and Murphy are assumed by Society to be mated makes the situation all the more complicated. They should present themselves as a team, especially if they seek to gain the unwavering trust of Society.

The easy thing to do would be to let Morven take the blame and be subjected to whatever punishment Murphy decides. But Serena suspects there is a bigger underlying issue that needs resolving in order to avoid future complications.

Serena looks up at the giant Undine. His eyebrows are lifted in the center, but they slope down to the outside, causing worry lines to show around his eyes. His grip on his trident is so tight, his hand is turning white.

"Tell me, Morven," Serena addresses the guard. "Before I sent you to Rayne, when was the last time you had eaten?"

Morven glances down at Serena before answering the question. "I'm not sure, exactly, your majesty."

Serena crosses her arms. "You are a very large Undine, Morven."

"Yes, your majesty." He is looking straight forward again.

"The largest of all Undine, I'd say."

"Yes, your majesty." He shifts his weight back and forth on his feet.

"I can summon Rayne to know for sure, but I think it's safe to say one of your size requires more volume of sustenance than the average Undine."

Morven's eyebrows stitch together.

Serena gives him a moment; there were a lot of complex words in that sentence.

Finally, Morven speaks. "I…suppose, your majesty."

"So I ask again—when was the last time you ate, before visiting Rayne?" Serena uncrosses her arms and clasps her hands behind her back.

"It had been two moons, your majesty." Morven doesn't hesitate this time.

Murphy's head whips to the side and he stares at Morven, open-mouthed.

The large guard glances at his boss, his empty hand twitching. "I'm really sorry," he says, then looks at Serena. "My deepest regrets, your majesty. I accept whatever punishment—"

Serena holds up her hand, stopping him. "Why did you go so long without fulfilling some of your own basic needs?"

Now Morven's lower lip is quivering. "Normally I can find something in between rounds, but I was on a double shift patrolling borders, and there's no…" Morven trails off, hesitating to mention that only dead corals border the kingdom. No one likes to say out loud that the Undine realm is dying.

Serena looks at Murphy.

He nods at her, then turns to Morven. "Take your place in line."

Morven performs a flank, but his turn is slower, and his chin lowers as he marches to rejoin the rank of guards.

There is nothing more to be said. Murphy will have to take into account the state of the environment, even when performing basic functions such as assigning rounds.

Serena looks at Murphy, then inadvertently glances at the small door carved into the side of the Great Hall. It is the entrance to the chambers in which the pair retires each night, together. The continued exhibition of them being paired supposedly helps endear Serena to the people since Murphy is a long-standing authoritarian figure, whereas Serena is not.

They will talk more later.

Her eyes flit from the shadowed entrance straight to Kai. It is an involuntary reaction. Serena does it each time she looks at the room. Kai never meets her gaze; he keeps his eyes straight forward, giving no sign he is even aware of her.

Behind Serena, Nerin clears her throat, breaking the one-sided exchange. "The council approaches."

Chapter Three

As the council filters into the Great Hall, Serena takes her place at the throne and Murphy marches the guards back into formation of two ranks on either side of the high platform.

The order in which the council appear is telling. Sarafina, the head gardener, and Evandre, the scientist, walk in first. By all accounts, the pair should have been the furthest away, working to stop the deterioration of the corals lying on the outskirts of Society's borders. Instead, they slink around the mainstream of Society with their closest assistants, like a swarm of jellyfish congregating in the warm waters. Serena watches Sarafina's yellow and Evandre's purple move forward in unison. They are the colors of royalty—the most prevalent colors in the former king's tail.

Purple and yellow, both vying for the throne, but passed over for Serena's dark blue scales which lie flat and inconspicuous against the waters of the ocean that surround Society.

Serena takes a deep breath, forcing her back straighter. She can hear Nerin's hum of approval behind her.

Next to enter is Zayla, Serena's former Caste Master, her gold scales glittering against the minerals in the cavern walls and ceilings. Zayla herself brought to light Serena's Absconding charges, and she has kept her distance from the new queen since the crowning.

The next two council members enter—Hailey Sage-Brush, the healer, and Isadora, the psychic.

Together, they remind Serena of the Aurora Borealis. Hailey's bright blue-green painted across the inky black northern skies—the same inky black as Isadora's scales.

Serena studies her aunt Isadora. Of course, Serena didn't know they were related until recently, when the king revealed that Serena was his own daughter, and not the orphan she was raised to believe she was.

Look for the one called Alaric. I must know about him. Isadora's words after she sentenced Serena to visit the werewolf camp still nag at Serena. Why such an interest?

Sarafina clears her throat, drawing Serena's attention back to her.

Studying Sarafina from head to scaled toe, Serena determines she doesn't appear exerted with the kind of swim it takes to get to the dead corals, and probably hasn't for some time.

"The status of the corals?" Serena asks.

Sarafina glances at Evandre. Protecting the corals is the only duty Serena has tasked the pair since she was crowned. *The utmost importance for the welfare of Society*, she remembers telling the two.

When Sarafina looks back at Serena, she folds her hands and relaxes her shoulders. "We are monitoring them," she answers.

Serena frowns. Hard to monitor the corals when you are always so far away from them, but Serena doesn't speak the admonishment aloud. Along with constant reminders to sit up straight and keep her teeth away from her lips, Nerin impresses upon Serena the importance of remaining in the good graces of the council. A slighted council member can turn Society against Serena quicker than an Ungainly can drown.

Instead, Serena smiles at Sarafina and Evandre. "I'm confident you will solve the problem. Such a feat would assure Society that you have their best interests in mind during these trying times."

"A wonderful idea, your majesty," Nerin speaks up at Serena's side. "In fact, we will announce the mission during next Assembly. I think the equivalent of such an important task can be assigned to each of the council members. It will be the perfect opportunity to demonstrate their ability to serve their new queen as well as guide Society into the new era we face."

Serena smiles. If anything, it is the opportune method to force a resistant council to operate.

Forced smiles and nods run up and down the line of council members; some openly glare at Evandre and Sarafina, as if it is their fault in the first place.

The slight sound of shuffling feet draws all eyes to the arched entryway as Cordelia enters. Her burgundy scales have become the most recognizable color among the Painted Maidens and the more she withdraws, hiding away from Society in her own cave, the more prevalent they are when she shows herself. Dark claret scales smolder beneath her golden waves of hair, like a subtle warning, telling those around her to back off.

And they do.

The Great Hall is not crowded, but a clear path unfolds in front of Cordelia as Undine step away. Serena's gut clenches in sympathy. She is all too aware of the chill that snakes down your spine when too many eyes are upon you. Serena feels it when she takes the throne, though it seems to subside with practice. She remembers the full brunt of it each time she made the trek to the front of the Great Hall during her trial and subsequent punishments.

Cordelia's striking blonde hair, woven into a tight braid that hugs the nape of her neck, draws cursory glances, as it always has. But now Serena's eyes always travel down to the bulge of her belly. Today, it looks even bigger. The inevitable swell is a constant reminder to Serena; the Undine are running out of time.

Cordelia fixes her stare on the floor in front of her and bends her knees in a curtsey.

Serena stiffens at the awkward moment. Less than a year ago, Cordelia was the popular one in their caste, always at the front of their traveling formation while Serena stuck to the back.

When Cordelia straightens, Serena takes a deep breath. "You are well?" she asks.

"I am, your majesty," Cordelia answers with a slight bob of her head.

Serena's eyes travel down to the bump again, she can't help it.

Folding her hands over her stomach, Cordelia clears her throat. "You requested my presence, your majesty?"

"Yes, I would like to discuss the impending birth—but I didn't quite expect an audience," Serena says, her eyes flitting to the council and coming to rest on Sarafina and Evandre. Sarafina looks down, running deft hands over her scales, but Evandre holds Serena's gaze.

"We can have the discussion in your own quarters, if you'd like. Or even mine—" Serena cuts herself off when Nerin nudges her with her elbow. "Or not," Serena mumbles, gritting her teeth. No one but Murphy and the queen herself are allowed in the queen's quarters. "But I'd like the Head of the Guard to be present, along with the Healer," Serena motions to Murphy and Hailey.

"It's fine, we can discuss it here, your majesty," Cordelia says, her voice calm.

Serena nods to Murphy, who sends two guards to the entrance of the Great Hall. The discussion won't be interrupted by curious passersby.

As soon as they take post, Serena looks back at Cordelia. "Are you scared?" she asks. The words are out of Serena's mouth before she can stop herself.

The room goes silent. Even condensation from the stalactites hanging from the ceiling ceases to drip.

Cordelia's eyes widen slightly, and Serena watches one hand tighten over the other. "I know birthings haven't gone well in the past, before the Maiden's Massacre," says Cordelia. "But I have faith in my queen and council."

"You know only what Society chose to reveal to the Temporal Caste," says Serena, her voice going soft. "Most of it has been kept from us so that we face this event..." Serena gestures to Cordelia's stomach. "Willingly and with minimal stress."

The two Undine were part of a larger caste together, thirteen in all, who together made the youngest Undine of Society. With other attempts at mating and birthing thwarted by werewolves, or mother and child falling victim to the sheer amount of stress during unnatural birthing circumstances, there had been no more calflings.

Zayla steps forward, raising one finger. "I'm not sure the council would agree with revealing the gruesome past to Cordelia."

"I'm not sure the council made the right decision keeping it from us," Serena snaps back, her words clipped.

Zayla's golden scales flash under the minerals of the cave. As both Serena's and Cordelia's former Caste Master, Zayla can't feel good being schooled by her students.

Serena sighs, realizing she was more harsh than she intended to be.

"It was the king's decree," says Zayla, voice low.

"Under whose guidance?" Nerin steps beside the throne. "We were all there to advise the king, and he made his decision. If Serena wishes to reverse his decision, it is her prerogative. We will support her and give counsel only when asked."

Zayla defers to Nerin, bobbing her head and stepping back, much more quickly than she would have to Serena. Despite the change in leadership, Nerin at least has remained a constant reminder of how the hierarchy works.

Satisfied, Nerin steps back and turns to Serena. "Is this what you wish? All you have to do is allow Cordelia access to the King's Library."

Everyone turns to Serena, waiting for the decision in silence, but Serena's eyes fall on Cordelia. "I will leave the decision up to you, Cordelia. This birthing will not follow policies set forth by myself or the council. We will all defer to the mother. If you wish to read the histories residing in the restricted section of the King's Library, you have my permission. But you must make your decision soon. The passageway to the archives is..." Serena glances down at her stomach. "Narrow."

The Undine have nine full moons from mating to birth. Six have already passed.

Cordelia blushes. "Thank you, your majesty. I will decide soon and let you know."

Serena nods, and can't help but look up at Nerin. The Queen's Second presses her lips together, but the edges of one side turns up in approval.

Serena lets out a slow, quiet sigh. "You may go," she says to Cordelia.

Cordelia curtsies, and turns on her heel. Before she exits the Great Hall, Serena beckons for Kai. He approaches and kneels in a bow before the throne. It is exaggerated, his head almost touching the stairs in front of him and lasting longer than it should.

Serena has to resist rolling her eyes. She knows he has to keep up appearances, but bowing before her makes the relationship awkward, whether he is poking fun in his own way or not.

When he finally stands, Serena gestures with her hand for him to approach. He moves up the stairs, and kneels again. This time Serena does roll her eyes. She leans forward to whisper. "Follow her, and convince her she must go to the King's Library. Prepare her with some of the history beforehand, if you must. Just enough to pique her curiosity."

He lifts his head and raises an eyebrow at Serena. This close, Serena can feel his breath caress her cheek and wrap around her neck.

"Pique her curiosity?" he asks.

"Yes," Serena closes her eyes, forcing air into her own lungs. She wishes she kissed him when she had the chance, back at the beach. What else can she say to keep him close? She can't think of anything, and the council's eyes miss nothing. She sighs in regret. "Go now."

Kai straightens, only to bend again in a deep bow. He turns with a flourish, descends the stairs, and performs another bow. By now Cordelia has left the Great Hall, and Kai has to trot out after her, holding his trident in front of him like he is charging to battle.

Serena laughs, but slaps her hand over her mouth after she realizes what she's done. She coughs into her hand, trying to mask the break in appropriate court composure. Feeling a touch at her shoulder, Serena turns up to look at Nerin.

"The queen needs her rest?" Nerin says.

Serena isn't sure if it is a question or a statement, but she nods then pushes herself out of the throne. "I shall retire," she informs the council.

They each curtsey, and Murphy calls the guard members to attention as Serena descends the stairs. *One, two, three, four, five, six.* Serena counts each time she goes up or down. It helps keep her nerves at bay.

Turning to the only other arched doorway besides the entrance to the Great Hall, Serena glides past the council, feeling their heads turn to watch her as she passes. Her pace quickens, and she is grateful she isn't bound to the throne until high tide comes in like the king was.

Behind her, Murphy gives orders to the guard. He will follow Serena in shortly, which is another reason Serena sent Kai away. She needed an excuse to spare him from watching that again.

It should be Kai following me in every night, Serena thinks for the hundredth time.

Chapter Four

The small arch gives way to a short tunnel about the size of Serena's old cave on the outskirts of Society's underwater mountain. She pauses at the end of it as she always does, considering sleeping in the snug confines of the tunnel instead of the massive chamber that was once her father's sleeping cove.

Even after almost six months of forcing herself to sleep here, she still can't get over how unfamiliar it feels—even more so than the oversized throne. Her fingertips linger against the tunnel wall as her eyes scan the room. Serena imagines it represents what the kingdom looked like on the outside of the mountain, the part that had to be destroyed in order to hide its presence from curious Ungainlies.

Pillars carved with swirling pictures and etchings in the ancient language stretch from floor to ceiling. Around the circumference of the room, small coves are sculpted into the walls. They are just large enough for each member of the Queen's Guard to remain close during times of threat. To Serena's knowledge, they've never been used, except by her. She prefers a small cove to the massive bed carved from rock occupying the middle of the room. Like the tunnel she still stands in, the cove is small and almost cozy. Its constricting walls take away the colossal sensation of emptiness the rest of the room holds. It is too much like the Great Hall, packed with every Undine in the kingdom under the open air suspended over them, waiting for Serena's voice to penetrate the space with decrees, guidance, reassurance, strength, and everything else Nerin preaches the monarch should do.

There is too much emptiness in this kingdom.

Serena closes her eyes and steps forward, letting her fingertips fall from the tunnel walls. Crossing the open space quickly, she reaches out with her other hand until it meets with the rock of King Merrick's bed. A giant column formed when stalactite met with stalagmite, melding together. Unlike the other columns squared off around the cavern, this one doesn't structurally support the room. The only thing it supports, or used to, was a sleeping king.

An area was chipped out of the bottom of the column, leaving only four thick posts on each corner to keep the entire structure from crashing down. Serena begins circling the bed, stopping when her arms wrap around one of the posts. Footsteps echo down the tunnel, and she turns to face Murphy. She fails to convince her arm to let go of the post.

Murphy enters the room, stopping just outside of the tunnel.

Serena holds her breath, waiting for his first words.

Will it be a reprimand or praise? Usually it sets the tone for the rest of the conversation.

"You should not question my authority in front of my men," he says, standing rigid with his trident perfectly parallel to his form.

Letting out a slow sigh, Serena prepares herself for the argument. But defensive words don't come. Instead, she turns, sinking down onto the rocky bed. She holds the post even tighter and leans her head against it. "I'm tired, Murphy." *And I'm not cut out for this.*

At. All.

Her unspoken words hang in the air between them like dead weight. Murphy strides forward, cutting through the tension as efficiently as a shark fin on the ocean surface. When he comes to a stop in front of Serena, she expects a rough jerk to her feet. Maybe even a good shaking. Sometimes harsh words and fierce actions are all Murphy seems capable of.

Instead, he turns and sits beside Serena. She leans away to look at him, mouth open. Sitting on the king's bed would be unheard of for anyone, and she can only imagine the punishment Murphy might dole out to one of his own for doing so.

He sits rigid, leaning forward still on the balls of his feet like he might dart up any second. His eyes jump around, taking in the new view of the sleeping rock. He twists to look behind him and up.

"Poseidon," he says, almost to himself.

Serena's eyes flit up to the carving at the top of the bed. The sea god stands erect with one arm raised. His beard hangs past his chiseled chest, and a tunic falls loose around his waist. It is the same drawing looming over the Undine prison.

"No wonder you don't want to sleep here," Murphy murmurs.

The sound of shuffling feet echo from the tunnel and a shadow passes over the opening. Serena and Murphy both jump to their feet.

They are supposed to be mated, but neither can bear the thought of being caught together on the king's bed.

"It's just one of the guards taking his post," says Murphy.

They both let out a breath.

"Not Kai..." Serena says.

Murphy shakes his head, turning toward her. "I know you have feelings for each other, but they can't be displayed in public. It would seriously harm both our reputations. Your relationship with Kai will have to wait."

Serena sighs. "I know, but Murphy...we can't wait forever."

He nods, looking at the tips of his trident. "We'll figure something out. Maybe stage an elaborate break up scene," he says, one side of his mouth curling up in a crooked smile.

Serena laughs. "That would be fun."

"But after I ensure Society is willing to obey you, no matter what."

Her laughter dies out, and the heavy weight of silence settles in again.

Murphy clears his throat. "Society will be in enough turmoil as it is—we need to make sure the majority of the Undine are behind you before we...split. That was the reason for our pairing, anyway."

"The king had it all planned out, didn't he?" Serena asks. "The punishments, naming me Werewolf Liaison, and even my..." She glances at Murphy. "Mate. He had my whole life arranged before I've even had a chance to live it."

Murphy lays his large hand on Serena's shoulder. "Your father had to face choices no father should ever have to face. Take the opportunities he left you and do something meaningful with them."

Serena forces a smile up at Murphy. "I'll try—but I'm not sleeping in this bed."

Laughing, Murphy pats Serena on the shoulder, twice. "Come on, I'll hoist you up into your favorite nook."

The pair walk to the wall, Serena closer to Murphy than she has to be. The room doesn't seem as enormous that way.

A single trident stands against the wall, marking her sleeping place. The weapon is the smallest of its kind. It has three, sharp tips, but the curve on the outer two prongs is deeper, and the center prong is the longest of the trio. Instead of a smooth single pole as the stem, the trident twists, briefly separating into two spiraling rods which merge back together at the bottom.

Combined from the melted tridents previously carried by Kai, Murphy, and Serena's best friend, Ervin, the gold is mixed with magnesium alloy, a rare metal extracted straight from seawater that takes a lifetime to collect.

Murphy clasps his hands together and bends down on one knee. Serena places her foot in his palms and he stands, hoisting her up to one of the higher coves meant for sleeping guards.

She pulls herself in then leans out to grab her trident as Murphy passes it up.

He holds onto it a tad longer than he has to. "You've been warned to keep your trident by your side."

"I've had plenty of warnings, Murphy Air-Spirit," Serena yanks the trident from his hand. "You can't expect a girl to remember them all." Serena runs the pad of her thumb over a mark etched into the stem of her trident. It is a double circle—the shape above smooth and whole, and the shape below choppy. A full moon and its shadow falling upon the ocean. It is Moon-Shadow, and it is her mark.

"A girl, no…" Murphy backs away from the wall. "But the same does not apply to an Undine queen." A few moments pass while he stands, still looking up at her. "Are you going to assign me a mission, too?" he asks. "To demonstrate my ability to serve my new queen?" His tone is higher and his words clipped, mimicking Nerin's voice. He is trying to lighten Serena's mood, and it works.

She smiles, thinking of the middle-aged maidens. "Murphy, you could fail every mission I give you and still hold the hearts of most of the Undine."

"The very reason why we need to hold up appearances of being paired," he winks at her.

Serena sighs, rolling over on her back and taking her trident with her. "Between you and your mother, you are going to make a great queen out of me."

Murphy rests his hand on the edge of her sleeping cove. His voice goes soft. "You already are a great queen, Serena. But not everyone can see that yet." His hand drops and Serena hears light footsteps brush over hard rock across her chambers to a smaller adjoining cave, one that has been Murphy's living area for as long as Serena has been alive.

"Thank you, Murphy," she whispers to herself.

Chapter Five

Serena walks down the short tunnel, dragging the walls with the pads of her fingers. It is some sort of comfort after a long night in the king's chamber. Murphy's chamber was dark when Serena climbed down from her nook. He was probably out making rounds after only a few hours of sleep. Yawning, Serena pauses to stretch just before the tunnel opens up into the Great Hall. It is unfortunate timing. The two guards at the entrance come to attention and make a coordinated, precise turn to face the queen just as Serena is in mid-stretch, her trident overhead, and her face contorted into a lopsided, open-mouthed yawn.

One of the guards begins his bow too quickly and the other hesitates before giving his. The result is a pair of bobbing heads like buoys in rough waves. Snapping her mouth shut quicker than she can bring her hands down, Serena is left with a pressing lump in her throat of a suppressed yawn. She tries swallowing it down before she speaks.

"I'll assume you are my escorts for the day?"

They both nod.

"Murphy is assigning two of you now?"

They nod again.

"I see…" *It will be much more difficult to give two guards the slip when I feel the urge to surface.* "Well, have you eaten yet today?"

Two vigorous nods.

Serena crosses her arms, staring them down. She won't let Murphy bully everyone, especially when he isn't even present.

The nods slow and stop until the guards begin to shake their heads.

"Well, come on. We can all visit Rayne together."

The walk to Serena's childhood home—the orphanage turned diner—doesn't bring back any nostalgic memories. Everything has changed, right down to the two brawny guards trailing either side of her. The hall that is traditionally left empty is now packed with Undine, entering or leaving Rayne's diner. Maidens squeeze themselves against the wall as Serena passes, barely able to make room for the queen and her entourage.

Inside the main dining hall of the orphanage, the long wooden table that once served dozens of orphans now holds twice the amount of adult Undine, laughing, gossiping, and passing food bowls amongst one another. They sit shoulder to shoulder on the benches running alongside the table. Smaller, round tables now line the edges of the room in order to seat more.

Steam and smoke bellows out of the kitchen from the cooking fires, carrying with it the smell of clean water—a touch briny—and cooked seaweed, making Serena's stomach rumble. Rayne bustles through the steam to place another bowl of noodled kelp on the table. Hands reach for the slightly crunchy, almost translucent cuisine and Rayne deftly bats them away.

"Spoons, maidens. I'll not have you grabbing at my creations like a horde of ravenous crabs." Rayne turns down her lips at the group but gives an appreciative nod when they each grudgingly reach for their utensils. Rayne's eyes float up, spotting Serena, and her mouth turns into a full-on grin.

Weaving her way in between tables and chairs, Rayne walks toward Serena with open arms. At the last second, Rayne remembers her place and bends in a curtsey instead. The smile is still wide on her face. She gestures to the long table. "I still don't understand why the sudden push to use Ungainly instruments."

"It's just…a precaution is all," says Serena. She doesn't necessarily want to reveal she is training her people to live above ground—at least not yet.

"It's unnatural," grumbles Rayne.

Serena smiles. "Nonetheless, thank you for helping implement the policy, and thank you for not making clear it was my guidance."

Rayne crosses her arms.

"Besides," says Serena. "They aren't all that complicated. They're spoons." She sighs, watching one of the maidens look at her upside down reflection in the utensil while running her fingers through her hair.

"Perhaps I should…" Serena takes a step toward an empty spot at the table. That small movement draws all eyes, and the maidens stand upright so quickly one of the benches tips over.

Serena goes tense, drawing her shoulders back into her spine. Eyes darting from one maiden to the next, the entire room is at a standstill, unsure of how to handle the awkward situation Serena has just created. She remembers they rarely saw the king off of his throne—and now here is the queen, ready to dine with them.

Rayne clears her throat. "Um, your majesty— right this way, please."

Turning on her heel, Serena follows Rayne to a table set up one step above the rest of the room in a small, carved-out nook. The tension deflates in the dining hall behind her.

"You aren't one of them anymore, Serena." Rayne pulls out a chair for her.

"I never really was." It is Serena's turn to grumble as she sits down. She tries balancing her trident across her lap but it sticks too far out from the under the table. Next she tries leaning it against the table, but it keeps tipping to one side or the other. Serena raises her eyebrow at Rayne. *See!?*

Sighing, Rayne takes the trident. "Ronan already thought of that." She leans it into a small, carved out notch at the back of the table. Rayne returns her own raised eyebrow. "A Queen does not have to go it alone. There are those that will look out for you, if you'll just let them. Now, I'll go get you some food." Rayne turns on her heel and bustles away before Serena can object.

"The guards too, please," Serena shouts after Rayne.

Returning with a plate full of steaming food, and one bowl of sea-lettuce soup, Rayne sets them down in front of Serena and takes the chair opposite her. Serena picks up her own spoon, glancing at the guards who are each balancing a small plate and eating while standing.

"This is something new." Serena pokes at a clump of thin, dried algae that looks like twigs.

"Hijki," says Rayne. "You put them in your soup."

Serena pinches a few off the top and drops them in her bowl. They expand as they soak. Serena spoons some into her mouth. The Hijki is still somewhat crunchy and it adds a vibrant mix of salty and sweet to the soup.

"It's good, very good," says Serena, taking another bite. She gestures to the open room, buzzing with low chatter. "So, what have you heard?"

The old orphanage isn't just a place for Undine to grab a quick bite. It is a common meeting area to catch up with neighbors away from the formalities of the Great Hall, and Rayne is privy to all the information.

"Everyone is mostly chattering about the missions you will assign the council, and how it will affect their personal lives," says Rayne.

"Good," mumbles Serena. "It will keep their minds off the werewolves."

Rayne gives Serena a pointed look. "That is one problem that is not easily solved."

"Easier than getting this salmon into me, I hope." She flicks her spoon at a nori roll on her plate. It unravels, revealing thin strips of raw salmon inside.

Rayne's lips go tight. "The plants around the kingdom are becoming more and more limited, Serena. They are *dying*. You are going to have to get used to eating something else sooner or later. We all will."

Serena holds up a flabby, pale pink strip of meat, wiggling it in front of her face. Her mouth turns down in distaste. "If the corals go, so do the fish. So unless we are willing to migrate, we are going to have to figure something else out."

"We've tried that before, Serena. You were too young to remember, but maidens got very sick in other waters. Some even died." Rayne picks up a spoon, turning it in her fingers watching light refract off the smooth silver. She snorts. "Seems we do better in The Dry than in other waters."

"Exactly," says Serena, making a pointed glance at the spoon. Leaving the salmon untouched, Serena finishes the rest of her meal in silence under Rayne's watchful eye. Finally, Serena pushes her chair back, stands, and grabs her trident.

"We need to start growing herbs and vegetables again. Have you seen Sarafina yet today?" Serena glances around the room, the Head Gardener won't be far from the Great Hall.

Collecting the dishes from the table, Rayne shakes her head. "No—but, what do you plan to do? We can't grow in The Dry with the wolves patrolling."

"We have to find some way to make it work," says Serena, catching the attention of the guards who wolf down the last morsels on their plates.

"I'm thinking that is too much for you to take on," says Rayne, handing one of the guards Serena's leftovers.

"A job for Sarafina, then." Serena smiles, already walking out and debating to herself if she should break the news to the Head Gardner or if Nerin should.

"Have a good day, your majesty!" Rayne calls out after her.

Serena turns, almost forgetting the formalities. "Thank you, mother Rayne—your creations were delicious as usual."

They curtsey to each other. For a second, Serena almost feels like she is a child back in the orphanage, playing a make believe game of royalty. The illusion is pulled out from under her like a rug once she realizes every eye in the dining hall is on her. Serena clears her throat, addressing the rest of the Undine. "Carry on and…try the Hijki."

Serena turns on her heel, trusting the guards' heavy footsteps behind her to drown out any snickers.

Chapter Six

The swim to the archives takes Serena and her guards around the backside of the Undine mountain, on the western side of Vancouver Island. The majority of the path is surrounded by dead coral forests. Refusing to let any Undine ignore the problem further, Serena slows down while they swim over the cavernous wasteland. The guards are uncomfortable and keep inching forward. Each time their heads move level with Serena's shoulders, she glares until they fall back into position.

I won't be bullied into ignoring the problem either.

When they reach the narrow tunnel leading up into another mountain and the archives, Serena motions for the guards to stay behind. They oblige, partly because there is no other exit from the archives, but most likely because they don't feel like passing through the small tunnel on full stomachs.

Navigating her way through the tunnels, with darkness all around her, and the walls squeezing in, Serena feels freedom. A wide grin spreads across her face. Shoulders back, duck head, tight turn to the right. Maneuvering in the pathway took some relearning with her new trident, but the archives are always worth the trip.

As the end nears, Serena pins her arms and her trident to her side. Rolling her body as efficiently as a wave, Serena propels herself faster. Dimmed light from the archives entrance cavern blinks into view. One last thrust with her fins, and Serena breaks free from the water. She tucks her body into a tight ball, doing one summersault and then opening up again as she reaches the apex of her jump. Her fingers reach out toward the cave ceiling and just barely scrape hard rock.

Smiling briefly, Serena bends at the waist, piking for the dive back in. She straightens her body just as she enters the water, barely making a splash. When she resurfaces, it is only her head bobbing out. She can't get out of the water quickly enough, excited that she is finally able to touch the ceiling. Her own little challenge—one she had been practicing for months.

Transforming from fins to legs, Serena pulls herself out and throws on the robe and slippers required to enter the archives. She leaves her trident standing against the wall.

"Mariam!" she calls, struggling to get her arms in the robe. Serena stops by the catalogues, tying the sash around her waist. "Mariam!"

"Tsk, tsk," Kai comes from around one of the large columns with his finger to his lips.

Serena smiles, closing the distance between them quickly. His raised eyebrow stops her in her tracks. He nods his head to the other side of the library, and Serena follows his gaze. Cordelia sits at a table, bent over a book, with Mariam behind her pointing out passages as they both read.

"She actually came…" whispers Serena.

Both of the maidens look up. Caught off guard, Serena gives a slight wave. Mariam knits her eyebrows together, and shoos Serena away with a quick gesture so Cordelia cannot see. Serena nods, pulling Kai out of their view.

"Look," Serena says, holding up her scratched finger.

"What?"

"I did it, I touched the ceiling in the entrance cavern." She pushes up on her toes, then settles into her heels just as quick, unable to contain her excitement.

Kai smiles, and the hard line of his chin and cheekbones soften. He leans in, so Serena is forced to take a step back straight into one of the cave walls. The nook carved out to hold books is too big. Some of the books scrape as they are pushed further into the nook.

"You are still obsessed with touching the ceiling? I thought you gave up on that."

Serena's finger still wavers in the air between them. She bites her lip. "I need some fun in my life."

Kai's mouth turns down in a teasing frown. "Come on, Serena, you can think of something better than that." He kisses her finger, his warmth running down her arm and straight into her belly.

Her body goes slack, giving in before she really needs to. She sinks further into the books as he continues to press forward.

"Come on, Kai – a queen sometimes needs help, too."

"You want me to show you how to have fun?" His lips are inches from hers now. The ridges forming the top of his lips brush across hers.

"You have my permission," she whispers back.

He closes the distance, lips pressing into hers. Serena flattens her hands on the cave wall behind her back, using it to push forward into him. He doesn't give, meeting with the same intensity.

She allows her hands to creep up his sides, tugging at the robe he wears. She paws at the thick fabric folds, desperate to find his warm skin underneath. When she finally finds her way in, she feels scales, not skin.

"Tsk, tsk," she mimics him. "No scales allowed in the library."

"Your majesty," he mumbles into her hair, his lips grazing her neck up to her ear. Chills run down her spine. Slowly, he retracts the scales underneath her fingertips. As her finger glides up following the curve of muscle over abdomen, more scales retract.

Encouraged, Serena places both hands under his robe, palms pressing against him. Up and down his front, around his sides, and over his chest. His scales disappear at her touch until there is only skin.

She looks up into his eyes, forest green muted with flecks of golden brown around the edges. Serena suddenly can't stand what little space is between them. She wants Kai, and she wants all of him. Leaning in until their lips touch again, Serena wraps her arms around his waist. Her leg rises slightly and snakes around the thick of his calf. She can feel his hand gripping the back of her neck, holding her in place.

A loud cough signals another is approaching. Their eyes fly open in only a moment of hesitation before they jump apart. By the time Mariam rounds the corner, Kai and Serena have their backs to each other studying the spines of the books in front of them with vigor.

Mariam crosses her arms at the pair. "I don't mind opening up the archives for your secret affair, but the least you could do is keep it under wraps while someone else is present," she hisses, glancing at Kai's open robe.

Kai follows her gaze down, then fumbles with his sash, cinching the robe closed. Behind him, Serena is quickly trying to realign the books on the shelf that reveal the outline of her thin form.

"She entered the King's Library?" Serena asks Mariam, changing the subject.

Taking a cue for his dismissal, Kai wanders out from the shelves.

Mariam waits for him to go, then nods. "She did."

"How is she taking it?"

"She has a lot of questions, particularly those that involve maidens abandoning their sons."

Serena fixes the last book, then turns to look at Mariam. "Some think this is a mistake—that it will stress her so much that the delivery won't be successful."

Stepping toward Serena, Mariam places a hand on her shoulder. "Some are stuck in the past. Which is why you are equipped—better than any—to lead us. Don't doubt yourself, girl." Mariam's rounded brown eyes gleam with intensity.

Serena doesn't say anything, but nods her head.

"Okay…" says Mariam, not entirely reassured. "Why don't you go talk to her?" She moves aside and nudges Serena forward.

Still fighting off heat waves from kissing Kai, Serena takes a deep breath. She walks toward Cordelia hunched over a book at the table, and is grateful Kai has found something else to do within the archives, out of sight.

"Thank you," Serena says. "For taking my offer to access the restricted section."

Cordelia looks up at Serena, eyes wide. "Oh, yes your majesty." She coughs. "Of course."

Serena sighs, and pushes a chair next to Cordelia. Her old caste mate stiffens, as though she might jump out of her own chair.

"We aren't holding court, no need for formalities," assures Serena as she sits down. "I just want to talk."

Cordelia swallows, and nods. "Okay." Her eyes wander down to the book and she closes it.

There are not elaborate etchings or jewels on the cover. Serena knows what it is about— werewolves.

"Maidens did not have it easy back then," Cordelia says, giving a nervous laugh.

"Poseidon's Curse," Serena says. "You can ask Mariam about it. Almost all available maidens were required to participate in a selection and a pairing, and so many of them lost their calflings."

"I don't understand," Cordelia runs one hand down the braid at the nape of her neck. "Why did it all happen?"

"The environment changes. When we couldn't keep our male calflings alive in the water, we came up with another solution."

"But, werewolves?"

Serena nods, tracing the edges of the old book with her thumb. "Our own children, our only hope, who became our protectors and then…"

"Our destroyers," Cordelia finishes for Serena.

Images from books depicting the night of the Maiden's Massacre flash through Serena's head.

"Listen, Cordelia." Serena places a hand over her former caste mate's arm. "There is a lot at stake here, and others will try to push their will onto you. If you aren't careful, you will drown under them. I wanted you here because you have to know all the facts, and all that you might face in just a few short months. These are your choices."

"Thank you, Seren—er, your majesty." Cordelia swallows hard.

Serena smiles. "I know, it still sounds so weird."

The maidens each give a nervous laugh, interrupted when a small piece of paper folded into itself lands on the table between them.

Serena grabs the note, looking up directly into one of the ceiling shafts filtering sunlight into the cave during the day.

"What is it?" Cordelia asks.

Brushing bits of cave debris off the note, Serena glances at Cordelia. "Whatever it is, it came from The Dry."

Serena slowly unfolds the paper.

We need to meet. Moonrise tomorrow.

Drawn in the corner of the slip of paper is a small, yellow wolfsbane flower.

Serena looks at Cordelia, eyes wide. "It's from Liam."

Chapter Seven

"Absolutely not. No way." Kai crosses his arms and lifts his nose in the air, channeling Murphy.

"I'm pretty sure it will be safe," Serena points to the small flower sketched into the corner of the note. "It's like...a signal for peace."

"How do you know it isn't a trap?" asks Kai.

"Liam could be on their side, Serena," says Mariam, taking a softer stance next to Kai, but a stance nonetheless. "Or they could be using him to get to you. Or—"

"How would you go anyway?" Cordelia asks, still sitting at her table in front of an open book.

All three heads turn her way.

"I mean," she shrugs. "Even if the note were genuine, he can't expect you to just walk out on the shore with the patrols spotting you."

"How she gets there doesn't matter because she is not going," Kai's words float past Serena like background noise.

She looks down at the note, studying it. Cordelia is right, there has to be some clue.

Serena peers closer at the flower, holding it up to what light is left shining through the same hole the note came down. The stem has odd, diagonal lines penciled in.

"Rope," says Serena, interrupting Kai. She looks up at the narrow tunnel burrowed into the ceiling, past the mirrors reflecting the light. "He'll send rope the same way he sent his note."

"Oh, of course," smirks Kai. "Because those tunnels are way too small to send any of the guardsmen up with you. It's perfect." He throws up his hands, walking away. He pauses, turning back around. "You aren't going—and that is final, your majesty."

This time his use of her title isn't sexy at all, it is outright infuriating. "He is my twin brother, Kai Forest." Serena raises her voice, allowing her hair's bioluminescent glow to light up in agitation. "And werewolf or no, he is the only family I have left." Her voice cracks at the word 'family', and Serena can see Kai's eyes transform from angry slits to sympathetic ovals. It hurts Serena more than anything, because she knows he wants to be closer—he wants to *be* her family.

"Come on." Serena glances up at Kai. "Let's at least go tell Murphy."

Serena says her goodbyes to first Mariam, then Cordelia, trying to recall an air of formality and reserve before she has to report back to the Great Hall. Leaving together, Serena follows Kai out of the archives. They pause to de-robe, turning their backs to each other. As much as Serena wants to watch, she keeps her eyes steady on the dripping stalactites. If she squints hard enough, she thinks she can make out the scrape of her fingernail driven into the grime of the ceiling next to the sun hole.

Behind her, she hears Kai's robe fall to the floor.

Focus, she thinks. *Not here, not now.*

He slips off his padded slippers, taking a painfully slow time about it.

You are a queen—act like it. Besides, you are still mad at him.

Finally, Serena hears a splash in the water. She lets out a breath she didn't know she was holding.

Hanging up her own robe and slippers and retrieving her trident, Serena quickly dives in after Kai. She follows his light brown tail, sticking close and expecting him to lengthen the distance between them with his speed any moment.

Concentrating on the arduous turns and twists of the narrow tunnel, Serena arches her back, preparing for the hairpin curve above. It is one of the larger spaces of the path, but if you take it quickly enough momentum will carry you through the rotation. But just as she is whirling around at the bend, Serena slams into Kai, who is waiting as still as stone.

"Umph!" the air is forced from her lungs and her eyes go wide. Her trident floats to the bottom of the small cavern.

Before she can bounce back off of Kai, he grabs her arms, pinning her against him.

"What—?" she gasps, momentarily forgetting they are still underwater. Only bubbles come out.

Pressing through the agitated fizz, Kai takes Serena's mouth with his own. Serena squirms, unable to forget that either Cordelia or Mariam could come through any moment, not to mention the guards that are supposed to be waiting at the entrance.

Kai wraps his arms around her waist, propelling them both up to a small air pocket at the highest point of the space. When they break the surface, they are both breathing hard. It is dark, but Kai's green eyes are so clear they almost glow. Within the constricting space, their foreheads touch.

"What are you doing?" asks Serena.

"If we can't be open about our relationship in front of others—if I have to guard every move I make around you, every glance, every expression—then I am going to steal as many moments with you as I can."

Under the water, Kai intertwines his fingers with Serena's. He brings one of her hands up, kissing her on the knuckles and allowing his lips to brush across them, his breath lingering on her pale skin. "Will you allow me these small indulgences, your majesty?" Miniscule water droplets cling to his lashes. He brings his hand to her hip and squeezes, waiting for her answer.

Running her other hand up his bared chest, Serena bites her lip and meets his gaze, trying to convince herself to be as bold as Kai. Her fingers wrap around the nape of his neck and she pulls him even closer, the tip of her nose skimming across his. "As long as you promise to never call me 'your majesty' in private again."

She feels him move, tracking him by his breath against her cheek, then her ear. "Agreed," he whispers. "Serena…"

Her name on his lips sends chills racing through her body. She tilts her head back, meeting his mouth again. He presses his palms into the small of her back and she responds by wrapping her tail around his. Her spine heats under his touch. Flames flare up her shoulders and neck, fizzling out as they sink down into the cold, dark water together.

Pressed against each other, Serena opens her mouth and feels his tongue slide over her lower lip. Need overtakes her, and she wants more of him. She presses back, gripping him tight— almost frantic that he might pull away any second.

Their tails brush the rocky bottom of the passageway releasing trapped air pockets. Bubbles float up, tickling the pair with froth and foam. The effervescence fuels desire and Serena loses track of how long they are bonded together.

Finally, they draw apart. One more quick kiss on her cheek, and Kai bends to retrieve both their dropped tridents. He hands one to Serena and nudges her forward. Reluctantly, she allows herself to be guided through the rest of the tunnel first. Occasionally reaching out to tease the tips of her fins, Kai's distraction causes Serena to lose focus and she bumps into the walls more often than her first time in the tunnel.

Lighter waters ahead come into view, and by the time Serena emerges she has small scrapes along her shoulders and back. They help to rein in the raging fire still burning in her stomach, chest, and head. The icy ocean water does its part, too. By the time they exit the tunnel and face the guards standing watch, Serena is composed…mostly. Loose strands of hair float into her peripheral view as if they are waving and shouting out, 'look what she just did!' Frantically, Serena pushes them back, trying to smooth them down behind her ears.

A short shrill whistle rings out from behind Serena. The guards in front of her nod their heads at Kai's command, then turn and leave. Once they are out of eyesight, Kai moves in front of Serena, helping her tuck the loose strands back into her thick braid.

Smiling, Serena nods her thanks. They are close and Serena wants to kiss him all over again, but they are in the open now and have to be careful. Kai moves away, strong enough to allow the moment to pass. Serena frowns as realization of her weakness sets in.

Not good, she thinks as she watches Kai's back end swim away. *But at the same time, way too good to pass up.*

* * *

Once they are back into legs and walking the halls of Society, Serena slows her pace, pulling her shoulders back. Kai falls behind, trailing her like any guardsman would. Their presence is formal, but inside Serena deflates. She doesn't like hiding behind this mask almost all the time, especially next to Kai.

Heads bob as Undine bow into full curtseys when Serena moves by. Passing another hallway, Serena hears a slight grunt. She retraces her steps, Kai moving back almost in synchronization.

The oldest male undine stands against a wall, arms crossed.

"You speak Ronan?" whispers Kai.

"Fluently," answers Serena. "Come on, he has something to show us."

The pair follow Ronan to the smoky room of the armory.

Formalities curtailed in the vacant workshop, Kai leans into Serena. "You don't suppose he's going to let us hide behind the fire and—"

"Kai!" Serena elbows him in the ribs.

Ronan turns an ear but does not look at the couple. Instead he moves around his workbench, pulling at something on the ground. Kai follows to help, ushering the old Undine out of the way before giving one strong tug. Several translucent panes balanced on a wood contraption scoot into view.

"What are they?" asks Serena.

"Shields," answers Ronan. "To block the Ungainly weapons."

Serena curls her toes in, feeling the pain of a bullet ripping through her foot all over again. It wasn't the worst wound endured during the King's Massacre, but definitely not one she would be anxious to experience again.

Running his hand over the outside pane, then rapping on it with his knuckles, Kai smiles. "Bulletproof? How did you manage it? Have you tested them?"

Ronan runs a gnarled knuckle across his upper lip.

Serena smiles to herself, the old man cannot be made to answer quickly. Growing up, she bore witness to his evasion of Rayne's most severe interrogations.

"Alternating panes of glass and laminate," responds Ronan, his words gravelly.

Serena steps forward to touch the invention. "Amazing what you can find floating around in the ocean."

Ronan grunts.

Glancing at Kai, Serena pushes her luck. "We can use them, you know—for a visit to Liam."

"They wouldn't fit up the tunnels," Kai shakes his head.

"There are other ways to The Dry…"

Kai narrows his eyes.

"Just saying," shrugs Serena.

"What you choose to do with them is up to you," Ronan says, hoisting one upright. "But there are five of them."

Kai moves forward, poking and prodding at the glass, then testing its weight. "Can we put straps here, and shape them smaller?"

"To create shields?"

"Yes," says Kai. "Too cumbersome for running, but if we're trying to hold our ground, on say a beach…" he trails off.

The pair bend over one of the pieces, mumbling as they consult with each other.

Shifting impatiently from foot to foot, Serena huffs. "Kai, I have a meeting with the council. Shall I report that you are otherwise occupied?" she asks.

"Please do," Kai says, eyes still running down the edges of the gleaming glass.

"Okay," says Serena. "Be careful."

"Always am," Kai responds, finally looking at her.

"That's my line." Serena smiles, touching his shoulder lightly in farewell. It is all she will risk, or at least deem appropriate, in the presence of Ronan.

Chapter Eight

"I have your missions," Serena announces. She stands as part of a circle along with the rest of the council, minus Kai, in the middle of the Great Hall. Instituted by Serena almost right after she took the crown, the meeting setup is more productive than all of them craning their necks up at her on the throne. They tend to be more candid with her when she isn't surrounded by reminders of monarchs past. Besides, standing instead of sitting keeps conversations short and to the point. Even Evandre finds it harder to prattle on when she is shifting from foot to foot instead of sitting comfortably on her bum.

Sarafina clears her throat, glancing between Serena and Nerin. "I find it odd that after years and years of traditional leadership policies, we are suddenly doing things differently. I'm sure that—"

"Years and years of tradition?" interrupts Serena, her jaw clenched and her hand squeezing the trident by her side. "The corals turn to skeletons around us, we haven't birthed a calfling in eighteen years, and yet you suggest we stay the course?"

"It doesn't mean we need to break *all* customs," Sarafina shoots back. "After all, look where it got the king."

"Are you blaming his death on me?" Serena raises her voice, squaring her shoulders with Sarafina. She flashes her trident in front of her, reminding Sarafina of her position.

Sarafina's eyes widen slightly as she attempts to recall decorum. "No, your majesty."

The moment passes, one that will most assuredly not be escaping any of the council members' memories any time soon.

"Forgive me for interrupting." Isadora steps into the circle, her black scales glittering like the cave minerals cast into the ceiling, giving an impression of the open night sky.

Everyone turns to look at her as she rarely speaks at council meetings.

"I believe the path the king chose was due to…several things. It was unfortunate, admirable, suspicious, and perhaps unavoidable. Characteristics that seem to overshadow the lives of every noble family member." Isadora looks at Serena and smiles.

Serena steps back into place, nodding for Isadora to continue.

"You all know the legends; Alpheus, Leucothea, and Proteus. And don't forget Dagon, the avenging devil of the sea. It seems King Merrick fell right into place in a long line of tragedies, but one that paves new paths for the Undine." Isadora turns in a slow circle, making sure to look each council member in the eye as she speaks. "And from what I've seen so far, Serena is bold enough to charge down that path, headfirst, with one goal in mind. Securing the future of the Undine. And if we, her trusted council, the collective leaders of Society, are not brave enough to follow…" Isadora pauses, turning to look at Sarafina and lowering her voice. "Then we are already doomed."

Sarafina's shoulders sag, silenced by a psychic and a seventeen-year-old queen.

Isadora lowers her eyes, then turns to Serena. "I understand you request words with me, your majesty.

I will remain in my cave the rest of the day when you are ready to speak."

"Thank you, Isadora."

A talk with Isadora is long overdue. After the king's admission that Serena is the true heir, the tragedy of his death pushed aside the fact that Isadora is Serena's aunt—and the twin sister of Serena's mother, the deceased queen.

Isadora curtseys, then turns and takes her place back in the circle.

Nerin clears her throat. "As you were saying, your majesty—the missions?"

"Yes, thank you, Nerin." Serena turns to Sarafina and Evandre first, always standing side by side. "You are well aware of yours. The corals. Except now I require an update every third moon—"

"Will you have time for that your majesty?" Evandre interrupts. "I mean, you are difficult enough to pin down as it is."

Serena smiles. "Not an update to me, Evandre. An update to the rest of Society—or to all those who care to attend. They will be held here, in the Great Hall, at the setting of the moon. My presence is not required."

Evandre and Sarafina exchange a glance.

Serena turns to Zayla. "Zayla, with the graduation of the temporal caste, and no more students to teach, I have wondered what you do with your time. It seems you have taken a liking to working with Rayne in the kitchens, working to feed the entirety of Society. It seems your desire to nurture has not escaped you."

Zayla nods slowly.

"I charge you, along with Hailey…"

Society's head doctor lifts her chin in response.

"…with ensuring Cordelia's success in birthing a healthy calfling and to furthermore increase our chances for more."

One corner of Zayla's mouth goes up in a wry smile "That is an awfully difficult position you put me in, your majesty," she says, looking at Serena, then Hailey. "But one that I would be honored to fulfill."

"Thank you, Zayla and Hailey. I will speak with you more on the subject later." Serena turns to Isadora. "And for Isadora, who manages to see all for who they truly are, I entrust the future of the Undine into your hands."

"The future of the Undine?" Isadora asks. "I can only see potential paths each life might take, not that of whole societies."

"I understand," Serena nods. "But I have to tell you that I suspect one of those potential paths might put every one of us in The Dry—permanently."

A chorus of resistance breaks out, the loudest of all is Evandre.

Isadora holds up one hand, and the group silences. "I've seen enough myself to believe it, and I will do as you say, your majesty." Isadora bobs her head in a curtsey again. She is being way more gracious than Serena has ever witnessed, even in front of the king.

"Nerin, my trusted Second," says Serena, motioning over her left shoulder. "We have already spoken on your duties. Nerin is charged with unity of the Undine. As word gets out about our prospective fate, as it no doubt will—" Serena glances at Evandre and Sarafina. "—we will become more divided than ever. We will need a peacekeeper, and Nerin has already played this role many times."

"As you say, your majesty," says Nerin. "Which leaves only the male members of the council left to task."

Serena clears her throat. She did not have time to talk it through with Nerin beforehand.

Murphy steps forward. "May I make a suggestion?"

Hesitating, Serena isn't sure she wants Murphy to assign his own duties. It would be unfair to the rest of the council members. She bites her lower lip. *Are we going to butt heads again?*

"A suggestion as to Kai's duties," explains Murphy.

"Please—let's hear it." Serena says, releasing a slow breath.

Murphy comes to attention. Standing straight, he is two heads taller than anyone else there, and twice the width. "The safety of the queen should be his top priority."

Serena's heart quickens. *What is he doing? Does he know about the note from Liam already?*

"Although it is of course already the responsibility of the guard, the queen has proven a difficult...charge," Murphy says.

Careful, Murphy.

"And with the prospect of increased time in The Dry, I would feel more at ease with one specific individual shadowing her at all times."

At all times. Kai will be with me all the time. A part of her wants to jump up and hug Murphy, another part of her wants to slap him across the face. Kai will be within reach on a constant basis, but not being allowed to touch him in front of anyone else will be pure torture.

"Agreed," says Hailey, on Murphy's right.

Evandre and Sarafina are quick to jump in, followed by everyone else with a chorus of agreement.

Serena sighs. To deny him now would be to deny the entire council. Nerin nudges her, well aware of what Serena is considering. Hesitantly, Serena speaks. "Very well, Murphy. It will be so. And now that leaves your assignment." *And I am not going to take it easy on you.*

Murphy shifts from one foot to another. The movement is subtle, but Serena takes a moment to revel in it.

"I bequeath the Head of the Guard with safety of...everyone else," she says. "You are to patrol the borders of our kingdom yourself—at least twice daily, as well as make the rounds throughout personal caves. Ensure the kitchens are safe...and the armory."

His mouth drops open, and Serena smiles at his lapse in bearing.

"And Murphy—don't forget about the archives."

The mission will keep Murphy plenty busy and away from her and Kai so at least she won't have to deal with that awkward trio. Briefly, Serena thinks it may be too harsh, but then again, so was his suggestion.

Murphy steps back into line, his lips tight. "As you say, your majesty."

"Council adjourned," Serena snaps before there can be any disagreements. "We'll meet again tomorrow so you can present the outline of your plans to me. And Murphy? Please let Kai know I will be waiting for him in the archives at moonrise." Serena turns to Isadora. "I will speak with you now."

"As you say, your majesty. Please follow me."

Acknowledging the farewell curtsies of the rest of the council with a bob of her head, Serena falls in line behind Isadora. Her scales are as black as Serena's hair. As they leave the Great Hall, Isadora releases the scales along her shoulders and neck. The formal dress is not required out of court. Serena watches as Isadora's scales sink into pale white skin. There isn't a trace of blood as is common when other Undine retract their scales. Squinting closer, Serena can see a crisscross pattern of pinkish scars along her back and shoulders. It is the same pattern as her scales, as if she has done it so much, Isadora's skin is permanently marked.

Isadora flips her hair back behind her shoulder. The thick braid covers much of the scarring.

"You have never been to my chambers, your majesty?" Isadora asks, keeping her eyes forward as they walk deeper into the cave system.

"Just once, with my caste but other than that no, I…um, the necessity never rose. But I understand the king took your council."

"Some, but it was the queen that was always more open to my visions."

"Of course," says Serena.

"After my sister's death," Isadora continues, "the king saw me less and less. I think I reminded him too much of her…" Isadora trails off so Serena has to strain to hear the last few words. She parts the beaded curtain suspended from her door and gestures inside. "Please, let's talk."

Serena slides past Isadora, beads hitting her shoulders. The cave is dark and Serena stands in the middle as Isadora moves around lighting candles.

Serena watches the psychic closely, studying her features and movements for some glimmer of recognition for the mother she doesn't remember.

"Please, take a seat," says Isadora.

Serena chooses a stool made out of driftwood and sits. The wood is surprisingly smooth at the seat.

"Dulse?" Isadora holds out a bowl of craggy, copper-colored, sheets. "I am told you don't eat enough."

Serena stiffens then declines the food.

Shurgging, Isadora pulls up her own stool in front of Serena and they both take a seat, slowly. The bowl of dulse sits in between them. "Your hand, please."

"Why?" asks Serena, curling her fingernails into her palms.

"It is my way," says Isadora, holding out her own hand.

No wonder my father stopped seeing her, thinks Serena. Nonetheless, Serena extends her own hand. It is immediately enveloped in rough, scratchy palms as Isadora begins to pry and massage each of the grooves surrounding Serena's knuckles.

"As you know, twins are extremely rare in Society," says Isadora. "The ancients have always said twins are a sign of change—for better or worse. We made quite the splash in Society, your mother and I." Isadora smiles to herself, still kneading away at Serena's hands. "Once we twins were born, our family's status was elevated. Dad was on the king's council, himself. So when it came time for the pairing, of course your mother and I were top picks. King Merrick, who was allowed to choose a mate at any time, mind you, went straight for your mother..." Isadora trails off, her hands going still.

Serena waits a moment, then attempts to bring her back. "What about you? Didn't you end up with someone?"

Isadora's drifting eyes snap back to Serena. "Me?"

Serena nods.

"After your mother was paired with the king, not many bothered to ask about me."

"You didn't answer the question, Isadora."

"No, I didn't." Isadora begins kneading again, but her movements are jerky and the tugging on Serena's fingers borders on painful. "I was paired."

"But you didn't want to be," encourages Serena.

"Well, now who is the psychic here?"

"I'm sorry." Serena says. "But you said you'd answer all my questions."

"Yes, well." Isadora straightens her back. "My mistake." She folds her hands in her lap, sighing. "No I didn't want to be paired. In fact, I made it very clear during the Choosing Ceremony. But with one twin already spoken for, the males were very persistent. I eventually gave in—Adrian was his name." Isadora lifts her chin and straightens her back. "He's dead now."

Serena narrows her eyes. "Why didn't you want to mate?"

"That…is a question that no one else has bothered to ask, not even your mother." Isadora slumps. She reaches out to trace the rim of the dulse bowl with her fingertips, but doesn't attempt to eat any more than Serena does. "It was because I saw what would happen to our sons if we did. I saw what would happen to *my* son." Tears begin to swell up as she shakes her head. "I became with calfling, and it happened anyway. He is no longer with us."

"I'm sorry, Isadora. I can't imagine what it must feel like to lose a child."

Isadora runs a shaky hand across her eyes. "Not quite what it feels like to lose a parent, I can tell you that much."

Serena nods, conceding the point. "Hopefully, we will not let Cordelia experience the same. Have any visions come to you on her or her calfling's future?"

"Yes, as a matter of fact, they have." Isadora stands, folding her arms across her midsection, and walking away from Serena.

"Well?" prods Serena.

Isadora stops and looks over her shoulder. "It will be a difficult birth, Serena. And if not played out right, there is no future for her calfling."

Chapter Nine

After leaving the psychic's quarters, Serena doesn't have long to think about Isadora, or Cordelia, or complicated birthings. As soon as her shoulders cross the beaded curtain, Murphy, with two guards behind him, is at her side issuing orders.

"We need to convene the council," he says.

Serena turns on her heel, almost at the expense of getting run over by Murphy in the process. He stops short, but the pair are standing so close she has to crane her neck back to look him in the eye. "The council will be busy with their assigned missions," Serena responds. She pauses, considering which crisis he is actually referring to. "What is this about?"

"The note," he says.

"Oh…that," Serena waves a flippant hand in the air.

Taking a deep breath, Murphy pauses for a moment to calm himself. When he opens his eyes again, he steps back to lend space to Serena. "Apologies, your majesty, but in all my time serving the kingdom, no monarch has ever been so willing to put themselves in such danger."

"Then—"

"I cannot—I will not—allow that tradition to break while I stand guard," interrupts Murphy.

"I think—"

"The very idea is unfathomable," Murphy says, his voice loud. "When do you plan to even go?"

Serena's cheeks go hot with all the interruptions.

"Stand down, Murphy." Her words echo off the walls of the large, empty cavern, and the silence that ensues is even louder.

Serena is acutely aware that even the low whistle of the guards breathing behind him has ceased. "Please do not underestimate my understanding as to the gravity of the situation. We will work together on this, but if we want to help Cordelia, I must go to The Dry." Serena searches his eyes for some hint of comprehension. "She doesn't have much time left."

Murphy crosses his arms and raises his chin.

This isn't working, thinks Serena.

"I'm going to be honest with you, Murphy. The one thought running through my head right now is…how would the king have handled this situation?"

Murphy relaxes his stance a bit, his interest piqued.

"You know exactly what he would have done. He would have raised his voice, he would have slammed his trident into the ground, and he would have used every last ounce of his weight to push his agenda first."

Pausing for several seconds, Murphy gives the slightest nod, acknowledging the king's ruling style.

"But as you see, I don't have nearly the weight to throw around. And I will not bang my trident against the ground for fear it may actually hurt my wrist…"

Murphy smiles at this.

"…and I don't have the voice to scream and shout. Instead, they say I have my mother's voice—a singing voice."

The insides of his eyebrows lift in a small slip of grief at the mention of Serena's mother.

"There is one thing I do share with the king, and with you, even. The resolve to protect our people and ensure our survival. But I can't do that hiding away in caves." She takes a step closer to him, laying a gentle hand on his arm. "Let me do this, Murphy. Liam is my brother—I will be safe."

A moment more of silence and Murphy gives the slightest nod. "As you say, Serena." The informal name amidst the formal tone is not taken as an insult, but rather a sign of trust—like Liam's wolfsbane.

"Thank you," says Serena. "I will be standing by in the archives, waiting for Liam's rope when the time comes."

"But—"

"Shall we retire and converse on the subject after we've each had a chance to mull it over?" She turns her back to him, reveling at the opportunity to interrupt him. "I will need your guidance on this, Murphy."

"So be it." Murphy sighs, following her through the Great Hall to the small arched doorway leading to their joint quarters.

Murphy pauses in the Great Hall, giving assignments to the guardsmen and rotating their shifts.

Entering her chamber alone, Serena takes a deep breath to calm her nerves. Seeing Liam again will be somewhat of a welcome release. To her, both Liam and the forest have always represented freedom from The Deep. It is a notion needed now more than ever in her new position.

But what news will he give her? So far, Alaric has not allowed the Undine to even approach the beaches, despite the king's sacrifice. It makes King Merrick's last brave and selfless gift to his daughter completely null and void.

The thought boils around in Serena's head, heating her cheeks again. Her hands began to shake, aching for an outlet to release her anger, and her breathing grows ragged.

Stop it, Serena tells herself. *You can't make any good decisions in this state.* She takes another deep breath, laying her trident against the king's bed and sitting herself until her hands stop shaking.

There are only a few moments of privacy. All too soon, Serena can hear heavy, but hesitant footsteps coming down the short corridor to her chamber.

Murphy must be in a mood. But is he in a mood to apologize, or to fight?

She stands quickly, folding her hands behind her. When his shadow grows long into her room, she glances at the floor. "Murphy, I'm—"

Interrupted by a clearing of the throat, Serena looks up.

Kai stands in the entrance, not Murphy. His wide green eyes don't wander around the room and he remains still, one foot slightly behind as if he may turn and bolt from the room. One hand jitters at his side.

"Kai…" is the only word Serena can think to say. He's never been in the room before, at least not with her.

Finally, he turns, squaring his shoulders with hers and committing to his place. "I am here as designated by my new mission," he says. "It looks like we'll be spending a lot of time together."

As he says it, high tide hits and ankle deep water rushes in, bathing the floor in velvety blue ocean. It mutes the immensity of the empty room, drawing the pair closer together even though neither one moves.

"This is about as high as the water gets," Serena says, folding her arms over her mid-section. "It doesn't reach the top of the bed."

Lame, thinks Serena. She forces her hands down to her sides again.

Kai smiles, flashing white teeth behind full lips, and all Serena can think about is kissing them.

This is going to be so hard.

"So...scales not needed," he says. Before the sentence is finished, the first of the light brown armor he donned in The Dry is retracted from his neck and shoulders. Underneath, his skin is darker than Serena's, like he has been at the surface too long. His frame isn't as broad as Murphy's, but it is wrapped in sinewy muscle. Kai is the fastest and most agile guardsmen Serena knows—and she has seen them all in action.

He walks toward her, scales disappearing at a rapid rate, leaving behind a solid chest and a defined abdomen.

A trickle of salt water follows the chiseled clefts in his midsection. The scales are so low, Serena can see his hip bones as he passes her. She peers out from behind one of the rock columns at the corner of her sleeping area. Armor disappears up his ankles and calves, the muscle underneath gliding up and down like the stealthy, calculated movement of a shark.

Serena's mouth drops open, one hand squeezing the rock at her side. *This is going to be very, very hard.*

"Is this good?" Kai asks.

"Huh? What?" She has to tear her eyes away from his legs, the scales have retracted all the way past his knees.

"Here—this sleeping nook. Is it okay if I sleep here?"

It is the very one Serena chooses every night, but for some reason she can't bring herself to say that. Instead, she nods, still hiding half her body behind the rock column. Her mouth feels bone dry.

Resting his trident against the wall, Kai hoists himself up to the sleeping nook. Serena retreats altogether behind the column as he has his back turned. She can hear him slide the rest of the way into the nook.

"Have I scared you off? You still there?"

"Hmm," she manages to mumble.

"Well then, goodnight Serena Moon-Shadow, Queen of the Undine."

There is a short pause while she swallows, coaxing her vocal chords to work. "Goodnight," she manages to squeak without looking at him again. She sits on the bed she has never before slept on, her fingertips still scraping across the rock.

Serena's eyes shoot back to the entrance as Murphy walks in, tall and cocky. Barely slowing down, he nods in her direction with a sly smile. "Sleep well, you two."

She narrows her eyes, her hands itching to go for his throat. He did this on purpose—knowing sleep will be almost impossible for her. Murphy disappears into his adjoining chamber and Serena is again alone with Kai.

She scoots back on the bed, bringing her own trident with her. When she lies down, she keeps her eyes straight up, refusing to look at Kai until she has her breathing under control.

Instead, she stares at the etching of Poseidon who stares right back at her. She can't help but remember her time in prison. She feels like she is in prison now, or even worse than prison. She is under constant scrutiny. There are always eyes watching and they are more judgmental than Serena guesses Poseidon's ever were. Now with Kai in the room, she isn't even free to pace, nor to toss and turn in the oversized bed—not without having to answer his questions.

As the candles in the room begin to sputter out, one by one, Poseidon's eyes glow back at Serena. She would love to ask him some questions. *How would you deal with Alaric? Would he even dare betray you? If I sacrifice myself to the wolves, who would lead the Undine into The Dry when the ocean grows too poisonous for them?*

In the course of a never-ending list of worries running through her head, the minerals that make up Poseidon's eyes begin to twinkle. One eye more so than the other, so that it looks like the sea god is winking at her. Serena thinks of Arista, the other prisoner released when Cordelia helped Serena escape. Arista hasn't been seen or heard of since, though the guards have been searching when time allows.

Just add it to the list, Serena thinks, sighing and turning on her side. She curls into her trident, running her finger over where the three prongs are melded onto the stem.

"Do you always sleep with your weapon?"

Serena freezes, amidst her rambling thoughts she almost forgot Kai was there. It is difficult to discern his detailed features in the dimming light, but Kai is lying on his side looking at her, his shoulder rising and falling with slow, controlled breath. Slowly taking her hand from the trident and tucking it under her side, Serena bites her lip, hoping he can't tell she is doing it. "My weapon usually stands where yours does right now. I prefer sleeping in the smaller nooks; they remind me of home."

Kai pats the hard rock beneath him. "There is plenty of room still."

She can almost see the smile on his face.

"Not for me *and* the trident—which would definitely have to be in between us should we share the same nook."

Kai laughs out loud. It fades away and the room falls into a comfortable silence.

After a few minutes, Kai breaks it with a soft voice. "Why did you task me with guarding you—as my mission?"

"I didn't."

"Oh," says Kai, disappointment tingeing his remark.

"It was Murphy," Serena turns on her back, staring at Poseidon again. He reminds her of Murphy, all bulky muscle and chiseled features, but she doesn't see the allure that other Maidens do. "I think it might be him finally consenting to our union, or at least a step in that direction."

"Well…"

"Well what?" Serena asks.

"I might have had words with Murphy about it."

"What kind of words?" Serena props herself up on her elbow, staring at Kai.

"You know, heated…words."

"Kai! What did you tell him?" Serena knew all too well that if you pushed Murphy too hard in one direction, he'd push back ten times as hard.

Kai shrugs. "I just let him know I am reconsidering my position as Second in Command."

"What? Why?"

"I think it holds complications if we are ever to have an open relationship together. Anyway, he wasn't too happy about it."

"You'd give that up to be with me?"

Kai props himself up on one elbow too, looking at Serena. "Would you give up the crown for me?"

She almost laughs out loud. "Kai, if I could give up the crown, it would have been done not long after it was given to me. But for all the reasons to do it, you are at the top of the list."

More candles have flickered out, and now Serena can't see Kai at all. She nestles her head into the crook of her arm, scooting her trident close to her.

"You should name it," Kai says, so softly Serena can barely hear him.

She rests her hand gingerly over the stem of the weapon. "Did you name yours?"

"Yes, but…it's sort of personal."

"Okay, I'll think about it."

"And Serena?" asks Kai.

"Yes?"

"Stop biting your lip."

Chapter Ten

Serena tosses and turns most of the night. The combination of the oversized, unfamiliar bed of rock, and the cold weapon may have something to do with it, but she can't help but keep glancing over at Kai. He is very still through the night, almost annoyingly so.

Doesn't he at least snore? Serena thinks with contempt. *Oh no, do I snore?* She clamps her hand over her mouth as if a snore might escape any moment. Yet another reason not to fall asleep. Even so, exhaustion sets in and as the last of the tide trickles out, Serena drifts off to a restless sleep, dreaming of wolfsbane and walking, talking tridents.

Once she blinks her eyes open again, the candles are re-lit and the room is bathed in a soft light. She hears a shuffling behind her and her eyes fly open, darting to Kai's unoccupied nook.

"Don't worry, still here," he says from the other side of the room.

Serena sits up. "I wasn't worried, I was…" *hopeful.* But she doesn't say it out loud.

After lighting two more candles, Kai gestures to the end of the bed. "Rayne made us something to eat."

Yawning, Serena grabs her trident and scoots down to the end of the bed, next to a plate of food. Kai meets her, sitting down on the other side of the plate. His fingers pop as he stretches and yawns; he is not nearly as tense as Murphy always is around the bed.

Serena catches herself staring at his calves. They are scaled once again, and she isn't sure if she is relieved or disappointed.

"Eat," urges Kai.

Glancing down at the plate, Serena finds half of it is covered in salmon bits. *Oh no, is he going to try to force fish down my throat, like Rayne does?* "It's a lot."

Kai smiles, turning the plate so the fish is on his side and the vegetables are on hers. "We'll share, then."

Breathing a sigh of relief, Serena picks up a strip of agar-agar. The almost translucent strip of red algae turns to jelly in her mouth. Slightly sweet and a little salty, it is one of her favorite breakfast treats.

"Hungry?" Kai asks.

Serena glances down to find she has finished her side of the plate, but Kai is slurping up the last of the fish bits, too. "So…" he puts his arms behind him, leaning back on the bed. "What do you want to do now?"

Serena feels giddy. She runs the pad of her finger along the smooth edge of the plate. "I don't know. What do you want to do?"

He shrugs. "Well, the council is in the Great Hall, waiting for you."

"The council?!" Serena practically shrieks as she jumps from the bed. "Why didn't you say something?" She brings forward more scales so they climb up her neck right to her chin. Her formal garb for the Great Hall.

"You needed to eat," Kai furrows his eyebrows, confused, as if it is a silly question.

The jolt back to reality is annoying. A moment ago, the pair were acting as if they had an entire day ahead of them with endless possibilities. Now Serena needs to face the council and already someone is nagging about her eating habits.

"Do they know you are in here?" she asks.

"A few saw me walk in with the tray," Kai stands, handing Serena her trident and grabbing his own. "But you are my assignment now, so they might as well get used to it. Right?" He winks at her.

"Right," she says, squeezing her trident as a flutter moves from her stomach to her chest. "Just—try not to do that when I'm standing in front of them."

"Do what?" Kai asks, following her down the short tunnel to the Great Hall.

"You know very well what," Serena hisses back. His winks, smiles, and general gestures throw her off her game too easily.

"As you say, your—"

Serena gives a low, guttural grunt as a warning.

"I mean," corrects Kai, "Serena." He swoops around in front of her, causing Serena to stop short. Bending in a sweeping bow, he lifts her free hand and kisses her on the knuckles.

There, in the shadowed hallway between the Great Hall and the royal chambers, Kai presses his lips to Serena's hand gently, yet insistently. He runs his thumb over her knuckles then stands.

"There—that should get us through the day." Spinning on his heel, he steps into the light of the Great Hall and bellows. "Make way for the queen!"

It is completely unnecessary, as only the council stand in the Great Hall. Low mutters of conversation die down. Murphy openly rolls his eyes at Kai.

"Make way I said!" Kai yells at Hailey, who looks thoroughly confused, practically on the other side of the room.

She takes a step back anyway.

"Thank you, Kai," Serena says, coming up next to him. She lowers her voice, "if you'll just cut it out—now…"

"As you say." He doesn't smile, though she can see the humor in his eyes. The green shade almost twinkles with laughter.

She clears her throat, trying to keep her cheeks from flushing. "Good morning," she says to the council.

"Good morning, your majesty," they echo in disjointed harmony.

"Any urgent matters?" Serena asks, approaching the group.

"Each of the council members special missions have been announced to Society," says Nerin. "There is a general feeling of…concern as to why these assignments have taken place."

See, it's working already, thinks Serena. "Thank you, Nerin. I will address it directly with the people during next Assembly." Serena turns to Evandre and Sarafina. "Your report on the corals?"

Evandre remains silent, looking at Serena down her long nose.

Sarafina's mouth drops open. "A report? There's been no time. I haven't even been to see them yet—"

"Not been to see them?" Serena's eyes grow wide, and Nerin's spine goes stiff enough for the both of them. "What have you been doing?"

"As…as the head gardener, there are matters to oversee, food is growing scarce and—"

"Food is growing scarce because our corals are dying!" Serena slams her trident down on the rocky floor. The echo booms throughout the cave, reminding her of her father's temper. Most of the council shuddered when he brought the trident down.

This time, they do not.

Instead, they look at her with wide eyes and lips pressed tightly together.

Breathe Serena, she thinks. *You cannot rule with pure aggression.*

Closing then opening her eyes, Serena looks at Sarafina. "If you fail to reap food from the oceans, you'll need to start new gardens in The Dry. You can speak to Hailey and Rayne about which seeds you have to work with."

"Me? Go into The Dry? After all that's happened?" She asks, almost frantic. "How could I possibly be expected to make the journey enough to successfully grow a garden, and live to tell about it?"

Serena smiles. "Tell me Nerin, did the king hold a vote with the council on whether or not to name me Werewolf Liaison during The Choosing?"

"He did," Nerin folds her hands in front of her, looking at Sarafina.

"And may I venture to guess that Sarafina's vote was yes?"

Sarafina's eyes dart from Nerin to Serena, like a half moon perch evading a shark.

"It was," answers Nerin.

"And thus I will extend the same courtesy," says Serena. "It is your turn to give it a try."

"As you say, your majesty," Sarafina's voice is so tight, Serena swears she must be gritting her teeth.

"Any more reports?" Serena asks the rest of the group.

"You didn't ask the status of my assignment," Kai raises his hand, eyebrows lifted in an effort to look eager, but Serena can see the twinkle in his eye.

"As long as I am standing before you, alive and well, I give permission for you to omit your report, Second in Command."

"As you say, your majesty."

Out of the corner of her eye, Serena can see Sarafina purse her lips in a pout. Serena opens her mouth to say something, but Isadora interrupts.

"A word, your majesty?" asks Isadora.

Serena starts with Isadora suddenly by her side. "Oh, yes. Um, the council is adjourned."

Isadora motions to the side of the room. "As you may or may not know—depending on how studious you were during your divination sessions in school, positive energy is almost essential in foreseeing the future."

"Yes." Serena nods. "I remember something like that." During her visit to Isadora's cavern, Serena had been more interested in the various jarred substances on the shelves than in Isadora's lecture.

"Then you may remember that hydrocoral, the orange shade similar to the Sunbeam family color, is vital for dispersing negative energy."

Serena has seen the decline herself in the disintegration of the coral forests. There is barely any hydrocoral left, like the Sunbeam family.

"It makes it very difficult for me to foresee the future," Isadora's voice has gone high.

Serena turns her full attention to Isadora. Her long, slender fingers are as jittery as her voice.

Narrowing her eyes, Serena can see small wisps of hair escaping from Isadora's braids.

"Are you okay, Isadora?" Serena steps toward her, lowering her voice. The woman looks bone-tired and wrought with worry. For a moment, Serena feels a pang of loss for her mother. Sisterly empathy, wisdom, and support might just be what Isadora needs. Unfortunately, Serena doesn't do empathy very well.

"Me?" Isadora gives a nervous laugh. "Yes, child… er, your majesty. Please forgive me." Isadora bends to curtsey then hesitates, as if she is unsure it is the right thing to do.

Serena frowns, suddenly wishing she would have told Liam about Isadora, and that maybe she should tell Isadora about Liam. Just the knowledge that more family is out there might make all the difference.

Isadora finally decides to complete the awkward curtsey. She takes a deep breath, smoothing black scales down her midsection. "To be honest, hydrocoral is also used in the transformation potion. Which may or may not be needed directly after Cordelia's labor."

Serena nods. "Let me speak with Hailey, and see how much time we have. We'll come up with a solution."

If it were up to Serena, no transformations will ever take place again. But if the newborn calflings are dying, there might not be a choice.

"Thank you, your majesty. Time is of the essence, of course." She puts her fingertips of one hand to her temple. "Time grows short for everyone. As you know, the full moon—and your eighteenth birthday—

are within the week. It is Alaric's deadline. Do you think he will honor the deal, then?"

Tiny, iridescent scales along Isadora's black body armor emerge, then disappear just as quickly. It is a sign of stress, the body's natural reaction to ward away danger. Serena is able to see her own image reflected in Isadora's scales, her black hair is the same shiny color. A disjointed thought about the colors that run within families comes to Serena. Sometimes it is obvious, like the Sunbeam family and their bright orange scales. Sometimes it is more subtle, the color transferring as with Isadora's scales and Serena's hair. But no one else carries the inky black they do. Serena hasn't seen it anywhere else except…a cautionary thought nags at Serena. She has seen the black in another place, a place where it didn't seem to belong because it is surrounded by brown—the light brown color indicative of males in both Undine…and werewolves.

Alaric.

Serena gasps, stumbling back. "You…you…you're," Serena points her finger at Isadora.

Look for the one called Alaric. I must know about him.

Heads turn toward them, and Kai and Murphy are standing beside Serena before she takes her next breath. "You're his…" she manages to stutter out again.

"His mother," Isadora finishes for her. She has finally stopped jittering, her shoulders sagging.

Kai and Serena exchange glances. "You said your child is dead," says Serena.

She shakes her head. "I said he is no longer with us."

Sinking to her knees, Serena presses her hand to her mouth. *If Alaric is Isadora's son, then that makes him my cousin.* She shakes her head.

"Your majesty?" Someone calls out and Serena feels hands lifting her back to her feet, supporting her wavering stance.

My cousin, she thinks again. *And the king's nephew. His own nephew murdered him.* A wave of anger and nausea slide through her stomach. "Isadora is Alaric's mother. Put her under guard. She must be watched at all times."

Murphy and Kai move toward Isadora, large hands grasping above her elbows.

"No," Isadora shakes her head, putting up her hands. "I mean, yes I'm his mother, but it's not like I support what he does." Desperation spills from her voice.

"Don't...don't put her in the prison," says Serena.

Kai and Murphy loosen their grips on Isadora, but don't let go completely.

"Just watch her. You are confined to your quarters, Isadora."

The guards guide Isadora out of the Great Hall, her black scales flashing one last time. Another wave of nausea washes through Serena.

"Maybe you should come to my quarters," Hailey offers, approaching Serena.

"No," says Serena. "I'm okay," she glances at Hailey.

Hailey glances to the archway in which Isadora disappeared, surrounded by guards. "I've said it before, that woman always seemed a bit...off..."

Hailey trails off under Serena's gaze. "No offense, your majesty."

"None taken," Serena closes her eyes, thinking of Alaric. *My cousin.* "Apparently everyone in the family is a bit off."

Hailey clears her throat and runs her palms down scales on her midsection, but refuses to acknowledge Serena's comment.

Time to change the subject. "While we're here, why don't you fill me in on the progress of your mission."

"As a matter of fact, Zayla and I examined Cordelia yesterday." Hailey lowers her voice. "She is showing signs of going into labor prematurely."

Serena bites her lip. "How soon?"

"She is due two full moons from now. The first, as you know, is in four days. She will surely drop but there is always a possibility she will go into labor early.

Hailey's words press down on Serena and the pressure is worse than when bottoming out in The Deep. "And if that happens?" asks Serena. "The chances that the calfling will survive?" Serena is careful not to use the plural form, she doesn't want to reveal just yet that Cordelia has a difficult labor ahead of her.

Hailey hesitates before speaking. "Not very good for the calfling or the mother. It would just be too soon."

"We've been working round the clock on some medicines and such to help," says Hailey. "But if we had some wolfsbane seeds, we could try to recreate the transformation just in case. Of course, Isadora knows the recipe for the potion better than anyone else," Hailey adds, keeping her gaze solidly on the wall behind Serena's shoulder.

Serena sighs. "Well, as she is confined to her quarters, she'll have nothing but time to work on it."

The Great Hall empties of everyone but Serena and Hailey. The guards are no doubt busy working out how to add Isadora to their already overbooked shifts.

Serena turns to leave. "Let me know if Isadora becomes uncooperative."

"Are you going to the dining hall?" asks Hailey.

Serena suspects it is more of a suggestion than anything else. She furrows her eyebrows. "No, I have a meeting."

"A meeting?"

"At the archives," says Serena, walking away.

It   isn't   a   complete   lie.

Chapter Eleven

The sky is clear, and the surface of the ocean calm. Serena can tell by how far the moon's light pierces into The Deep. She cuts through the rays, well aware that she may have missed Liam's rope by now—it is well past moonrise.

Twisting through the narrow tunnel toward the entrance to the archives, Serena tries to bury Isadora away in her thoughts. She rockets through the space where Kai stopped to kiss her. Serena swears she can still taste him on the bubbles nipping at her mouth. This time, when Serena breaks the surface at the entrance pool, she leaps so high she can place her entire palm against the cavern's ceiling. A giant splash, then she surfaces again, nose breaking the surface first.

Smiling, Serena dons her boots and robe and walks into the archives. Two of the guards stand waiting for her with Cordelia next to them. Neither Murphy or Kai are anywhere to be seen.

"Cordelia," Serena says, startled. "I didn't realize you'd be here."

"She never left, Serena." Mariam says, gesturing to the werewolf book. "She's still reading."

"Have you eaten anything?" Serena asks Cordelia, trying not to glance at her growing midsection and estimating how much bigger it will get.

Nodding, Cordelia glances at Mariam. "She's making sure I take care of myself."

"Yeah, she's good at that," Serena says, her lips tipping up in a smile at Mariam.

"And you, your majesty?" Mariam asks. "When was the last time you ate?"

Serena shakes her head, looking up at the narrow skylight above them. "The fate of my next meeting may very well depend on the size of my waistline." Before Mariam can comment further, Serena turns to the guards. "Has Kai or Murphy been here yet?"

"No, your majesty," says one as they both come to attention. "Murphy and Kai, along with a number of other guards will be in The Dry, standing by for your meeting."

"They may be waiting awhile. I very well could have missed my ride already."

A thick rope uncoiling from above hits Serena on the shoulder.

The guards raise their eyebrows, almost in sync.

Serena sighs as the rope swings slightly back and forth in front of her. "I guess I didn't." She looks up, grabbing the rope and giving it a slight tug. "Well, if I'm not back in an hour, don't come after me."

"Serena, wait!" Cordelia steps forward.

All eyes turn to her, and for a moment, she looks sheepish. Serena can barely place her as the most popular Undine in their caste a year ago, confidant and social. "I mean to say…be careful, your majesty."

Serena nods her head, understanding Cordelia's fears. Right now, Serena is the only person that might be able to negotiate a safe birthing event for Cordelia.

"Always am," says Serena, with a quick smile at Mariam. It used to be Mariam sending words of caution before Serena went into The Dry.

"Did Murphy or Kai say where they would be out there?" Serena asks, handing over her trident.

One of the guards shakes his head, tentatively taking the royal weapon. "No, they just said they'd remain concealed."

"Let's hope so," Serena mumbles, looking up at the rope. Placing both hands directly above a thick knot level with her face, she pulls to test its sturdiness. The rope responds; it is yanked upward with Serena dangling from the end. Serena considers letting go but Cordelia, the guards, and the books are well below her within a matter of seconds.

Instead, Serena takes a deep breath, steeling herself for the narrow shaft above her. Her heart pounds so loudly she can hear it in her ears. There is no time to debate whether this is a trap or not. Her elbow bumps the mirror reflecting sunlight down into the archives, and as the opening of the rocky tunnel first scratches at Serena's shoulders, she can hear the mirror shatter on the ground below.

Sorry, Mariam.

Moonlight blossoms across Serena's face, and she releases the rope. She stops the inevitable fall by forcing her hands and feet against hard rock. Sharp divots shred their way into Serena's palms. She still slides down and a grunt escapes her lips as she pushes outward even harder. She finally comes to a stop just as her heels touch the end of the tunnel. There are at least a hundred feet between her and the next hard surface.

"Okay!" Serena yells down, already her body is shaking with exertion. The whistle of her weapon glides through the air. She leans to one side, allowing the trident to pass through. It sails through the opening and into the starry night. When she hears the three pikes strike the dirt, Serena climbs again. The chasm narrows at the top and she latches onto fist-size grips jutting out of the walls. Dirt and debris fall away as she scrambles the rest of the way up. When her next reach hits feathery-light shrubbery instead of rock hard wall, Serena heaves herself into The Dry, inhaling a breath of musky, fog-laden air.

"Nice robe."

Serena turns at the voice behind her. "Hello, Liam of Clan Werich." Pausing, the ends of her mouth turn down in a frown. "May I have my trident back?"

Part II

Liam

Chapter Twelve

Liam wakes to the smell of stale beer and blood. He lies still, enduring the scents crawling around the room several minutes before he cracks open his eyes. A small bag full of thick, crimson liquid hangs next to his bed. The tube running from the bag to his arm ushers the blood away, separating it from Liam's veins.

He sits up, cursing. Another few minutes and the bag would be full.

What would happen then? Overflowing, a reverse process, dangerous air bubbles in my blood stream...I don't know but I don't want to find out, either.

Fingertips scraping across the gritty floor, Liam's hand closes around a clamp, picking it up and using it to pinch the tube closed. The last of the blood trickles into the bag, then the tube goes clear. Swinging his booted feet off of the bed, Liam closes his eyes and grimaces as he withdraws the needle from his vein. One slow breath, and it is out.

A small spurt of red trickles down the inside of his arm. He stands, a wave of blackness threatening to overtake him. The room rolls in front of him. Dirty dishes in the sink, curtains drawn tight against his tiny trailer windows, and empty beer bottles littering the floor. Liam steadies himself against the flimsy wall.

His boot hits something, and a sealed bag of blood slumps over.

As his head clears, he glances at three more small sacks of his blood.

Alaric went too far this time.

By all accounts, Liam should not be standing. But his body adjusts well to the lack of sanguine fluid.

Is it because of the wolf inside, or because I've been doing this for almost a year?

Unhooking the most recent bag from the hanger on the wall, Liam walks to the sink, tempted to dump it out. He pauses, considering it, but Alaric would just make him endure the torture all over again. Instead, he removes the other end of the tube from the bag and seals it shut. He throws a jacket on and collects the rest of his blood donations.

The trailer door swings shut behind him as he leaves. The nights are getting colder, and his breath hangs in the air in front of him like an ominous mist. Walking past the other trailers in the park as quickly as he can, Liam ducks his head, keeping his mouth tucked into his jacket.

He tolerates Alaric because he has to. He is bound to the clan, and can't seem to go further than a few miles before feeling stretched too tight, like he might rip right through the middle if he doesn't return. Having tried leaving on several occasions, he knows the feeling all too well.

Only two more sets of a trailers to go. He'll drop the box in front of Alaric's door, then will be free to head to the bowling alley down the road. It is his only true escape from Alaric's rule. Even though Alaric's henchmen go there whenever they aren't on duty, Liam can hide away in the kitchen.

Working hard to lighten his steps and go unnoticed, Liam even holds his breath as he slinks up to the trailer. He sets the shoebox of blood bags down silently and turns his back on it. The shadows of the trees beyond reach out to him, beckoning for Liam to move faster. He lifts his head in response, practically stretching out his neck as if when even his nose touches the darkness he'll be free from the trailer park.

"Liam," growls a voice behind him.

Liam stops short, resisting the urge to hunch his shoulders. Already he can feel wiry hairs prick their way through skin at the base of his neck. Turning, Liam nods his head. "Alaric."

"Goin' somewhere?" Alaric asks.

Light from the trailer blares out from behind Alaric, and Liam has to squint to make out the features on the clan leader's face. Ever since the King's Massacre, Alaric keeps tabs on the camp and everyone in it, regulating their schedule almost like a prison.

"I can hear you grindin' your teeth," says Alaric.

"I'm goin' to work," says Liam, making a concerted effort to relax his jaw. "It's on the schedule, and I'm not on patrol tonight."

"Well if you ain't on patrol…" Alaric smirks, his teeth flashing white. "You have time to talk." He gestures to the door swinging open on the trailer.

"A few minutes," Liam mumbles as he walks past Alaric.

Alaric snarls at Liam's brush-off. Of all the members in the clan, Alaric has the least amount of control over his anger, and therefore his wolf.

Alaric picks up the shoebox of Liam's blood and throws it on the small kitchen counter. Inside, Liam's nose crinkles with the smell of old pizza boxes. The trailers are old and musty anyway, several of the clan members sleep outside when the weather is fair.

"Beer?" asks Alaric, reaching into the darkened door of his refrigerator; the light bulb has burned out.

Liam leans against the sink, crossing his arms. "Work, remember?"

"Oh, come on. All anyone does there is drink. Besides, you need to replenish." Alaric throws him a bottle.

Liam leans to the side as it grazes his cheek, catching the bottle with a solid grip.

"I go there so the clan can take half my paycheck, and so the Canadian government can take the other half."

Alaric shrugs, taking a large gulp of his own beer. "Someone has to make money for the clan; most of us are out there every night patrollin' the beaches."

"Or I don't know," Liam turns away looking out a window up at the moon. "We could not patrol the beaches."

Alaric snorts. "What? And give those split tails full run of them, just so they can make more fish head babies and abandon half of them for us to inherit? Think of how many shifts you would have to work to feed all those mouths."

Liam rubs his temples. Alaric's scenarios make no sense, but it is useless to tell him that. After spending the past five years arguing with him, Liam doesn't want to waste his time any more.

"Why did you call me in here, Alaric?" he asks.

Alaric takes another drink, staring at Liam over the cold glass bottle. "I want you to talk to the girl; I have a message for her."

"I don't think the girl wants anything to do with me—she'll never trust me again, not after what you did to their king."

"She doesn't have to trust you, Liam. Just find a way to deliver a message."

Liam considers Alaric. "What's the message?"

"The offer still stands. The girl for the beaches. I want the debt fulfilled."

Mouth dropping open, Liam stutters. "I—but…the king sacrificed his life. The debt has been repaid."

Alaric's lips curl up in a cruel smile. "Hardly."

Liam feels his eyes go wide. *This man is never gonna stop.*

"Listen," Alaric reaches in for another beer, popping the lid open against the counter. "Them sea hippies are in a bind. One of them is preggers, and they need a beach to give birth. Why they can't do it anywhere else is beyond me."

Liam grits his teeth again. He has already explained it to Alaric several times.

"Anyway," Alaric continues, "Serena is in a position to negotiate. She's taken over for daddy."

"How do you know all this?" Liam asks. As he says it, movement at the back of the trailer catches his eye.

Alaric follows his gaze. When he looks back at Liam, he is smiling. "A mermaid traitor."

Liam's nostrils flare, picking up a scent that has been there all along. The smell of the sea is unmistakable. How did he not notice? "Who is it?"

"Names ain't important. For now we can call her…chum."

Yep, I definitely need to speak to Serena.

Liam downs the rest of his beer in one large gulp and throws the bottle back at Alaric. He has to move just as Liam did to dodge the bottle.

Alaric catches it with one hand, not bothering to hide the grimace on his face.

"I'll deliver your message," says Liam, heading for the door. "Don't send any of your goons to follow. There won't be any negotiations if we scare her off at the first meeting."

"Wouldn't dream of it."

Liam pauses, one hand on the door. "I'm serious, Alaric."

Holding his arms up innocently, Alaric smiles. "Hey, this is your rodeo. I'm hands off."

"Give me a few days to figure out how to do this," Liam says. "I'll let you know. Enjoy the blood."

Chapter Thirteen

Outside, Liam heads in the opposite direction of the bowling alley. He flips open his cell phone and calls work.

"Hey—tell Connor I'll be a little late tonight."

"How late?" The voice on the other end of the line sounds agitated. "Danny is shooting his mouth off again about the clan to a human."

Liam sighs. He has broken up plenty of conversations where a pack member is trying to reveal who he really is, especially after several too many drinks. Usually the humans who are listening are just as drunk as the member so nothing ever comes of it. "Just give him a couple free games of bowling. Set him up at the far end with someone else from the pack so they keep to themselves."

"Should I report it to Alaric?"

"No!" Liam runs his hand through his hair, silently chastising himself for the outburst. "I mean, I'll take care of it with Alaric." Liam used to report the incidents, but after members showed up the next day with bruises, black eyes, and broken bones, Liam keeps it to himself. It was the first small step to earning the trust of some in the pack.

Liam flips the phone closed before the voice on the other end can argue. Shoving it in his back pocket, Liam heads in the opposite direction of the bowling alley. He'll only get a few hours on his timecard tonight, but Liam doesn't want to wait and give Alaric a chance to follow him to Serena. *Better to take care of it now, when Alaric isn't expecting it.* As Liam walks, he digs in his jacket pocket for a pen and paper. He scribbles out a short note, careful about what he says.

Keeping his ears perked for other wolves in the area, Liam slows until he is sure he isn't being followed. The closer he gets to the water, the stronger the smell becomes; salt and sand, wet rocks and damp earth. It reminds him of the traitor Undine in Alaric's trailer.

The note crumples in his clammy hand, and he keeps checking to make sure his sweat isn't smearing the writing. He walks all the way to the cliffs—to the very spot where he shifted in front of Serena. He will never erase the look on Serena's face from his mind. He can still feel his fangs pushing their way through his gums, see his own blood dripping on her shoulders and face. Watching her eyes go wide and her pupils dilate with fear only increased his urge to let the wolf loose. He remembers a blow to his gut, then flying through the air. He blacked out after that; he doesn't even recall the landing. But he woke up on the same cliffs with the rising sun and a splitting headache.

From then on, Serena had no reason to trust him. *I wouldn't trust myself either, stupid.* He shakes his head. *I lost control as easily as Alaric does.*

He pauses at the edge of the cliff, looking out over the ocean. He's been here many times since, listening for Serena's call. But after the King's Massacre, the death of their King—of her father, of *his* father—Serena disappeared into The Deep, the one place Liam cannot follow.

The pull of the ocean teases him forward, a powerful force. Now he wonders if the pull never really was the ocean—maybe it was his sister, Serena, all along.

Liam considers bottling the note and tossing it out into the waves. But there would be no guarantee Serena would end up with it. It could be intercepted by any Undine—or even the traitor.

What is the one place Serena is guaranteed to be? Finally, it comes to him. Liam turns with a smile, heading for the same place he planted the shrub over the archive sun shaft in order to lure her out all those moons ago.

* * *

After delivering the note, Liam still cannot bring himself to go straight to the bowling alley. Though it is escape enough from the trailer park, plenty of the clan will be there. Stinking of stale beer and sweaty clothes, loud and drunk members barely keep the secret of the clan under wraps.

Trudging through the forest, Liam zigzags around larger trees, brushing away the flora that snags on his clothes if he gets too close. It would be much easier to traverse the forest as a wolf, but he doesn't have the heart to change tonight. A clearing in front of him opens, giving Liam the impression of a black hole. Charred flowers lie in clumps on the ground, their bright yellow coloring forever muted by several gallons of gasoline and one match. Though the smell of ash has long since been washed away by the rains, even the trees surrounding the patch remain burnt on one side.

No longer afraid of the former wolfsbane patch, Liam cuts straight through it. What is left of the flowers is crushed beneath his boots. He would never have come to know Serena as well as he did had she not had the protection of the small, yellow flowers. He recalls their short conversations, Serena surrounded by layer after layer of the poisonous blossoms.

Lashing out with his foot, he kicks through a pile of mush. "Damn it!" he yells to himself. *How did it all go so wrong?* He set out to unite the two species, but only managed to drive them further apart.

Hands on his hips, chest heaving in anger, Liam looks down at the wilted, blackened ground. Sprung free from his outburst, a tall yellow flower stands straight up, several bell-shaped blooms hanging from one stem. A dim glow of hope burns in Liam's chest and he takes off his plaid shirt and bends to pluck the flower from the ground. It is fully grown; the petals hiding away the secrets to the next of its generation. Liam wraps the flower gingerly and moves across the rest of the dead patch, a spring in his step.

A half an hour later he emerges from the trees and peers out at a small, wooden shack, the ocean practically lapping at its door. A thin stream of smoke rises cautiously from the chimney.

The old man is home.

Liam perks his ears. The fire is going inside but there is no subtle whine of electronics. No radio, no dishwasher, not even a space heater. The old man lives simply, but not even the clan resists modern amenities. Liam taps lightly at the door. Loose on its hinges, it rattles against the frame.

No answer.

Pulling open the screen door, Liam tries the handle of the large wooden door, the brass tinged with cold. He steps inside, closing the door behind him. Squinting his eyes, Liam scans the dark room. Only the faint glow of the fire on one side of the large living room lends light. A glint of metal to the side of the fire catches his eye.

"You know we can see in the dark, right?" Liam asks. "But even if we couldn't, that rifle is reflectin' light from the fire."

A form steps forward and the muzzle lowers.

"That you, Liam? You scared me half to death."

Judging from the shaky steps the old man takes toward his armchair, and the score of wrinkles sagging off his skin like he has been in the water far too long, death very well could be knocking at his doorstep next.

"You need to keep this place warmer, Cecil." Liam walks over to the fire, throwing another log on to stoke it.

"Can't." The old man pulls a blanket over him and coughs, spittle flying from his mouth until he is out of breath.

Liam waits until the coughing fit subsides. "You sick?"

"Don't know," he says, wiping his mouth with the back of his hand. "This town ain't got any doctors worth a damn."

Snorting, Liam throws another log on the fire. "Wouldn't know."

The wolves can't risk seeing a doctor and being exposed for what they are. The only form of medical care they have is Darcy, an outsider who married into the clan. She is the only human Alaric has ever allowed, probably thanks to her nursing degree, and to the fact she has given birth to a werewolf pup. The family has three of them running around now; they are the only pups since Liam was born and deposited on Cecil's docks.

"Quit wastin' all my wood!" barks Cecil.

Liam raises an eyebrow. "You know, for a human you growl pretty well."

"I can't go out scouring for wood—my hip don't work right in this cold," Cecil says, tightening the blanket around his shoulders.

"I'll bring you some," Liam brushes his hands off on his pants.

"The less you come around here, the better. I don't want that Alaric followin' you. Don't trust him, ever since he burnt down that bane patch. Could smell it from—" Cecil cuts off at another coughing fit.

"If Alaric is comin', he'll come. Hiding out in the dark with a gun pointed at the door ain't gonna to stop him." Liam walks around the room switching on lights and turning on the only space heater the old man has. "You got any tea?"

Cecil snorts. "Tea? I ain't no old woman. Grab them beers out of the cooler."

Liam smiles, rubbing the stubble on his chin as he makes his way past worn furniture and piles of magazines to the kitchen. Turning a full circle twice in the small kitchen and not spotting the cooler, he opens the fridge. Inside it is dark and there is no cold blast of air, but a small cooler sits on one of the shelves. After retiring as a fisherman from the swamps of Louisiana, Cecil came up to Canada to start his scuba business. The southern accent he still maintains has transferred to the wolves he raised, and is a constant reminder that the old man isn't from around here; it's one reason why Liam enjoys his company so much.

Pushing inside the cooler, Liam digs through the ice. "Don't your customers stay with you here, like, for a whole week at a time?"

"Who do you think I'm savin' on electricity for?"

"Maybe you need to raise your rates," Liam says, popping the tops off the bottles against the kitchen counter. He hands a beer to Cecil.

"Trust me, I have. I keep it primitive and expensive. The trips below are dull, yet still they come," Cecil says and takes a swig of beer, a bit of it dribbling down his chin.

Liam shifts a pile of scuba gear and take-out trash to one side of the couch. A plume of dust and dirt puffs out as he sits. "Seems to me you might not be up for scuba divin' for too much longer."

"Ha," Cecil snorts. "Haven't been below in ages. I got a couple interns that take them—though I still create the dive plans. Someone has to make sure no one gets too close to them mermaids."

"Do the interns know?"

Cecil shakes his head. "No, been hoping one of them shows an open mind, that I might pass my role on, but so far no luck."

"Well, there haven't been any close calls, so far as I know."

"Except your girl, there—Serena—is making it harder. Used to be I could count on the full moon to tell me to stay away from the beaches and out of the water. From what you tell me, she don't exactly play by the rules."

"No, she doesn't," Liam says, leaning back on the couch. He can't decide if he is proud of the fact, or annoyed.

"Not that I'd mind runnin' into one or anything. Them creatures kind of remind me of the bayou. But, it ain't just the divin' I have to worry about. I have connections with the town council that keeps other scuba divin' companies from doing business here and keeps the fishin' to a minimum. Those connections won't be so willin' to do favors for a nineteen-year-old intern."

For the first time, Liam can spot lines of worry on Cecil's forehead through all the wrinkles. "I have a guy—good with people and good with politics. He's trustworthy. Why don't you start introducin' us to those people. Maybe we can help out there."

Cecil looks at Liam for a long time, gritting his teeth. His breath whistles in and out over his dry, cracked lips. Finally, he leans back in his chair, pulling the blanket up higher under his chin.

"I've kept the secrets of these waters and these woods for so long..." He shakes his head. "It's my life's work—besides the scuba business. I don't want someone to screw it all up."

"Cecil—"

The old man holds up a hand, cutting Liam off. "I suppose if anyone is capable of keepin' your secrets, it would be one of your own."

A long silence passes, the sizzling and popping fireplace making the only sound. Cecil is smiling to himself.

"What?" Liam asks, looking into his empty beer bottle.

"It's just, I remember you—you were my last. They left you at the end of my pier. One night after the full moon as they always did. I still check, you know. Just in case."

Liam's grip grows tight around his bottle at the story of his abandonment.

Cecil continues anyway, eyes drifting up, lost in his memories. "For some reason, you seemed special to them. And no wonder, if you were the last."

"Why...did I seem special?" Liam keeps his eyes pinned to the bottle, but his fingertips move up to the crescent moon-shaped birthmark on the side of his face.

"Because," Cecil leans forward, eyes glittering with sudden life. "The king delivered you. The king! I saw him myself—my first and last full grown mermaid, uh, merman—"

"Undine," Liam mumbles.

Cecil doesn't hear. "Only one I ever saw. He had it all. The crown, the trident. Like a Greek God." Cecil leans back sighing. "He watched me, from a distance. Made sure I wrapped you up, took you inside. All night, as your tiny, fragile body endured the transformation from the potion they had already given you, I heard him out there. Oh, he was quiet alright. But the surfacing and diving back under was constant. He seemed so agitated that I expected a trident to come sailing through the window and straight at my head any moment."

"Has he been back since?" asks Liam.

"No," Cecil says, raising a knobby finger at Liam. "You were his son, weren't you?"

Liam nods slowly. "Just found that out, myself." There are a few more moments of silence while Liam works past the lump in his throat to speak. "He's dead now."

"How?" Cecil lifts his eyebrows in surprise.

"Alaric."

A low, guttural growl emits from the old man. "That low-down son-of-a-bitch! I knew he was sour from the moment I laid hands on him. He was the first I discovered. I picked him up at the end of the pier, stayed up with him all night and watched him transform. That very morning I walked to the water, makin' a promise to a calm sea that I'd watch over him—and you know what he did?"

"What?"

"He threw up on me—right after I made that promise!"

Liam's eyes go wide, and a laugh escapes his throat.

"It wasn't funny! That boy was a hellion growin' up. Havin' raised him myself, you'd have thought he'd turn out better." Cecil looks at Liam with serious eyes, then finishes off his own beer. "Ran off when he was fourteen. I'd thought I'd seen the last of him. And didn't mind so much as I had two other boys to look after by then. Five years later, he came for them, too. I woulda put up a fight, but my business had taken a turn for the worse, and well, you know…"

"Yeah." Liam says, leaning forward in his chair to set his own empty bottle on the floor.

"Should have kept you, though," Cecil murmurs, starting to drift off to sleep.

Liam stands, taking the empty bottle from Cecil. "No—it was better that Alaric raised me. Otherwise I wouldn't have the first clue on how to bring him down."

Cecil snorts. "You just be careful, you hear me son?"

"I hear you," Liam says, retrieving the two empty bottles and setting them on the counter next to a dozen others. He tries changing the subject. "Liam, Alaric, Connor—what's with all the Irish names, anyway?"

Cecil pulls a blanket over his legs, nestling his head back into a cushion. "My nana was from Ireland—straight off the boat and into the swamps…"

The fire begins to smolder out, but Liam pushes back a pile of magazines sitting too close to it anyway. By the time he walks outside, closing the door softly behind him, the old man is snoring.

Chapter Fourteen

Clouds roll over the moon, giving it a hazy, silver glow. Liam's beast stretches beneath his skin. It hasn't been out for a while now, and needs a release. The birthmark on the side of his face burns, reminding him what Alaric told him once:

Seems you have a special affinity with the moon.

Liam will never forget those words. They are seared into his brain, the same way his birthmark sears him each time he shifts. It hadn't taken long for Alaric to discover Liam could shift at will, without the full moon and without any Undine fear induced pheromones permeating the air.

But it wasn't until Alaric began injecting Liam's blood into other wolves, that Liam had started building his own, secret army—one that would eventually take Alaric down. After just a few doses, Alaric had a dozen wolves that could change at will. It does not bode well for the clan, for the Undine, or for anybody.

Just thinking about it causes a few spiky hairs to emerge along the back of Liam's neck. They cut through his skin like the dirty needles Alaric injects into Liam's forearms.

The bowling alley will survive without me a little longer, Liam thinks. *I need to run.*

Just as he gives himself permission, the burning sensation fire-balls out from his scar and onto his scalp, chest, and legs; it envelopes his entire body then sinks in until even his bones combust in the inferno. Liam can barely feel his bones stretching and popping behind the searing pain blazing throughout his cells.

Lifting his chin to the moon and clawing at his own skin, Liam rides the tidal wave cresting into insurmountable agony. At the apex of the swell, when Liam swears he can reach up and touch the moon, blackness takes over.

Not but a few seconds later, the werewolf opens his eyes, and it is Liam stretching underneath the skin, cautioning the animal when necessary, and pulling back on the beast when he can.

Liam always had more control over his wolf form than others exhibited. If it weren't for Alaric playing the role of the Alpha and keeping them in line, the others would run rampant every full moon. But Liam never needed Alaric's orders to act as a governor; he simply chose to follow the pack leader.

Not wishing to jar the old man from his sleep, nor attract any undue attention, Liam chokes back the howl rising up from his chest. Instead, he runs.

Ears perked, he begins with a slow gallop. His padded feet fall like dominos on the soft earth, one right after another. His tongue lashes out. The one habit Liam can't seem to break as a wolf is the constant licking of his nose. He doesn't understand the urge to keep it wet, yet he continues to do it. It is as necessary as breathing and he swears he can taste snot for days after.

He sniffs the air, sensing a clear path ahead and picking up speed. The wind whips against him, pulling at his fur. Though his whole body is covered with it, the hair is thicker around his chest, neck, and head—like a lion's mane. The pelt around his midsection and upper legs is slicked back and lies flat against his skin.

The forest grows thick with trees and Liam darts around them, zigzagging his way toward the higher cliffs. The thick smell of brine and salt drifts past Liam's nose, as though the ocean itself has stepped into the forest. Digging his yellowed claws into the earth, he skids to a stop and turns, sniffing the air. It isn't just any Undine, it is the traitor he smelled at the back of Alaric's trailer.

Liam pulls his lips back in a snarl and his ears flatten against his skull. Strong haunches sink to the ground then shoot forward like a spring, propelling Liam toward the smell. In an instant, the prey's heartbeat quickens and it is running in the opposite direction. Fear permeates the air, overpowering the odor of brine and salt and Liam relinquishes rein to his wolf.

The beast runs faster, saliva dripping off his fangs in anticipation of a kill.

No wonder we turned against the Undine, Liam thinks inside. *After we ran off all the humans and wildlife, there was nothing else to play with.*

When he catches sight of bioluminescent hair whipping behind a tree, a new burst of energy rockets down his body. The beast closes the distance quickly. When the Undine maiden is in full view, he squares off his shoulders. Thick muscles go tense and his almond eyes blink once. Head down, he leans back then jumps forward. Leaping through the air with claws extended in front of him, Liam stretches his neck out, mouth wide.

The maiden jumps up, latching onto a tree branch above. The beast's fangs scrape against scaled legs, just enough to get one teasing taste, then her feet are hoisted up into the tree. Before the wolf hits the ground, he tucks. Liam slams into the Earth, spraying dirt and dead leaves all around him.

Growling, the wolf flips to his feet, but Liam pulls back on his beast before he attempts to leap again. He is trying to comprehend the maiden's speech. Only she isn't speaking, Liam realizes with a grimace. She is laughing.

He stalks around the tree, his sinewy muscles still tense, waiting to pounce. The maiden moves as he does, keeping her face in the recessed shadows of the tree. Liam can't even get a good sense of what color her scales are.

"Is this how the Werewolf Liaison eluded you?" asks the maiden.

You mean the queen, Liam thinks, another snarl pulling at his lips.

The maiden takes a bold step forward. "If anything happens to me, dog, Alaric will not be pleased. I am too valuable to him right now."

Liam lunges, clawing at the bark of the tree to get higher. He roars, snapping his jaws at her feet, just inches from them.

She gasps, and crawls higher into the tree. She is on another branch by the time Liam thumps into the ground again. He regains his footing, stalking around the tree furiously as he listens to her heartbeat settle, resuming a steady beat.

"How about this," she yells down. "I know how to get to your precious Serena. Unless you leave right now, I will go straight to her and make you wish you never met me."

Liam whines out loud, though he tries to tell himself the threat is idle. He looks up at the maiden, aware he won't get at her unless he shifts back to his human form. Even then, she has the advantage higher up in the tree.

"Believe me, wolf, I can get closer to her than most."

Another scent catches Liam's attention. More werewolves, and judging from their hyped up, earthy scent with just a tinge of Liam's own blood, they are Alaric's henchmen, on patrol.

The maiden is looking in the same direction. "Better make a quick decision," she taunts.

Liam shakes his mane and comes to the base of the tree. He lifts up on his hind legs, resting his front paws on the trunk. Staring up one last time in the tree, he narrows his eyes, trying to get a good look at the maiden. He has to know who she is so he can tell Serena.

But she shrinks back into the shadows again, pulling a bow and arrow from the quiver on her back. "Leave," she tells Liam, voice hardened as she nocks her arrow.

Huffing, Liam pushes off the tree and lopes away into the bushes. He halfway expects an arrow in between his shoulder blades, if the maiden is in anyway as good as Serena with the weapon. But it doesn't come. He puts distance between himself, the maiden, and the incoming wolves, hoping they don't catch his scent.

The run back to his clothes and his phone goes quickly, his thoughts occupied with how he may have just put Cecil in danger. If the maiden followed him to Cecil's place, she would report it to Alaric. Visits to the old cabin are forbidden. Liam shifts back into his human form—the change not nearly as painful, but almost as exhausting—and dresses.

Damn, he thinks, looking down at his clothes. *Ripped again.* He picks up his cell phone; at least he didn't crush it this time. Liam will have to grab a new set of clothes before he goes to work, but a naked man walking into the trailer park is not an uncommon site, especially now that most wolves can transform at will. First thing to do when he gets to work is set up a watch schedule to protect Cecil. *The old man ain't going to like that.*

Chapter Fifteen

"On patrol tonight?" Connor raises his nose to the air as soon as Liam walks into the bowling alley.

Scratching the back of his neck, Liam shrugs. "Just out runnin'."

"Lucky bastard," Connor says, burying his nose back into his glass of beer. He is one of the pack who refused a blood injection, which is how Liam grew first to like him, then to recruit him to his cause. "And here I sit, drinkin' away the itch that can't be scratched until the full moon."

Behind the bar, Liam fills a clean glass with tap water and slides it over to Connor. "You know how we can solve that little problem."

"No thank you," mumbles Connor, begrudgingly putting one hand around the glass of water. "Might get AIDS or something. God knows what's runnin' through your veins."

Liam chooses to ignore that half-hearted attempt at an insult. "Not so busy tonight," he nods toward the only three lanes occupied. Despite the lack of occupants, the building smells heavily of smoke and sweat.

"Nah," says Connor, swiveling his stool around, leaning one elbow against the bar. "But lane twenty is stuck again."

"Christ, that's the third time this week. It's those new sixteen pounders you ordered; they knock the whole apparatus loose back there," Liam gripes, already grabbing the tool kit and walking around the dilapidated bar.

"Hey, Liam." Connor looks at him with heavy, reddened eyes. "See lane twelve, the one standing back a bit?"

"Yeah?"

"We're thinkin' of bringing him in."

"What the hell would he do? We ain't never busy enough, except on league nights—"

"Not bringin' him to work here, idiot," Connor slurs.

"Oh." Realization dawns on Liam, and he sets the took box down with a heavy thump. "What do we know about him?" Liam can barely recall which trailer he claims at the park. "How do we know he's not loyal to Alaric and just sniffing out information on his behalf?"

"I checked into him—he's golden." Connor smiles, then falls off his stool. "I got it, I got it." He stumbles while picking himself back up.

"Yeah—you're instillin' loads of confidence..." Liam trails off, looking back at the new guy. He walks to the machine to get his ball, and as he bends over the logo on the back of his work shirt is displayed.

Doug's Pier: Docking and Rentals.

"Okay, Connor." Liam watches as he makes a strike. "He could come in handy. Let's start him with a few simple tasks."

"You're the boss." Connor raises his glass.

Laughing, Liam heads down to lane twenty. Technically, at the moment, Connor is the boss.

* * *

It has been only one night since Liam dropped the note down the hole for Serena. By sunset, Liam is walking the shores, staring out into the ocean.

Did she get the note? Even if she did, will she come?

The waves offer no clues and the briny air coming off the sea only teases him. He stares out until he convinces himself to have faith, then visits the burned wolfsbane patch, searching for more flowers. He manages to find several, and begins collecting them in a basket left behind by the Undine.

Armed with as much wolfsbane as he could find, Liam heads for the forest just as the sun sinks from the sky. He waits near the hole behind a large, fallen pine tree feeling like the wolf awaiting Little Red Riding Hood, except now the wolf has the basket.

Liam raises his nose and sniffs the air. He senses at least three separate Undine in the area; male, by the scent of them. Liam keeps to a crouch though he is under no impression they don't smell him as well.

All at once, the night air grows thick with tension, and a slim, golden trident sails out from the hole in the ground. It is followed by a small blue-scaled hand clawing out. Liam smiles. It's as if the wolfsbane has brought him luck.

He rises slowly, hands further out to the sides than necessary as he enters the clearing to show he has no weapons. Before Serena emerges fully from the hole, Liam bends to pick up her trident. There is a scuffle in the bushes across from him and five sharp arrows emerge from the leaves, pointed at Liam.

He shakes his head, hoping his eyes aren't flashing red. He bends his knees, reaching behind him for the basket. Tilting it forward and presenting his wares to the arrows, he hopes the archers behind them get his meaning.

I mean her no harm.

The seconds stretch out. Serena's heavy breath breaches the air, adding to the tension.

Finally, the arrows move back. If Liam squints hard enough, he can still make out the tips trying to pawn themselves off as leaves.

He takes a deep breath, and watches her crawl the rest of the way out of the hole. "Nice robe."

When Serena turns, Liam's breath catches in his throat. Silver swaths of moonlight glide over dark blue scales, as if she has brought the ocean itself ashore. All Liam wants to do is find a way past those armored scales, wrap his arms around her, and give her a giant hug—making up for all those he missed out on.

Serena is saying something. Swallowing hard, Liam attempts to smile and hopes Serena buys it. "You look…taller, Serena."

Jackass. She looks so much more, but taller is the best you can come up with?

Liam twirls Serena's trident in his hand, the pointed tips gleam under the moonlight. It feels feather-light in his hands, but Liam is not fooled. He has seen the way it rips right through a ribcage. It is a sturdy weapon and reminds him of the claws that lie in wait underneath his knuckles. "I come bearing gifts." Liam pushes the basket of wolfsbane toward her.

She leans forward to look, the long black braid falling off her shoulders as she does. "I thought you burned all the patches."

He stops twirling the trident and fixes her with a hard stare. "To be clear, I didn't burn anything."

"Your people did." Her voice matches his cold tone, growing colder by the second.

"Under Alaric's orders, but not everyone in the pack agrees he's leadin' us down the right path anymore."

"Is that why you summoned me?" Serena asks. She slowly bends to pick up the basket, eyes still darting from Liam, to her trident, and back again.

Liam shakes his head, turning the trident once again. "No, not really."

Serena looks into the basket she holds. It is filled to the brim with wolfsbane flowers, each one containing the possibility to start a new patch.

"You should know there are more of my people here, watching you," says Serena.

"You should know," says Liam, picking up the trident so the full weight of it rests in his palm, "that none of my people are here." *And thank God for that.*

He holds the trident out at arm's length toward Serena. She steps forward, extending her own arm. It is scaled down to the wrist in full armor. When she grasps the stem of the trident, just below his hand, he doesn't let go. Neither moves; neither relinquishes the trident. He raises his eyebrow at her, waiting. Finally, she begins to retract her armor. Scale by scale, the ocean disappears beneath skin, hidden away like Liam hides his wolf.

"Thank you for trustin' me," says Liam, letting go of the trident.

Serena nods, and Liam notices she does not step back. Instead, she brings the weapon parallel to her body and raises her chin to look into his eyes. "You are my brother, after all."

One side of his mouth curls up in a smile. "Born to the same people, under the same moon, yet both of us abandoned by them."

A ribbon of bioluminescent glow shoots through Serena's hair, from her crown to the tips. "Our father was facing difficult choices."

"So you've forgiven him, then?" He turns away, as if he is indifferent to her answer, but he still looks at her out of the corner of his eye.

The question causes Serena to flinch. "Have you?" she asks.

Taking a deep breath, Liam turns his back on her—pacing to the tree line, then returning. "In the pack, we are raised to hate the Undine with every hair on our body—every hair when in wolf form," Liam says, emphasizing his point.

"That is a lot of hair," mumbles Serena.

He ignores her comment. "We were abandoned at birth because we were found unworthy of the seas, cast aside like gutted fish remains. Alaric reminds us of these things at the gatherin' durin' the full moon. For my whole life, hatred of the Undine has been shoved down my throat."

"Our male calflings were dying – parents had no choice," Serena says, trying to make him understand. "They had to force the transformation and give their sons to the Earth, or watch them die."

Liam shakes his head. "A detail Alaric likes to leave out." He kicks at the dirt under his boots.

Serena crosses her arms. "Then how did you find out?"

"The old man, the one human link between the Undine and the werewolves," Liam looks in the direction of the cabin down the coast.

Serena follows his gaze. "I've never met him."

"No." Smiles Liam. "I suppose you wouldn't have. The Undine leave their sons with him. And he makes sure the infants get to the pack, safe and sound. I sought him out later," continues Liam. "Asked him some questions that he was more than happy to answer. Said I was the only one to ever come askin'."

"That is…kind of crazy."

"I know," Liam says, talking faster now. "So I started bringin' others to see him, but only those that were somewhat open to the possibility that Alaric might have been less than truthful with us." Liam pauses, looking at Serena. "What?"

She has a wide smile on her face. "Nothing." She tries to resume a blank expression. "It's just—you remind me of me."

Liam relaxes his shoulders and returns the smile. "Uh-oh," he says, teasing.

"So where does the pack stand now? Would they be open to an alliance with the Undine, instead of a war?"

"We are divided. Those of us that have our doubts followin' Alaric have begun to meet regularly. And the others—well, you understand we have to be careful. If word got back to Alaric, I don't know what he'd do, but it wouldn't be good."

"He doesn't realize what is happening?"

"I don't think so. He's cocky and arrogant, and he's been our leader for so long that no one ever questions him."

Serena shifts the trident from one hand to another. "And let's say he is completely blindsided. What's your plan? What are the next steps?"

Liam shrugs, looking up at the stars. "I don't know. I don't know how I want this to end, or if it could ever really end well. I was raised by Alaric, you know. On clear nights we would sit outside, looking up at the stars, and he'd tell me the legends of the constellations. Many of them have to do with the seas. Aquarius, the Water Bearer; Capricorn, the Sea Goat; Gemini, the Twins—and their unconditional help toward sailors; and Pisces, the Fish. It's like when the stars look down, all they can see is the great ocean covering all of Earth. It just makes you feel kind of, I don't know…left out." Liam gives a nervous laugh. "I don't know why I told you all that, it's just—half the pack is lookin' to me now and I don't know what to do."

"Is that why you wanted to meet?" asks Serena. "To ask me what to do?"

"No." Liam shakes his head. He takes a step back.

Serena narrows her eyes.

"I asked you here on Alaric's request."

As soon as the words are out of his mouth, Liam feels the pulse of her heartbeat quicken. It thunders through him, shaking his bones and pounding in his ears. Her fear triggers his wolf, and he falls to his knees, squeezing his own arms around him, trying to hold himself together. "Control yourself, Serena!"

Inside, his blood rushes to his major joints, as if it is pushed and pulled by the moon itself. Her heartbeat grows louder and faster, even more so as his shoulder blades begin shifting under his shirt. It is a self-sustaining cycle, one that each of them is almost powerless to stop.

"You're asking *me* for control?" Serena takes several steps back, holding her trident at the ready. "I can literally see your wolf emerging."

Liam expects a hail of arrows to pierce his heart any second. He tries listening for the telltale whistle cutting through the air, but he can't hear a damn thing other than Serena. Her breath rushing in and back out through her lips, the electrical buzz of her bioluminescent hair as she fights to control it, and the ever increasing drumming of her heart.

Suddenly, the familiar whistle of a trident cutting through the air catches Liam's ear. Forcing one eye open, he sees the flash of a gold spearhead sailing over Serena's head, directly for him.

In front of him, Serena thrusts her own weapon into the air and the pair of tridents collide. Pulling her tips to the ground with an expert flick of her wrists, the rogue weapon is forced down. It plunges into soft soil, spraying bits of earth across Liam's face.

"Stop!" Serena yells.

Liam just wishes she would stop. Transformation in response to elevated Undine maiden energy is much different than when Liam chooses to transform on his own. The fire isn't as great, which means he can feel every fissure in his bone split apart then meld back together. In front of him, Liam sees Serena facing off with her own kind.

The stampeding herd of Undine guards have obeyed, stopping short before they reach Serena and Liam. Their chests heave and their eyes dart wildly from Serena to Liam and back again. They hold panes of glass in front of them.

Bulletproof? They won't stop a fully transformed werewolf, though.

Still standing in front of Liam, Serena straightens, slamming the stem of her trident into the ground. "This is my brother—my kin. You are forbidden from harming him—tonight and any time thereafter." It is the first decree she has ever made as queen, and she hopes she's done it right.

Trying to ignore the blinding pain emanating from his joints, Liam focuses on the scaring heat on the side of his face. He channels energy toward the crescent mark, hoping to kick-start it.

Soon enough the burning takes over, enveloping his body. Both kinds of transformations collide, confusing his systems. Everything freezes, a self-preservation method. He knows he is in a state of half-transformation, and he wouldn't dare want to see himself, but at least he didn't go so far as to black out.

Breathing hard from the exertion, he takes a few shaky steps to stand by Serena's side. She tenses, but is thankfully able to keep any other adrenaline rushes at bay.

"You are…in control?" asks Serena.

"Think so," replies Liam. It hurts even to speak.

"You might as well tell me what Alaric wants," Serena says. "Quick, before you try to eat me."

The dry humor helps. His wolf calms, and he doesn't have to hold onto him quite so tight. "He wants you, Serena," says Liam. "Says the ultimatum still stands. If you give yourself to the wolves on your eighteenth birthday four days from now, he will honor your peace agreement. But if you don't, no pairin' or birth events will be allowed."

Liam looks each Undine guard in the eye as he speaks. Behind their glass shields, they won't even hold his gaze, they glance away after a few moments. Judging from the amount of heat on one side of his face, only one eye blazes red.

"Serena, you can't actually be considering this." One of the guards speak up. "Please just, come home now."

"Kai, just give me a second to talk this through," says Serena, stepping toward the Undine guard.

"He is half wolf right now," says Kai.

"I trust him, Kai." Serena says.

Several seconds pass. Finally, Kai lowers his glass shield.

From behind her, Liam can almost see the relief emanating off Serena in the way her shoulders relax.

"Thank you, Kai," she murmurs. "Here, put the flowers in your dry pouch and deliver some to Hailey and Isadora."

Serena turns back to Liam. "Please tell Alaric I will consider his request."

Liam nods, unwilling to take his eyes off the guards or their tridents.

"And Liam," Serena steps closer, lowering her voice. "Can you get your hands on a boat?"

Liam pauses, thinking about Doug at the bowling alley. He nods his head.

"Good," says Serena, turning back to her guards. "I'll come up with a plan and let you know. Thanks for not killing me tonight."

Liam snorts, wanting to thank her guards for not killing him, but his vocal chords are so twisted it still hurts to talk. Still, he needs to warn her of the traitor.

"You haven't told me," Liam says, the last word morphing into a growl.

"Told you what?" Serena asks over her shoulder.

"What it feels like to be royalty," he says.

Eyes wide, now she turns around. "How did you know?"

"Because your majesty, you have a traitor," Liam bends at the waist in a courteous bow then stumbles away from the Undine. With each step further away from them, he can feel the nerves that run hot underneath his skin settle. The wolf loses his hold over the human and before long thick, spiky hairs flutter to the ground. They leave behind soft pores in Liam's skin, ready for the next batch to emerge when he transforms.

Yellow claws dig into soft dirt, and with the very next step it is his bare feet sinking into the ground. He pauses at one of the marked trees, distinguished only by a particular smell, and digs for a cape under the foliage. Wrapping the cape around himself, he heads toward the docks mulling over the meeting in his head. It gave him two very important pieces of information. One is that Serena is willing to do anything for her people, and the second is that her people are willing to do anything for Serena. Neither is a good combination for what Alaric has planned.

Chapter Sixteen

"Gonna go swim it off?" Liam asks, startling the man who is staring out into the water from the docks.

Connor turns, steadying himself on the shredded, swinging rope—the only thing separating one world from the next. It isn't unusual to catch a wolf standing at the edge of the ocean, staring out like they may jump in any moment. No one knows if it is the water itself enticing them, or the mermaids in it.

For the wolves though, there is something else keeping them from the water. It is the feeling of abandonment they experienced not just as babies, but every day of their lives. They are outcasts, turned away from home before ever getting to know it. They are the betrayed.

Breakers push against the dock in an enticing rhythm. The low beat of frothy waves, the high notes of the salty spray, and the enchanting melody of the hum of life teeming just below the surface combine, almost forming whispers to a siren's song promising the seductive kiss of a lover, or better—the coveted kiss of a mother.

Liam shakes his head. *This pastime is dangerous.* More than one wolf has succumbed, committing suicide on the beaches believing their loved ones would escort them to sea in the afterlife. *No wonder we all drink.* He smacks Connor hard on the back, trying to shake them both from their reverie.

"Did you talk to Doug?"

"Yeah, man," Connor blinks, the words sounding strained. He takes a deep breath, makes an effort to peel his eyes away from the midnight blue water, and turns to Liam. "He's on the fence."

"How much did you tell him? I told you before, we have to be able to trust these guys before we bring them in." Liam runs his hand through his hair, pacing away.

"Relax." Connor holds up his hands. "I mostly just asked questions, getting a feel for where he stands in the pack. He has attempted to leave more often than anyone else, you know. More than even you."

"Yeah?" Liam turns around, his interest piquing.

"Yeah. I mentioned there might be an alternative. He seems open to it, but…"

"I knew it, I just don't have clout with these guys. Why should they follow me? What reason do I have to give them?" Liam kicks at one of the splintered wood planks.

"Please tell me you didn't just say that." Connor rolls his eyes.

"What?" Liam leans against a post.

"Despite the fact that you are the youngest here, you do realize most of these guys actually look up to you, right?"

Liam runs a tired hand over the stubble growing on his chin. "No they don't."

Connor nods. "Yeah, they do. Ever since you made it a habit of second guessin' Alaric, first at his teachin' sessions, then with his command decisions."

Smiling, Liam recalls the frustrated anger emanating off Alaric whenever a pupil starts up with the questions. "It mostly started just to get a rise out of him. Had to entertain myself somehow."

"Still," says Connor. "They were listenin'." He pauses for a moment, playing with the frayed rope, only causing more strands of it to become unraveled.

"What?"

"It's just, I think some of them need a final push. The desire, and the will for change is there—but they need some guidance. And it can't be with the heavy-handed reign Alaric uses."

"I know, I know. But what?" Liam asks.

"Well," Connor shifts on his feet. "I do have somethin' in mind."

"What?" Liam narrows his eyes.

More silence.

"Come on, Connor!" Liam says, on the verge of strangling his friend with the rope just to get him to speak.

"I promised a match."

"You—you…what?"

"A match," Connor repeats.

"Me?"

Nodding, Connor looks behind him, as if he might actually consider bolting if Liam doesn't take it well.

Now Liam scratches at his stubble with furious hands. There hasn't been a match in years. It is a stupid, chauvinistic practice the pack used to use to settle differences. Alaric made sure they were scheduled almost monthly, until a silent protest was organized by Liam—though no one knew it was him. Members of the pack simply refused to attend, and without the boisterous crowd cheering on the fighters and no bets being exchanged, fighter participation dropped.

During the last scheduled fight, the combatants actually stood in the ring, discussing the problem and leaving after a handshake. Although Liam wasn't there, because of the protest and all, he could just imagine the look on Alaric's face.

Now Connor is suggesting they start up the same archaic practice Liam worked to stop, just so Liam could recruit followers.

"There has to be another way," Liam says.

"I'm open to suggestions, man."

The silence stretches out, measurable by each wave beating against the pier. Somewhere underneath, a plastic bin is caught against the pillars. Pings ring out like a ticking timer, awaiting Liam's decision.

He shakes his head. "I don't need Doug's boats. I can find another."

Briefly, Liam considers using the Cecil's scuba diving boat for Serena's plan.

No, I can't risk his involvement in this any more than I already have.

Liam sighs. "Who would I fight?"

Connor shrugs. "I could arrange for it to be pretty much anyone you want. Someone easy, maybe…"

Liam raises an eyebrow in warning. "No. If the outcome of this match is going to win me any followers, I'll have to earn it. Get someone big."

"Shawn?"

"No. He is too likeable."

"Gary?"

"Too dumb."

"Who then?"

Liam walks to the end of the pier and sits, dangling his feet over the edge. "During the King's Massacre, once everyone made it to the beach…" Liam pauses, remembering staggering out of the woods just in time to see Alaric tear into the king. "Some of the guys talk about a few wrongful deaths that took place."

"Well, yeah," snorts Connor. "They were dragging us out into the ocean to be drowned."

"Not pack deaths, mermaid deaths."

"Oh. You mean like the king? Do you want to fight Alaric because of that?"

"I can't fight Alaric yet—he has to lose clout with the pack, first. I'm talkin' about Serena's friend, Ervin. It was Rand who killed him, right?"

Connor's eyebrows lift as realization dawns. "Oh. . . yes. He had the gun."

It's not that guns were specifically forbidden during the King's Massacre, but there is a certain amount of pride in facing off with an Undine guard and dueling without weapons. Holding one down just to shoot him in the face was disgraceful to the pack. Several members had a problem with what happened on the beach that night, but what Rand did was like icing on the cake.

"Rand and his little goon squad. They all had guns. Serena was shot, too," says Liam.

"And they just so happen to be Alaric's closest followers," Connor says. "You do this, you start to break down Alaric's reign of terror."

Liam skims his foot over the surface of the water, a bit of foam sticking to the underside of his boot. "Set it up. I need a chance encounter with Rand. Somethin' that will set us both off. You can step in and suggest it settled in a match. There needs to be lots of witnesses."

"So at the bowling alley?" Connor asks.

Liam nods.

Connor's shoulders sag. "You're going to smash something up, aren't you?"

Smiling, Liam looks up. "You've been meaning to demo the ball return on lane fifteen, right?" He hops up, slapping Connor on the back. "I'll get it done for you, boss."

Chapter Seventeen

As luck would have it, Rand shows up at the bowling alley the very next night with his crew. The last of the Ungainlies have left, but Connor keeps the alley open for pack members only— sometimes into the early hours of the morning. It's better if they cause trouble here rather than in town.

Rand and his group down three rounds of beer before even heading to the lanes. Behind the bar, Liam sends the drinks out laced with hard liquor. It doesn't take long before they are loud and out of control. The second time a ball goes crashing down the lane just as the sweep lowers to clear the pins, Connor nods to Liam.

Now is as good a time as any.

"Hey, asshole." Liam shoves a finger into Rand's shoulder. "Ask your crew to tone it down or I'll have to ask you to leave."

Rand turns around, a smile on his face. "Ask away."

Laughter rings up behind Rand. Liam furrows his eyebrows. Maybe he fed them too much liquor. They aren't in a fighting mood; it's just the opposite.

"Okay—leave," Liam says, crossing his arms.

"Maybe after a few more beers."

"Yeah, barkeep," one of Rand's friends peels himself off the torn vinyl seats and stumbles up to Liam. He pours the rest of his beer right on the floor at Liam's feet. "Looks like I need a refill. Why don't you run back there and get us another round."

More laughter.

"I'm cuttin' you all off," Liam announces.

The entire room goes silent.

"You're cuttin' us off?" Rand asks. "We've had three."

The pair continues to stare each other down. Liam doesn't answer but can see the muscles tightening around Rand's jawline.

Rand tries again. "Go and get us another round, or I'll—"

"Or you'll what?" Liam interrupts. "Shoot me?"

Behind Rand, several pairs of eyes go wide. Since the King's Massacre, Rand has defended his use of a gun several times. None of those conversations ended well. His temper kicks in before his wits do.

"Listen here." Rand raises a hand to Liam's chest.

Liam uses the chance to escalate the confrontation. He pushes Rand hard in the shoulders, and the brute tumbles back into his friends.

By now a crowd has gathered, shouting support for either side.

'Lane fifteen' Connor mouths silently over the crowd at Liam.

Liam rolls his eyes to the flickering fluorescent lights. As if it isn't obvious, the ball return is practically wrapped in yellow caution tape and has a large out-of-order sign—been that way for two years now.

Pushed back to his feet by the crowd, Rand's face is red with embarrassment, or anger—or both. He charges, feet stomping against wood-paneled flooring.

Liam hunches, his senses sharpening with the adrenaline running through his veins. Focusing in on the man lumbering toward him, Liam smells wolf hair emerge. He glances down at Rand's hands to see nails scrape against skin as Rand's claws grow long. Rand is an obvious recipient of Liam's own blood, and is transforming here and now, against a member of his own pack.

Time to put him down.

As Rand crashes into him, Liam wraps his arm around his opponent's waist. Using the momentum Rand already has, Liam follows it, swinging around and lifting the beast up into the air. He releases, but Rand continues to glide up. His jeans rip at the knees as bones break apart then meld back together, wider and longer. At the apex of the lift, Rand throws his head back howling, his snout already lengthening.

Rand drifts back down. Rearing back his fist, Liam feels the fire inside that wants to force his own transformation. Instead, he channels the energy down, twisting his hips as he thrusts his tight knuckles forward. The connection is a powerful hit. Rand flies back, straight into the ball return. The machine shatters underneath him.

Liam's vision has gone red, but once the color drains away, he focuses on the wolf barely moving amidst splintered wood, metal, and plastic. A cracked number sixteen lies aside the pile. Blinking, Liam looks beyond it to see the number fifteen ball return whole and untouched, a piece of the yellow caution tape waving, as if it is taunting him.

I missed.

Liam glances over the shouting onlookers to see Connor slap his forehead.

Oops.

"Enough!" Connor pushes his way through the group. He is fuming, and it is not an act. "You two are destroying my alley! You need to finish this the right way—in a match, and out of my alley."

Cheers ring up around Connor, the enthusiasm of the crowd for a match taking Liam by surprise. The sport was apparently missed.

"Fine." Liam bends over Rand. "Tomorrow night at dark."

Rand, completely transformed now, stirs, then growls up at Liam.

Wrapping a large hand around the muzzle, Liam squeezes it shut. "And no wolves allowed."

More cheers. They will fight against one another as men. Liam knows that trying to keep the wolf under control when adrenaline runs high is a huge distraction, especially when his own blood runs through both their veins. Finally, Liam can use that to his advantage.

* * *

As soon as Liam enters his trailer, chest still heaving from the fight and the run home after, he smells an intruder. "What are you doing here?"

From the corner where his armchair stands shrouded in shadows, four empty blood bags fly at Liam.

"I have more orders to fill," Alaric's says, his voice following the bags.

Liam leaves them where they flop at his feet. "Can't," he says, turning away, peeling off his jacket, and retrieving a bottle of water from the fridge.

"Can't...or won't?" asks Alaric.

Shrugging, Liam downs the rest of the bottle, making Alaric wait for his answer. He swallows and wipes his mouth with the back of his sleeve. "Cannot, will not, call it what you want. I've got a fight tomorrow. Besides, I can't give more blood so soon after—"

"A fight?" Alaric leans forward in the armchair so a swath of moonlight falls across his face. "You mean a match. Who with?"

Throwing the empty bottle in the trash, Liam buries his head in one of the cupboards moving aside empty cereal boxes, searching for food, and giving himself time to think.

"It's not Rand, is it?" Alaric asks.

Liam's chest deflates. "I made the challenge not ten minutes ago."

Alaric smiles. "Well Rand made a call five minutes ago."

Liam shakes his head. "Won't do him any good. No wolves allowed."

"Ah, so you're goin' bare knuckle with this one…"

"That's right. And no bettin', Alaric. I want to keep the match clean."

"Wouldn't dream of it." Alaric stands from the chair. "I mean, you're obviously set out to make a point."

Liam glances at him under thick eyebrows as he unwraps a granola bar. "Somethin' like that," he mumbles.

"I mean the guy has gotten a little out of hand lately. That new crew he has, runnin' around causin' trouble." Alaric paces the kitchenette, inching closer and closer to Liam.

All Liam can smell is trouble. Rand is Alaric's right hand man, there is no way he is selling him out.

"And their, let's say, prolific use of guns lately…"

Rumors floating around camp say that Alaric himself gave Rand and his buddies firearms during the King's Massacre.

Alaric nods. "Yes, I think this could work out well. Make an example out of him, but at the same time we'll put you in the spotlight."

Heat crawls up Liam's neck. He undoes the top button on his shirt, then rolls up his sleeves. He needs to distract himself with something before he hits Alaric. He turns to the dishes in the sink, crusted over with dried enchilada sauce and takeout Chinese, and flips on the faucet.

Alaric is still talking. "Hell, if you beat him easy enough, my blood orders will double."

As Liam scrubs at dishes, he looks down at the many scars on the inside of his arms from clumsy needles piercing his skin. *I look like a damn drug addict.*

"Everybody is going to want a taste of you, and soon I'll have the whole pack hopped up and able to transform at my command," says Alaric.

The plate Liam holds in his hands snaps in half. He throws it down in the sink, flips off the water and turns.

"What are you plannin' Alaric?" The wet sponge still hangs in Liam's hand.

Alaric raises his eyebrows. "I'm plannin' our species survival. We will grow stronger so we can continue the line."

Squeezing his fists, a stream of water rushes out of the sponge, slopping across the floor.

"Our species was never meant to be!" Liam yells, stepping toward Alaric. "We are the result of a desperate attempt from some fish people to keep their weak sons from dyin'. Why should we continue to thrive? What right do we have in this world?"

Alaric's lids lower. "Have you no pride? Have you forgotten everything I've taught you?" He sneers. "We aren't some wayward experiment—we have evolved from the sea, just like man did in the beginning. Except we are better than man, and we are better than our mothers and fathers who abandoned us."

Liam gives a short laugh, then turns around to throw the sponge back in the sink. "Dylan, Quinn, and Shane, plus at least half a dozen others—all dead because you have mommy issues. But you got your king—shredded him to bits. Yet it still isn't enough. You want more."

"We can't leave while these damn bottom feeders are left behind. I've tried, you've tried—we've all tried." Alaric turns banging his fist against the wall in a half-hearted attempt. "Can't get no further than town, most of the time." He looks over his shoulder at Liam. "Win this fight. Show everyone else what courses through your veins. Make them want it. If we can't leave these beaches, we will dominate them. And I need your blood to do that."

Without another word, Alaric kicks the empty blood bags toward Liam, and exits the trailer.

Leaning over on the counter, Liam buries his face in his hands. Now, if he is going to pull the clan out from under Alaric's boot, he can't let this fight happen.

Chapter Eighteen

Liam's multiple calls to Connor's cell and the bowling alley only result in voicemail—he knows Connor is fully immersed in putting the fight together and making sure almost everyone in the clan will be there with their wallets out, no matter how much Liam shouts 'no betting'.

The first light brings knocking at Liam's trailer door. It is a group of three, anxious to coach Liam in Rand's weaknesses. No need to guess which combatant they put their money on. It is noon by the time Liam can fend off all the well-wishers, bribers, coaches, and one prostitute from town that Liam is almost sure Rand ordered. He sent her on her way with gas money for the trip out. Guessing there will probably be a few more, Liam grabs his jacket and heads out.

Though the bowling alley isn't usually open for another two hours, Liam finds the parking lot full, the doors unlocked, and the place packed. There aren't any pins being knocked down. There is a large group around the bar pre-gaming the fight, and another large group in the arcade area, where Connor has set up a betting board. From behind everyone else, Liam scans the numbers on the board. Literally thousands of dollars stand to trade hands tonight.

Liam catches Connor's eye and jerks his head toward the kitchen. Handing off the dry erase marker to someone else who begins taking bets, Connor pushes his way through the crowd. The pair enters the back kitchen, where a cook is standing over the deep fryer.

"Out," Liam tells the cook.

After the door swings shut, Liam doesn't waste any time. "I came to tell you the fight is cancelled."

"Cancelled? Why?" Connor asks, unconcerned. He picks up an industrial-sized salt shaker and salts a batch of cooling fries.

"Because Alaric wants me to win."

Spoken out loud, the reason sounds stupid and childish. But of all people, Connor knows it is best to avoid anything Alaric wants.

He turns to Liam. "If I go out there and cancel the fight, do you know what will happen?"

"More fry orders?"

"Quit jokin' around, Liam," Connor slams the salt back down on the counter. "I've collected a lot of money. There'll be a riot of people going after what they've put in. There'll also be a lot of disappointed, and possibly angry werewolves. Cancellin' the fight now isn't going to put any numbers behind you—in fact, it'll probably lose you some."

Liam runs an agitated hand through his hair. "Where's all this money comin' from anyway? If the clan is so rich, why am I givin' away half my paycheck so I can live in a trailer park?"

Connor shrugs. "I'm not sure it is all come by legal means, and it definitely isn't all reported to Alaric."

Liam paces the kitchen. When the deep fryer beeps, he grabs a towel to wrap around the handle and pulls the basket of fries out. Hot oil splatters on his hand. "Dammit!"

Three long steps and he is at the sink, thrusting his hand under cold water. Connor comes up behind him, handing him a dry towel.

"It's too late to cancel, isn't it?" Liam sighs, taking the towel.

Connor gives a half-smile and nods slowly. "Why does Alaric want to you to win?"

"He thinks it'll convince the rest of the clan to take my blood," Liam mumbles.

"Wow...just wow."

"It can't go his way, Connor," Liam says, looking over his hand. It is bright red, but not seriously burned.

Connor rests a hand on Liam's shoulder. "We'll figure something out. Have a little faith."

* * *

The rest of the evening, Connor is too busy to consult with Liam any further. Not willing to face the crowd, go home, or even to run the forest for fear of coming across any more members of the pack, Liam stays in the kitchen helping to fill all the food orders.

The cook is a young teenager from town who doesn't ask any questions. He keeps his head down, his hands busy, and his ear buds in, which gives Liam some much needed privacy to sort out how to handle the fight tonight.

The evening passes quickly, and after the last orders come in, Liam and the cook run down the line of fryers. Flipping them off, Liam turns to the teenager and shakes his hand.

"Thank you."

The teenager gives him a confused look. "No problem, man. Um...anytime?"

"Sure thing, pal," Liam says over his shoulder, leaving the back way. The fight is supposed to begin in ten minutes, and Liam has finally worked out a solution. Everything will turn out all right, as long as Alaric doesn't get in the way.

The walk to the warehouse goes quickly. When Liam enters, he is encased in the crowd at once. Pack members give him last minute advice or simply a slap on the back. Liam makes his way through the crowd muttering his thanks. Cracked concrete gives way to a dirt floor, and there is a distinct odor of rusty nails.

"You got this?" Connor pulls Liam from the last of the crowd.

"Yeah." Liam rolls out his shoulders and removes his shirt. "Is Alaric here?"

"In the back. Staying kind of quiet."

"Just make sure he stays—and can see."

"Okay…"

"I'm serious. This'll only work with him here. Have you seen Darcy yet? We might need her."

"Not yet." Connor shakes his head. "You gonna let me in on the plan?"

Liam glances around, leaning in closer to Connor. But as soon as he opens his mouth, the loudspeaker blares with an electronic whine.

"Testing, testing—" The speaker cuts off with a bout of coughing after the announcer inhales a year's worth of dust off of the microphone.

With no time for explanations, Liam gives Connor an apologetic smile. Still stretching, he enters the makeshift ring which consists of old tires fashioned into a large circle. Half the fun of the fights is watching the contestants bounce off the ring after a hard hit.

"Okay fighters." Connor enters the ring along with Liam. "The rules tonight—no weapons, no wolves. Stay in the ring."

Liam lifts his eyebrow. Connor is to be the ref. Hopefully he doesn't stop the fight too soon.

"If you stay down for a count of ten, it's a loss. If you submit, it's a loss. I will accept a tap-out or audible statement as a submission. Got it?"

Rand nods, but Liam is too busy staring at the inside arms of his opponent. Fresh blood trickles down at least four pinprick holes. He's been given blood, a lot of it—and fairly recently.

"Liam? Got it?" Connor says louder.

Eyes blazing, Liam looks up at his opponent. Rand shakes his head violently as if he had a sudden caffeine rush to the brain.

"Hey," Connor shoves Liam in the arm.

"What?"

"You okay? You got the rules?"

"Yeah, yeah, I got them. Let's get this over with." Liam's entire strategy is thrown for a loop, but there is no time to come up with plan B.

"Fighters shake hands!" Connor yells out from the middle of the ring.

Liam holds his knuckles out, keeping his eyes on the ground. His best bet is to give Rand as much confidence as he can.

Rand knocks Liam's fist away, unwilling to endure a cordial exchange.

That confidence thing ain't going to be a problem.

A bell rings, and the crowd roars, shouting suggestions, encouragement, or obscenities at the fighters.

The noise is a distraction to Liam's hypersensitive ears. Tumultuous waves of sound roll around the arena, amplified by bare warehouse walls. Among them, Liam picks out one phrase.

"Watch out!"

Instinctively he leans his head back, narrowly missing Rand's swing. Liam doesn't expect his opponent to attack so quickly. But Rand is anxious to expend the pent up energy Liam's own blood gives him.

Wiping his face with the back of his hand, Liam focuses on Rand. He can't afford to make this look too easy. Rand attacks again—three lightning-quick strikes with closed fists.

Dodge, block, dodge. Liam fends off the assault then follows with a kick to Rand's midsection. The werewolf stutter-steps back, and Liam sucks in the air.

Time to take a hit.

His best bet is to make it look like he is getting cocky.

Something fancy.

Liam charges, landing a blow to Rand's chest—nothing too damaging. He spins, ducking under one of Rand's counter-swings. But Liam rolls right into the follow-up of Rand's other fist. He can see it coming out of the corner of his eye. *It is too low*, Liam thinks. He squats down further, absorbing the strike with the side of his face.

Hands out, and body twisting in mid-air, Liam catches himself on the ground. The bitter-tangy taste of dirt and blood fill his mouth. Spitting it out, Liam listens for footsteps behind him. Rand doesn't take advantage of the fall.

Idiot.

A sharp pin-prick sensation hits the butt of Liam's palm. Lifting his hand, he wipes at the dirt. It is a tooth. Liam runs his tongue over both rows of teeth; none are missing.

Getting his feet under him, Liam stands, making sure to step over the tooth from some long forgotten fight and grinding it into the ground with his boot. He wipes away the remaining blood trickling out of his mouth, and arches his eyebrow at Rand. "Had enough?" he asks.

Blinded by rage and adrenaline, anything Liam could have said would be taken as an insult. Liam can almost see the blood vessels in Rand's eyes expanding to a bursting point with another rush of blood consuming his veins.

Rand charges, and Liam shakes his head, feigning ill effects from the previous hit. Forcing his eyes to go wide, he angles his body to give Rand as much to work with as he can. Ducking his head, Rand shoulders Liam right below the sternum, and they both fly back into the tire ring.

The fall does nothing for the fight. They bounce right back up, still locked together. Wrangling shoulders and hips, Liam twists them both in the air so they land on the dirt, with himself on the bottom.

"Ten, nine, eight…" Connor shouts out from next to them.

With his chest struggling to expand under Rand's heavy weight, Liam sucks in a breath, emphasizing the wheezing noise through his cracked lips.

On top, Rand looks more stunned than ever, just now comprehending his advantage.

"Come on, hit him, man," Connor hisses in a lower voice to Rand. Then to the rest of the crowd, "seven, six…"

"Right," Rand responds, always a pro at taking orders. He closes his fists and punches Liam in the face. Three thumps for every number Connor spews out.

Liam keeps his hands uselessly out to the side, counting down how many more hits he'll have to endure. *Connor is going slow on purpose*, Liam thinks with a grimace. *I'll get him back for that.*

Heads move higher, popping in from all directions in Liam's peripheral vision. Behind them all, he spots Alaric, still watching. If his lips weren't so swollen, Liam would smile. He could practically hear Alaric's growl of displeasure.

The blows raining down on Liam's face altogether cease, replaced by a howl of anguish. With one eye swollen shut, Liam struggles to focus the other one on the fighter above him. Suddenly, the weight on Liam's chest is lifted as Rand falls to the side. He is convulsing, his entire body jerking. The howl tapers off and is replaced by gurgling coming up from his throat.

Connor holds up one hand, pausing the fight while he bends to Rand's side. Liam pulls himself to his knees, crawling to Rand's other side.

"Rand? Oh, shit." His eyes move from the recent injection sites to the eyes rolling to the back of Rand's head.

He glances at Connor over the convulsing body. "He took too much blood. His body is rejecting it."

Connor turns, yelling for Darcy. A shadow falls over the trio and Liam breathes a sigh of relief that help has come. The arena has gone silent. Darcy's soft but stern voice, issuing the life-saving instructions needed right now does not come. Instead, there is a gunshot blast—a short, piercing shriek that leaves Liam's ears ringing.

Rand's body goes still, a gaping hole tearing down the middle of his forehead.

Liam looks up in shock, right at Alaric. The pistol is still pointed in between Liam and Connor.

Liam was dead wrong. Alaric was hedging all his bets on Rand to win. Before the fight, he would've spread word that Rand was hopped up on Liam's blood. But the extra insurance he played by giving Rand a stronger dose was his downfall. Rand's body couldn't handle it. Instead of seeing his experiment fail, Alaric put an end to it.

"Let this be justice for disobeying my orders to bring pistols to battle." There is no round of applause or cheers, which is the usual response Alaric receives when preaching to his people. Alaric looks down at Liam, lowering his gun. "I couldn't let him win the fight. Besides, this way the punishment fits the crime."

Alaric tries to justify his actions, but it is too late. Everyone saw Rand's seizure. Without another word, Alaric turns and leaves the arena. Liam's hand squeezes Rand's lifeless shoulder, and catches Connor's glance.

They both know that Alaric has just lost a majority of his followers.

Chapter Nineteen

Liam stalks home, leaving the shocked onlookers to handle Rand's remains. Burned and returned to sea as soon as possible is how the tradition goes. For all of Alaric's preaching about shunning those who abandoned them, they always end up in the place from which they came.

Passing one of the double-wide trailers, the almost foreign sound of a female voice rings through the camp.

Darcy.

If she had been there, treating the seizure as soon as it happened, Alaric wouldn't dare push her out of the way just to shoot Rand. Liam growls, then turns toward the trailer, slamming open the door. "Where the hell—"

The scene in front of Liam stops him short. A battered and bloodied man lays across the kitchen table. Darcy bends over him, stitching a large gash in his shoulder, occasionally dabbing at blood with clean guaze.

"Zeke?" asks Liam, piecing together the swollen face.

"Mmph," Zeke mumbles.

"You look as bad as I feel," Liam walks in, shutting the door closed behind him with extra care as guilt settles in from his explosive entrance.

Zeke grunts. "Can't believe I missed the fight. Had a hundred bucks on you. Tell me you won, man." He strains his neck to the side to look at Liam. "You didn't win, did you?"

"Well." Liam rubs the back of his neck. "I look a hell of a lot better than the other guy."

"Am I gonna have another patient tonight?" Darcy asks, snipping the thick, blue string protruding from Zeke's shoulder. She ties it off, waiting for Liam to answer. The kids are looking over her shoulder. As the pack's only medical provider, they are used to bloody men strewn about their kitchen.

"No," Liam finally says. "Not unless someone burns themselves building the fire."

Everyone pauses, even the three kids glancing up at Liam with understanding in their eyes.

"Boys, go get ready for bed. It's way past your bedtime." Darcy points to the back of the trailer with a pair of bloodied clamps.

"But mom," the oldest pipes up. "You said we could stay up and watch."

"I'm done stitching, so go," she barks.

All three kids jump then slowly make their way to their rooms.

Once they are out of earshot, Darcy turns to Liam. "You killed him?"

The look in her eyes is not anger, it is pure disbelief.

"No, Alaric did."

"What?" Zeke sits up, grabbing his side and wincing in pain.

"Careful—those ribs aren't broken, but you have a lot of bruising there." Darcy dotes on her patient, but turns her gaze on Liam for an explanation soon enough.

Colin, Darcy's husband, comes in from the living room. "He interfered? That's like…breaking his most sacred rule in the matches."

"He's getting worse," says Liam. He nods to Zeke. "What happened to you?"

Zeke shrugs, then winces again. "Got jumped walking home from town."

"Wolves?" asks Liam.

"Nah, smelled like humans," Zeke says.

"I wonder if it was Alaric's doing, just to keep Darcy occupied and away from the fights," Liam says.

Just then, Robbie, the youngest of the three boys runs out to get a toy he left behind on the couch. As he runs back through with a fake sword, he takes a swipe at Liam. Playfully, Liam dodges, spins and taps the boy in the back with his boot, shoving him along. "Get outta here…"

A giggle follows the boy to the back of the trailer. Darcy and Colin smile at Liam before their lips turn down in worried frowns as they watch their youngest disappear back into his bedroom.

Colin shakes his head. "If you hadn't stepped in to keep our boys away from Alaric's *schooling*," he says the word while making air quotes with his fingers, "who knows what would be happening to our boys right now." He glances in between the swollen faces of the men who both suffered a beating tonight.

The three boys are an anomaly. Of a clan with almost fifty members, they are the only pups born naturally, not having suffered the transformation from fins to fur. And Darcy is the only human ever to give birth to a werewolf. Liam has managed to stave Alaric off so far, but it won't last.

"So what happens next?" asks Zeke. He gingerly touches a line of stitches across his cheek until Darcy slaps his hand away.

Liam shrugs. "First, we take care of our fallen. Then, I don't know…"

"We could try leavin' again," Colin offers. "Get you all out of here."

"No." Darcy shakes her head. "I don't want to put our boys through that again."

Liam has tried helping smuggle the family out of town twice. Each time, just as Liam and Colin begin to feel the pull to return, it seems the three boys feel it tenfold. A mother can only watch her children writhing in agony on the ground for so long. The attempt at dosing the boys unconscious until the bond was snapped didn't help either.

"Hell." Zeke slams his fist on the table that still supports his weight. "Why don't you just kill him and get it over with?"

"Kill Alaric?" asks Liam.

Zeke nods. "You know a wolf's intuition—we'll follow the alpha. The alpha just has to prove…you know, his alpha-ness, or whatever."

Liam shakes his head. "I have to be sure the rest of the pack is willin' to fall in line first. Otherwise, it would just create more fightin' while others try for the position."

"How will we know when—?" Darcy's question is cut off by a loud knock at the door.

Everyone in the room freezes, glancing at each other.

"Alaric?" Zeke tightens his fists. "He wouldn't dare show his face here."

Liam holds up his hand, letting the others know to stand down. He cracks open the door cautiously, then pulls open the door all the way. There are at least a dozen pack members standing outside.

From the front of the group, Doug steps forward. "What Alaric did tonight…" Doug trails off, shaking his head. "Well, we just wanted to let you know—whatever you need, we have your back."

The group takes a few cautious steps back, making room for Liam as he exits the trailer and comes down the steps. "You are all willin' to follow me, even if it means violatin' Alaric's orders?"

There is a chorus of grunts and nodding heads. Liam takes his time, looking them each in the eye.

"There are others, too," Doug says. "No one is happy with what happened tonight. But I'm not sure you have the support of the entire pack."

"How many?" asks Liam.

"Maybe about half. But with the roll Alaric's been on lately, it won't take much to turn the rest."

Liam nods. "Thank you. Keep this to yourselves for now. Even if you think you can trust the other wolves, we can't let Alaric catch wind of any gossip. His response will be rash and ruthless. Hang close to your trailers, and I'll send word of the next steps."

The group filters away, glancing at each other as they do. Liam feels it inside, they are unsure if they've made the right decision.

"Oh." Doug turns back around, tossing a set of keys to Liam. "Here."

"What's this?" Liam asks, catching the set in the air.

"For the office at the launch, and the lock box that holds the keys to each of the boats. Everything there is at your disposal."

Eyes wide, Liam nods his head in thanks. *Time to go get Serena.*

Chapter Twenty

The small boat skims over the surface of the ocean. There is nothing but inky black above and below Liam. The milky glow of the nearly full moon doesn't give enough light. It's as if the darkness is working to swallow the moon whole.

Liam peels his eyes from the compass on the boat's dashboard to study the moon. Only two more nights until Serena's birthday. Two nights until the deadline, and Alaric's ultimatum given to the king almost eighteen years ago. Once Serena is given to the wolves, Alaric will allow them to take back the beaches in peace. The king thought his own sacrifice would satisfy the debt, but he was wrong. And the mermaids would be wrong thinking Serena's sacrifice will be the last. Alaric will never be content—not as long as there are Undine left in the ocean.

Slightly off course now, Liam adjusts the steering wheel.

Come on Serena, where are you?

He has no doubt she can find him if she is listening, or that he could find her if she sends out a call. But what if something happened? Or what if she decided not to come?

He slows the boat and tries peering into the darkness, but the rolling ocean plays tricks on his eyes. His vision is no good out here. Catching movement out of the corner of his eye, he turns, heart racing. It is just an extra large wave. The boat rocks from side to side as it rolls underneath him. It would be only too easy for one of those mermaid guards to sneak up on him, or to leap from a wave and take aim with their trident or a bow and arrow.

Liam hunches his head down, as if that will help.

There is a rush of displaced water, unnatural to the movement of the ocean. Liam cocks his head. The barely discernable whine is running up from the ocean depths.

Liam turns, eyes scanning the surface. He feels so helpless out here.

Keep it under control.

Spiky hairs bristle under his skin, aching to be released. The whine gets louder as it nears the boat. The scar on his face burns, and his joints throb, anticipating the transformation.

Behind the boat, water explodes up and out, spraying in all directions. A form shoots up into the sky just as a growl emits from Liam's throat. But he has spotted the midnight blue scales, and by the time Serena tucks her body for a roll, he has managed to swallow down his animal instincts.

Liam turns back to the wheel, ready to rev the engine when she lands. He hears a dull but solid thud behind him.

"Show off," Liam says, smiling over his shoulder. He eases the throttle forward.

Serena takes a step back for balance. "You came alone?" she asks, glancing around the boat, casting suspicious glances at the storage bins.

"I said I would, didn't I?" he answers. *Though she didn't say as much.* There is no way to tell what follows them under the surface.

"Clothes." Liam nods toward a black duffel bag sitting on the floor next to him.

Cautiously, Serena edges closer to him. She is covered from head to toe in armor. Midnight blue scales glitter under the light emerging from behind dark clouds, as if it were a shadow of the moon itself, cast upon the ocean dark. The sharp, angular lines of her face aren't necessarily imposing, though they give her an air of mischievousness. She is thinner than most humans Liam has seen, but the definition of muscle in her spindly arms and long legs says she has some fight to her.

Serena bends to unzip the bag. A braid of pitch-black hair falls over her shoulders. Standing over her, Liam can see the bioluminescent glow of each strand near her skull as if it is anxious to run the length of her hair. Somehow, she keeps it under control, just as he fights to keep his wolf fleece from emerging.

When she stands, she is holding a light blue t-shirt and a pair of small sweatpants. Pinching them in between two fingers, she brings them closer and sniffs.

Liam holds back laughter, which turns into a snort. She looks truly appalled that she is about to don the outfit.

She glares at him. "I feel like you should turn around."

"Done." He is afraid he really will laugh out loud watching her try to struggle into the clothing. "So will this be a first—a mermaid wearin' human clothing?"

"So far as I know," she mumbles.

Liam hears her hopping around the boat, then stumbling.

"No wonder we call them Ungainlies—though unsightlies might be a better description," she says behind him.

Liam looks over his shoulder, and raises an eyebrow. He eases back on the throttle until the boat is only coasting.

"What?" she asks when he turns, crossing his arms.

"Unsightly is right," he remarks. She is holding out her arms as if large, inflated balloons are shoved up into her armpits. Her feet are more than shoulder-width apart, she pulls her stomach in, and her neck long. She is trying to abstain from touching as much of the material as she can.

"What?" she says. "It's itchy."

"It's just cotton," Liam shrugs.

"Why did you stop?"

"We have some work to do, especially if you are gonna pass off as a human. You are bein' way too obvious; lower your arms."

Serena obeys, but just by a little.

"Lower," he says.

A look of disdain crosses her face, and she drops them a little further.

He fixes Serena with his best stare. "All the way."

She takes a deep breath, and lets her hands drop to her sides. "There," she says, her eyes closed tight.

"Good. Now unclench your fists, open your eyes, and relax your face. Try not to look like you are holdin' your breath."

"That's what it feels like," Serena argues.

This is going to be harder than I thought.

"Promise me you will keep clothes on at all times, no matter how itchy they are. We can't hide you from the werewolves or the humans if you are showing off your scales or bare skin."

Serena rolls her shoulders in one, large circle, closes her eyes again, then stretches her neck. It looks as though she is giving herself a silent pep talk, coaxing herself through the process.

When she opens her eyes, the bioluminescence at her roots has winked out. Her spine is no longer as rigid as a trident—it is curved, like she is slightly slumping. Her shoulders are relaxed and even the sharp, angular features of her face seem somehow softer. She has successfully transformed into a passable human.

"Yes," says Liam. "Like that!"

"As you say," Serena nods.

His smile turns into a frown. "You have to stop sayin' stuff so…so…rigid."

For a split second, her spine stiffens, but she corrects herself and tries again. "Whatever."

"And now you sound like a proper teenager," Liam says.

"Thank you." Serena cocks her head. "I think. Now, shall we continue, or do you prefer to drift among the waves the rest of the night?"

Liam furrows his eyebrows. "No, I really don't. I have someone I need you to meet anyway."

"But I need to see—"

Liam opens up the throttle and guns the boat forward, effectively cutting off Serena and leaving the ocean behind as fast as the little boat will allow.

Serena settles herself in a cushioned bench at the bow, eyes peering into the water as if she can see beyond the mirrored surface. Reaching out, Serena stops herself just before her fingertips dip into the ocean. Instead, she takes a deep breath, steeling herself, and looks toward the fast-approaching shoreline. Sequoias and pines slice through the air, like a beacon guiding Liam home.

Her eyes don't linger long at sprawling Vancouver Island. Instead they float up, fixed on the waxing moon. It has broken through the cloudy sky with an intense glow. Liam's birthmark tingles under the midnight rays. He looks at Serena basking her own face in the moonlight and he wonders if her skin tingles under the rays too.

Within minutes, the boat is puttering into the docks. He doesn't have much practice with watercraft, and it takes a few tries to angle the starboard side into the pier. Flicking off the motor, Liam walks the length of the small boat, throwing ropes up on the wooden walkway.

Stumbling a bit as he does it, Serena laughs as she crosses the boat steps out onto the pier. "Where are your sea legs, Liam?" Serena jokes.

He doesn't take it as such. "Disappeared, when my parents abandoned me."

Serena pauses on the dock, shoulders hunched. Finally, she turns. "Apologies, I should not have said that."

Shrugging, Liam steps out of the boat to tie off the ropes. "It's okay. But now you are soundin' all mermaid-y again."

"What? Teenagers don't apologize?"

He smiles. "Not much. The better response would have been something like…'bitter much'?"

"I'll keep that mind." Her eyes scan the small hut sitting at the beginning of the dock, where the ocean ends and the land begins. "What is this place?"

Liam takes a deep breath, hoping this is going to go over well. "I like to think of it is as my second birthplace." He gestures, and the pair walk forward, side by side, down the pier.

Chapter Twenty-One

By the time Liam and Serena step inside the small hut, the sun is peeking over the treetops. Liam walks in with her close behind. The loud snoring lets Liam know they won't risk facing off with Cecil's rifle.

"He's the one?" Serena asks. "He looked after our sons when we gave them to the Earth?" She walks around the armchair in which Cecil sleeps, then bends to look closer at his face. "He received you?"

Cecil snorts and Serena flinches.

He shrugs, turning his attention to the fire. It is smoldering out. *Cecil must've gone through a good share of wood last night.* Liam smiles. *I'll have to get him more.*

"Why is he so wrinkly?" Serena asks. "Like Ungainly toes that have been underwater too long."

When Liam turns, Serena is extending one finger to the lines on Cecil's cheek. "Serena…don't!"

Cecil jolts forward, eyes flinging open, and jostling the rifle off his lap as he gasps. The gun lands on Serena's toe, the one Liam remembers being injured during the King's Massacre.

"Ow!" She lashes out, slapping Cecil across the face.

All Liam can do is bury his forehead in his hands.

"What in the Sam Hell?" Cecil starts, coughing after each word. He glances at Liam. "Who is this?"

"It's…Serena." Liam lowers his hand in defeat, all hopes of an amenable friendship gone out the gunshot hole.

Cecil glares at the mermaid in front of him. "Serena who?" But his gaze lingers on her face and her hair. He pushes himself to standing so he stares directly at her, his eyes opening in wonder, then slanting into acknowledgement. "She's one of them…well, I'll be." Staring at the fire, then back to Serena, Cecil narrows his eyes. "Why are you here?"

"I have to make peace with Alaric," she says.

Liam shakes his head in disbelief. He can't let her turn herself over to Alaric. *I have to keep Serena from going to Alaric, and keep Alaric from finding Serena.*

"Will he be at your camp?" she asks Liam.

Cecil snorts. "No sense in headin' for the noose just yet," he says. "How about somethin' to drink first?"

"I suppose if that is the polite thing to do," Serena glances at Liam who nods his encouragement. Resigned, she follows Cecil to the kitchen.

Liam walks to the window, pulling down one of the plastic vertical blinds to peer outside. Dawn is already creeping through the trees, pushing away shadows and calling forth the birds. No sign of any wolves.

"Poseidon be graced—I want one of these!" Serena exclaims.

Liam turns to find Serena and Cecil standing in front of the fridge, each with a bottle of beer in their hands. "A beer?" he asks.

She shakes her head, handing the open bottle in her hand to Liam. "No, the taste doesn't agree with me. I meant one of these." She points to the cooler. "Rayne has to dig holes in her kitchen until they fill with ocean water for cold food storage. I've stumbled into them more than once. Not pleasant, especially first thing in the morning. She would love this."

Liam puts the bottle to his lips, taking a drink. "I can get you some."

"Can you? I mean—it wouldn't be too much trouble?"

"Just gotta get over to the grocery store, they have plenty."

"It's that easy? They just—hand them over?"

"Well, I mean, I have to pay for them and all…"

Serena's lips part in wonder.

"What?" asks Liam.

It's just weird to think how everything you need is just so available to you," she shrugs. "In The Deep we have to make everything, or hunt it. Or hope it floats by in a pile of Ungainly trash."

"Let's consider it an early birthday present." He smiles, but it quickly fades as he realizes the dire consequences associated with her birthday. "Why are you here, Serena? What's your plan?"

She glances at Cecil, and in a matter of moments she is brought back into herself. Liam watches as her spine goes rigid. Her lips press together, and her chin tilts down. He can almost pinpoint a slight glow at the roots of her hair which lends a certain mystic ambiance to her appearance.

The most disturbing part for Liam is the shadow that falls across her face, darkening the skin beneath her eyes and emphasizing the tiny lines at the corner of her mouth. They are the type of lines that look as though they should not appear for several years to come.

"I need to make peace with Alaric because sooner or later, my people will by bound for The Dry. Our water is poisoned, I think beyond the point of recovery, and our food sources are dying—the corals are turning to bare bones."

"It's happening all over the damn world," Cecil grunts.

Liam looks at him in surprise. It's not like the man gets a newspaper. He doesn't even have a television.

"Half my life has been spent in the oceans," Cecil says, taking offense to Liam's questioning gaze. "It ain't hard to notice the differences from even fifteen years ago."

"Even so," says Serena. "We cannot seem to migrate somewhere safer, like many other sea creatures can do."

"Neither can we," mumbles Liam. "Believe me, I've tried."

"You can't leave?" Serena asks, mouth dropping open.

He raises an eyebrow. "You think we hang out for, what? The beautiful view?"

Now she blushes as her mouth snaps shut, the subtlest shade of pale blue running across her face. All Liam can think is there is no way she could blend in with humans.

She clears her throat. "Moving away from Society at first is just…cumbersome. Your whole body grows heavier, and you just start to feel so—"

"Tired," Liam finishes for her.

She nods.

"And you really just want to go back to your own bed," he continues. "Or…wherever you sleep."

She smiles.

"But if you can keep going, the feeling changes. The weight settles deep into your bones, and it—it—"

"Hurts," Serena finishes for him this time. "And then the pull begins. The further you go, the more spread out you feel. Like part of you has been left at Society."

"It gets tighter, and tighter. A thin thread that is about to snap." Liam shudders in memory.

"Has it ever?" asks Serena.

"What," Liam looks at her. "The thread?"

She nods.

"No. I've never made it that far."

"Me neither," she says. "I felt it when I was swimming out to find your boat. But I think it got better the closer you came."

"It's because you're leavin' the heart of the people," Cecil speaks up from his armchair.

Startled, Liam almost jumps. He forgot Cecil was in the room, and he certainly didn't remember the old man making his way to his chair.

Serena walks over to the old man, standing in front of the dark fireplace. "What do you mean 'the heart of the people'?"

Cecil just shrugs, staring at the fire with glazed over eyes.

"Like, where they live—their caves?" Liam offers.

"No." Serena shakes her head. "We migrated here; some say our kind came over all the way from the Atlantic. Our home now wasn't our original nesting grounds." Serena looks at Cecil again, her eyes narrow in concentration. "The heart of the people," she murmurs. "Our bloodline—the royal bloodline."

"That doesn't make sense," Liam says. "You are the last remaining heir; you have the blood. You still couldn't leave."

"But...I'm not the last remaining heir." Serena looks up at Liam.

His lips part, just slightly. He is catching on. "Because I am your twin brother."

"Two halves of a whole," Cecil whispers, drawing his blanket up to his chin. In the next few seconds, his eyes flutter closed and he is snoring.

Serena turns, grabbing the black bag that held her clothes.

"What are you doing?" Liam asks.

"We have to go," she says, walking to the kitchen. She stuffs a few bottles of water into the bag, then begins searching the cupboards.

"Wait a minute, slow down." Liam follows her, holding up his hands.

"Don't you see? The old man is right. It's us, Liam! I came to talk to Alaric, but maybe I don't have to. If we go together, we'll be okay. We have to try—we have to find somewhere safe for our people. Then we can come back and get them and—"

"Our people?" Liam asks. "They haven't been my people since they abandoned me on the dock, Serena."

Serena turns slowly, arms lowering to her sides. "I thought you wanted to help us."

"I do," he sighs, running a hand over his face. "But we have to do this the right way." He points out the window. "It's broad daylight out there Serena, and that t-shirt and jeans aren't going to fool anyone. If you want to travel, we'll do it at night when there ain't so many humans out."

"Ungainlies don't scare me, Liam."

He smiles. "Then you know nothin' of our world, Serena. Please, let's just wait until tonight. Besides, there are a few more I want to bring with us. I have my own people to look after."

Chapter Twenty-Two

"A few more?" Serena accuses Liam with narrowed eyes. She and Cecil come out from behind a tree to meet the group in the middle of the wolfsbane patch. It is the one spot close to the edge of the forest that Liam is sure Serena can find on her own.

The pair are half an hour late, though with the way Cecil wheezes by her side, Liam can understand why. "You don't have to come, old man," he says.

Cecil tries glaring at Liam, but the effect is ruined when a coughing fit takes over.

"Well, the truck is just a bit further," offers Liam in the way of an apology.

"Will we all fit?" asks Serena.

Liam watches her scrutinize the group. Connor, Zeke, Doug, and Colin all stand behind Liam. He agonized most of the day over a plan to slowly introduce Serena to his most trusted followers—who goes first, how to do it, how much time until he includes the next person in his secret. By evening he had a raging headache and was nowhere close to a workable plan. He decided to just do it all at once, and as soon as possible. They are running out of time.

His gaze moves from Serena, who seems to be taking the situation in stride, to his pack members. They are all already on edge after the fight.

Zeke stares at Serena with one eye, the other is still swollen shut. "I remember you from the King's Massacre," he says, licking his lower lip. He lowers his gaze. "I'm sorry about your friend. That, well, it just wasn't right."

"Thank you." Serena nods back. "There isn't much about this situation that is right."

"Preachin' to the choir, sister," smiles Doug. "Glad the boat ride went okay. I offered full use of my docks and watercraft to Liam, and I extend the same offer to you. Though I suppose you don't have much need for boats..." Doug trails off.

"You never know." Serena smiles back. "But thank you."

Liam releases a slow sigh of relief. *So far, so good.*

"Who's that, mama?" a tiny voice calls out from the back of the pack. Standing behind the five men is Darcy and her boys. Up three hours past their bedtime, the boys have mostly been subdued and quiet; the youngest is asleep and snorting, draped across Darcy's arms.

Serena lifts her nose to the air, staring at the family with wide eyes.

"They are...your young?" she asks to no one in particular.

Nodding, Liam steps aside so she can see them better. "You saw them when I showed you the camp before the King's Massacre. These boys are the only wolves born from a human mother."

"Their scent is different from the rest of you..." Serena starts, looking unsure of herself for the first time. "The wolf in them is stronger, yet more suppressed. Like they have better control."

"They do," says Colin, the hint of a prideful father's grin on his face. "No accidental transformations, not during the full moon—not even as babies."

"Yeah, but we'll see what happens with a mermaid so close," grunts Zeke.

"Yes, we will, but I shall do my best so as to not cause any problems," Serena shoots back at Zeke. Then her eyes flit to Darcy. "You have a beautiful family."

Darcy shifts from one foot to another, but holds Serena's gaze. "Thank you."

"We gonna stand here jabberin' much longer?" Cecil suddenly pushes his way through the group.

"He's right, we don't want to run out of night." Liam turns, motioning everyone forward with his arm. "To the left, Cecil—I parked at the West Coast trailhead."

Without a word, Cecil adjusts his heading and sets the pace for the group. It is slow, leaving Liam with time to agonize over every wayward sound ringing out from the forest. There shouldn't be any more wolves out tonight. Connor arranged for a series of complaints from certain members of the pack, all set to voice them at various times with visits to Alaric's trailer. He and his crew have a busy night ahead of him, so hopefully they won't get any interference. Nonetheless, Liam slows down to walk with Serena at the back of the group. He doesn't want to take any chances.

"Sleep good?" Liam asks, glancing at her out of the corner of his eye.

"A little," she says. "Had better luck on the floor than on one of those itchy armchairs."

Liam snorts. "I always wondered if the old man has fleas. Had an outbreak at the trailer park, once. Wasn't pleasant."

She raises a questioning eyebrow.

"Though I suppose you don't have fleas down in The Deep. I suppose you have no idea what fleas even are."

The conversation comes to an awkward lull. Liam scratches the back of his neck.

"So what's the plan?" Serena asks. "We just...see how far we can get? Because I can't stay gone—I have to come back for my people."

"Tonight is a test. We'll see if Cecil's theory about two halves of a whole is right." Liam clears his throat. The whole thing sounds a little cheesy. "And if it works, we'll leave Darcy and the boys somewhere safe and then come back to deal with Alaric. We can make runs every night if we have to, get everyone out who wants out."

"Are they in particular danger?" asks Serena, nodding ahead to Darcy and her boys.

"Alaric wants at them bad. Been tryin' to figure out the secret ever since the first was born. Every other time a woman becomes pregnant by one of us, she miscarries, or gives birth to a human child—to the right, Cecil!" Liam yells up to the old man stumped by a fork in the trail.

Cecil grumbles something then ambles down the path on the right.

"It's just—he's desperate to keep the pack going," Liam says. "Without having to rely on the newly abandoned." He glances at Serena.

Serena nods, her face softening. "I know how heavy a burden that can be."

There is a long silence as they walk, Serena's words hanging in the air between them. The scrape of boots against the ground grows louder when they reach the gravel-covered parking lot.

"Here we are," says Liam, nodding to the only vehicle there. It is a rusty pick-up truck and looks as though it won't even start.

"You've been takin' care of her," Cecil says, a wide grin spreading across his face.

Serena looks at Liam with an arched eyebrow.

"Should've seen it when he gave it to me," Liam mumbles to her. "Didn't even have all four wheels." He pulls a set of keys out of his pocket and tosses them to Connor. "Keep it slow. It's not like there are seatbelts back here."

Connor and Doug climb in the cab of the truck, while everyone else crams into truck bed. They sit shoulder to shoulder, Serena in between Liam and Darcy.

Serena leans in, whispering to Liam, "What are seatbelts?"

He sighs. "If we get pulled over, just please don't talk."

She looks like she has another question on the tip of her lips, but she squeezes them shut and nods.

Liam looks around at Darcy. As the truck engine sputters to life, the oldest boy falls asleep against her shoulder, and the youngest she has been carrying begins to wake up.

"We'll take it slow," he says. "If they start to feel any pain at all, we'll turn around at your word."

The deep crease between Darcy's eyebrows softens.

"Mommy?"

All eyes turn to the three-year-old boy in her arms.

"Shh, honey," Darcy whispers. "We are going on a little trip. Go back to sleep and I'll wake you up when we get there."

The boy doesn't close his eyes again. They are wide open as he stares up at the sky, stars littering it with bright pinpoints of light. Liam shudders, remembering the last time they tried to leave. Spasms overtook the youngest worse than the other two. He doesn't talk about it anymore, but Liam knows he remembers. Little hands tighten around his mother's waist.

"Do you know my friend, Serena?" Liam asks, hoping to distract him. There is a bump as the truck leaves the gravel lot and ambles onto hard pavement.

The boy's eyes shift from sky to mermaid as he realizes he is sitting next to a complete stranger. When Serena smiles at him, he shrinks further into his mother's chest.

Without a word, Serena looks away, staring at her feet stretched out in front of her. But the boy's gaze lingers on her, and Liam watches as it changes from fear to fascination. Liam can hear scales emerge before he leans forward to see them.

Only a few midnight blue scales emerge on her bicep; enough to take the shape of a five pointed star. The boy's eyes light up and he reaches out with a shaky finger. Serena glances at him, nodding her encouragement. Emboldened, he gives one of the scales a soft poke. The scale retracts underneath smooth skin. Serena wipes away the trickle of blood it leaves behind.

His eyes grow even wider. "Does it hurt?" he asks.

"Not as much as it used to." She shrugs.

"Oh, can you make a pirate ship?"

"Robbie," Darcy scolds her son.

But Serena just laughs. "That might be a bit complicated."

The wind increases as the truck picks up speed on the highway. The entire group hunches down.

"How about this?" asks Serena, almost nose to nose with the boy so he can hear her. Scales retract and emerge in different places and both Darcy and Robbie stare. Finally, the scales settle into a pattern. It is one long wave up and down her arm. It shifts, creating the effect of a rolling breaker in midnight blue. Moonlight glares against the scales, just as it would the surface of the ocean.

Robbie looks away. "The ocean scares me," he says.

The waves disappear into Serena's arm. "Why?"

"Sharks," Robbie says. "That eat you alive!"

Darcy laughs. "His older brothers, just trying to scare him."

"Oh, I wouldn't worry too much about sharks," Serena assures him. "They don't like the way people taste."

"How do you know?" asks Robbie.

"Because." Serena leans in further, whispering, "They told me."

"Oh," Robbie's lips round out. "Wow, you can talk to sharks?"

"In a way." Serena winks at him.

This late at night, the truck only passes a rare car traveling in the opposite direction. When the bright lights of a biker bar break up the monotony of the dark, Darcy and Liam exchange a glance. This was where they turned around last time. So far, no one feels anything.

Hope and excitement bloom in Liam's chest. Cecil is right; as long as Serena and Liam are together, no one is bound to the same spot. A thought crosses his mind, and he frowns. If the trick truly is Liam and Serena being together, what is everyone else feeling back at the park? Are they writhing in pain—pain that worsens as Liam and Serena move further and further away?

Liam leans over and bangs on the window separating the cab from the rest of the world. When Connor turns to look, Liam makes a motion holding his hand up to his ear.

Call.

They need to check in with someone back at the trailer park, and make sure everyone is okay. Connor can do it from the quiet of the cab.

But Connor shakes his head no, and points to the road ahead of him.

Blue and red flashing lights are dotted across the road in a barrier.

"What is it?" Serena asks.

"Police checkpoint," says Liam. "Probably looking for drunk drivers."

"Well, we're not drunk," says Serena. "Right?"

"Right," he responds. "But this ain't gonna go well."

Chapter Twenty-Three

"I promise I won't talk," she mumbles, staring at the blockade of five cop cars spread across the road.

A uniformed officer motions for Connor to pull over. As the truck squeaks to a stop, Liam watches an older gentlemen stumble on top of a chalk line drawn on the asphalt.

Here is hoping Connor didn't try calming his nerves before the trip with a few drinks.

"License and registration," barks out the officer before Connor even has his window all the way down.

As the men in the cab shuffle through the glove box, Liam glances at each of the passengers in the rear. The panic is clear on their faces. Though Liam suspects the authorities at least know of their trailer park, the clan takes great pains to steer clear of organized government. No one has birth certificates, passports, or social insurance numbers, and the generic documents they do have are all forged—like the license Connor is now handing the officer.

The officer takes a long time with the license, studying both front and back with his flashlight. He looks up at Connor, shining the light square in his eyes, then looks back down at the license.

"Richardson!" he calls out with a strong Canadian accent. "Come oot here, will ya?"

"What you got?" another officer responds, walking over.

Just as the first officer begins to hand over the license, lips forming a question, Richardson stops, staring at the children in the back of the cab. "Oh, no. Everybody out—now."

"Is there a problem?" Connor opens his door, one foot out of the truck.

"Not you!" the officers shout simultaneously.

"Sit back down, sir." The first officer closes the door for him, then hands the forgotten license back through the window.

"Officer, please." Darcy's voice is soft, but it cuts through the storm of male ego better than a strong howl on a silent night. "My boys just fell asleep, and they've had a rough day. I don't want to wake them."

"I'm sorry ma'am, but all minors have to be buckled in, aye? It's the law."

"Our minivan broke down up the highway," Colin chimes in. "This gentlemen here was kind enough to offer us a ride to the next motel we come across. And believe me, I know he's sober—I wouldn't let my entire family ride with him otherwise."

Robbie, still sitting in his mother's lap, whimpers, "Mom, my legs hurt."

"Hush," she says, "we'll take care of it in just a minute."

Liam and Darcy exchange a glance.

The old man performing his balancing act trips, crashing into the side of the truck.

"That'll put a dent in her," mumbles Cecil.

The group is momentarily forgotten as Richardson calls for more help with the drunk. He is growing more belligerent by the second, and additional officers only worsen the situation.

When the officer finally turns his attention back to the Liam and his clan, he looks resigned. He has bigger problems to deal with tonight. "I'm going to let you off with a warning this time," he tells Connor. "Next motel is two miles up—it ain't the Hilton, but I suggest you don't go no further than that until you have car seats for these kids, aye? A lot of drunks are out tonight, and they all seem a bit crazier than usual. Must be the full moon."

"The moon isn't full," says Serena.

Liam's heart stops. He stares at her in shock.

Her eyes go wide too, as if she can't believe she just spoke.

"What was that?" the officer shines the light directly in her eyes. Liam can see her pupils closing up almost instantly, but instead of shrinking circles, they go narrow like a cat's eyes.

"I just meant to say that the full moon is tomorrow night," Serena stumbles over her own words.

"You high or somethin' sweetheart?" Richardson asks, peering closer at her eyes.

Robbie shifts beside Serena again, rubbing at his knees, wrists, and elbows.

"Heh." Liam laughs, flopping his arm around Serena's shoulders. "New contacts. Kept losing her glasses."

Richardson turns off his flashlight, arching his eyebrow at Liam. "Just make sure she doesn't get behind the wheel—not tonight."

"Will do…uh, sir." Liam taps on the cab window. "We're okay to go—straight to the motel."

Liam lets out a slow sigh of relief as the flashing lights blink out behind the shadowing trees as the road curves inland.

"Mom, it hurts…" the oldest boy says. He has woken up, and he is doubled over grabbing his head.

"Oh, Aiden honey come here." Darcy hands Robbie over to Colin and wraps her arms around Aiden to whisper in his ear.

Liam exchanges a worried glance with Serena.

"Colin." Darcy looks up at her husband. "We can't do this again—I won't put them through it."

Colin looks at each of his sons, as if weighing the possibilities. They don't seem to be in unbearable pain. One is still asleep.

"Colin!" Darcy yells, exasperated.

"I know, I know—but we can't drive right back through the roadblock." He shifts Robbie on his lap. "We have to wait until morning—or at least until the cops are gone."

Glancing over his shoulder at the commotion in the rear, Connor steps on the gas, slowing only once the motel comes into view. He pulls in the parking lot, steering the truck well away from the office and from any other cars.

Piling out of the back of the truck, everyone lends a hand helping the boys. The only one that remained asleep suddenly jolts awake and pukes over the side of the truck.

"I'll get a room," Connor announces, glancing at the puddle forming on the ground. "And some extra towels."

Anxious eyes glance around the parking lot, but no one else is out this late.

Liam rubs the back of his neck. *This was a bad idea*. He takes stock of his group. Darcy and Colin are tending the boys as best they can, with Zeke's help. Cecil is bent over examining the dent in the side of the truck. Doug and Connor are at the office. Serena…*where is Serena?*

Turning in a full circle, Liam spots her still in the back of the truck. "Are you okay?"

She straightens from her hunched position, hand over her chest. "I don't feel anything." Pausing, she closes her eyes and touches her stomach, knees and head, as if making sure. "I feel perfectly fine."

Liam turns. "Zeke!" he calls him over. The pink and purple bruises on his face are ugly; it's a wonder the officer didn't ask about it. "You doin' okay?"

"No, man, not at all. I think adrenaline from when we were sittin' at the roadblock sort of masked it. But now it is full on. I feel stretched too thin, like my joints might pop out of my sockets any second." He leans over rubbing his knees. "I've never left before. Is this how it is every time? I'd take a thrashin' from Alaric's thugs over this any day. Every day, in fact."

Connor and Doug return, keys and towels in hand. "One room so we can stick together," He says, wiping a sheen of sweat from his forehead. "It's going to be a long night. The pain only gets worse the longer we stay away."

"Someone needs to stay close by the roadblock, so we know the moment the cops leave."

"I'll go," Zeke announces.

Liam nods. "Stay out of sight."

Zeke lopes off into the woods. Liam knows he'll have it easier, remaining that much closer to home. Besides, with a face like his it is better to stay in the shadows; the group doesn't need any unwanted attention.

"Someone should stay with the truck. Keep an eye on things from out here in case someone has seen us."

"Got it," Doug offers.

"Thanks," says Liam. "Come in and get me if you need a break. Everyone else, let's get inside."

Serena and Liam watch as Darcy ushers the boys in while Connor holds open the door.

"You don't feel anything either, do you?" Serena asks as soon as everyone is out of earshot.

"No," Liam shakes his head.

"I told you, two halves of a whole—keeps you pieced together." Cecil says from behind, startling them both.

"Yeah but just us? It's not helping anyone else." Liam narrows his eyes.

Shrugging it off, Cecil ambles toward the motel room where Connor waits, still holding open the door. "I never said anythin' about everybody else."

Chapter Twenty-Four

Once inside the small room, Liam almost immediately has Darcy, Colin, and their three boys settled in on the bed. The family takes up the entire queen-size mattress and is squished up against each other as it is, with the parents flanking either side.

"It's okay," Darcy says when Connor offers to ask for cots. "Being close like this will help them."

Cecil settles into the only armchair the room has to offer, claiming it as his own.

"I'm gonna hang here, help keep watch for a little while," Connor says, leaning against the wall and pulling down a section of the plastic blinds to peer outside.

Serena walks to the small kitchenette, which is still part of the same room—but at least it has a dark corner. She leans against the wall, then slides to the floor. She looks how Liam feels: tired, worried, and helpless.

He glances around the crowded room one more time. The boys in the bed aren't asleep yet, though they are trying. On either side of them their parents massage their legs and arms. Darcy holds a small trash can for any more vomit episodes. By the window, Connor appears relaxed, but the subtle shifting from foot to foot tells Liam he is uncomfortable. Cecil is already snoring in his armchair.

There isn't anything else Liam can do for anybody. They just have to ride it out until morning, hoping no more humans try causing problems for them. He sighs, then sits down in between Serena and the cheap kitchen counters. He tries smiling at her, and she does the same, but it is painfully obvious that both are forced.

A whimper comes out from one of the boys.

"I'd help them if I could," says Serena softly.

"I know," Liam pats her hand. "It's funny—of all the people that can leave…"

"It ends up being the only two that won't leave anyone behind," Serena finishes for him.

There is a long silence, then Liam removes his hand to shove it in his pocket. "Alaric can't know about this."

"I'm not sure I'm going to tell any of my people. If they know I can leave at any time, convincing them of my leadership skills is going to be that much harder."

"A secret then," says Liam.

"Can we trust everyone here?"

Liam nods. "I'll talk to them. They are gonna want to put this night far behind them." Liam yawns, stretches, then reaches up to grab a granola bar out of the complimentary basket on the countertop. He opens it and hands it to Serena.

"We should save it for the others," says Serena.

"Trust me, no one feels like eatin'." He holds the granola bar out to her.

She takes it, breaks it down the middle and hands half of it back to Liam.

They chew in silence, staring at the door to the bathroom in front of them. Its paint is cracked and peeling, and there is a long stain—probably coffee—running down one side of it.

"Do you like it?" Liam asks.

Serena runs her tongue around the inside of her mouth, then swallows a large chunk of the granola bar with a grimace. "It's awful."

He laughs. "I suppose you can't wait to get back to your salmon."

She shakes her head. "I don't eat fish."

"Seriously?" He looks at her. "You're like…a mermaid vegetarian?"

"Undine." She nudges him with her shoulder.

"So what do you eat?"

Serena touches the back of her head to the wall, a small smile forming on her lips. "All kinds of seaweed, cooked or raw—always better with a touch of salt. Sea lettuce soup with hijki. Nori rolls, if you can avoid the hidden salmon. And there is noodled kelp—not even the guards can resist Rayne's noodled kelp. A bowl of that can let me get to The Dry, unescorted."

"Who's Rayne?" Liam asks.

"My mother, or…at least the one who raised me," says Serena. "She runs the orphanage. Though with no more calflings, she has turned the orphanage into a dining hall. With her help we'll have all the maidens proficient in the art of eating with utensils in no time."

Liam furrows his eyebrows.

"I'm preparing them for life in The Dry," Serena explains.

"Ah, because of the…"

"Because our ecosystem—our home is poisoned. It is why Rayne is so desperate to get me used to eating fish. All the plants are dying."

"Eatin' fish can't be all that bad," tries Liam.

"That's not the point. Without the plants, soon there would be no fish. Already plankton are in decline."

"Which means less carbon dioxide absorption and less oxygen output."

"What do you know of it?" Serena asks, a teasing tone to her voice.

Liam shrugs. "We did some learnin' growing up."

"Oh," Serena says. "That's…good."

Liam sits up straighter. "What I know is that corals are disappearing faster than the rainforests. They are worried that ocean acidification might trigger some sort of mass extinction event; because it has happened in the past."

"It's already started," Serena mumbles.

"So what are you doing about it?" asks Liam.

She shrugs. "We're talking about growing more food in The Dry, if we can." She takes a deep breath. "My goal really is to prepare them to live in The Dry, permanently. Though I don't want to say it outright; it would create too much resistance. The Undine are really stubborn."

"Tell me about it," says Liam.

"Quiet your mouth," says Serena. "You are glad you met me; I know it to be fact."

"I thank Poseidon himself every night for the midnight-blue Undine standing in a circle of yellow wolfsbane flowers."

Serena yawns. "Yes, well, continue praying to Poseidon, because if things continue down this path, this midnight-blue Undine, along with the rest of Society, will be here for good."

Liam smiles, but can't help but think that wouldn't be such a bad thing. Complicated, of course, but not all bad.

"I have to get some sleep," says Serena, glancing over at the bed. It appears as though the family has settled down for the most part.

"Do you want the floor, or the floor?" Liam asks.

"Nope. I'll sleep in here," says Serena, walking onto the bathroom's cold tile floor and stepping into the bathtub.

"Oh—for the water?" Liam asks.

"For the privacy," says Serena. "Freshwater doesn't do it for me." She turns around. "Good night Liam of Clan Werich."

"Good night, Serena, Queen of the Undine."

Serena smiles and closes the door. Liam can hear the shower curtain rings slide across the metal bar. He settles back down against the wall and the thin, brown carpet. Bending one leg, he lays his forehead against his knee, wondering how he got to this point. Four werewolves, three kids, a worried mother, an old man, and a mermaid—all hiding out in a dingy motel room, afraid of what the humans might do to them should they be discovered. This isn't how he imagined his reign, and he is positive it is not how Serena imagined hers.

Chapter Twenty-Five

Something nudges Liam's foot, and his eyes shoot open. His brain works to catch up to his body, and finally he comprehends Darcy in the bathroom in front of him, helping Robbie as he expels the contents of his stomach into the toilet. Rubbing his eyes, Liam checks his watch. Five a.m. They made it through the night—kind of.

He stands to unwrap a plastic cup and fill it with water.

"Here," he says and hands the cup to Darcy.

She nods in thanks, sleep lining her eyes, and wrinkles creasing her forehead.

Pulling his hand away, Liam sees Serena pull back the shower curtain to peer out. She keeps the rest of her body behind the curtain, as if she were caught in the middle of bathing herself. The entire situation makes Liam uncomfortable and he backs away from the room. Turning to the kitchenette counters, he fumbles through the complimentary basket, looking for the coffee packet. The sound of crying stops him cold.

"I want to go home, Mommy."

"I know honey, we're going soon." Darcy strokes Robbie's hair.

"When?"

"Very soon, I promise." Darcy makes a pointed glance at Liam and the question hangs in the air between them. *When?*

He shrugs, trying to keep the desperation off his face. He confirms again on his phone. No missed calls, no texts. *Where is Zeke?*

The crying starts up again, and Liam runs an agitated hand through his hair.

Another sound echoes out of the tiny bathroom. It is another type of moan, but higher pitched, and it wavers as though it is trying to find its place in the world.

Liam watches Darcy and the child turn, confusion knitting their eyebrows together. Serena, fully scaled, peeks out further from behind the shower curtain. Dark blue scales frame her face, highlighting her darker shadows. Because of it her cheekbones appear more withdrawn, her chin slightly more pointed. The angular look is mystifying, and the boy shrinks into his mother.

Determined, Serena allows her lips to part further. She finds her harmony within the small space and she ascends a series of tones, each note soft but sustained into the next note, all melting together in a perfect melody.

Serena pushes the curtain aside, putting her entire scaled body on display. Opening up her lungs, the sonorous notes breeze past her lips. Her chest expands as she calls back in the air and pushes it out again, inserting layer and depth.

It is when she adds lyrics to the song that Liam has to grip the countertop just to keep himself from moving toward Serena. The words seem familiar, yet he can't discern what they mean, nor where one ends and another begins. Still, he feels as though if only he could get a little closer to their creator, he might be able to unlock their mystery.

Serena steps over the railing of the tub, closer to Robbie. With eyes wide, and chin tilted to look up at Serena, he moves toward her, letting go of his mother's hand. The pace of the song quickens; she is telling a story. Liam wonders if Robbie can understand it any better than he can.

Cocking his ear, Liam can almost hear an underlying base beat, growing slowly louder. Serena sits on the edge of the tub, so she is eye to eye with Robbie. The child doesn't look scared, just…fascinated.

Rich and vibrant, music envelopes the entire room like silk strands weaving their way around Liam's waistline, caressing his skin and pulling him forward. The story climaxes, notes pulling together in an interlacing ambiance. When the final sounds are released, Liam cannot discern the exact point in time in which they end. Long after Serena's lips are closed, he swears if he strains hard enough, he can still make out fragments of the song.

Laughter from a stranger passing outside of the motel room draws Liam from his trance. He turns to find Zeke in the open doorway, staring into the bathroom, as are the rest of the occupants of the room—Cecil included. Their eyes are pinned on Serena, bodies leaning forward.

"You heard the song too?" Liam asks Zeke. "From all the way at the checkpoint?"

"No," Zeke makes an effort to shake his head and eases back on his heels. "I came to let you know the cops have all left. But…" He licks his lips. "I would walk a hundred miles further, pain or no, just to follow that voice."

"That's a mighty powerful song," Cecil mutters, glancing at Serena.

"Come on, Robbie. Let's get you in the truck." Darcy straightens his shirt and steers him out of the bathroom.

"It's okay, Mom. I feel better now."

"Good honey, now go get your shoes on." Before Darcy follows him out, she turns to Serena. "Thank you—your singing was like none I've ever heard."

Serena shrugs. "They say my mother—or...our mother..." She glances at Liam. "Could sing like that too."

"I have to say, a voice like that might make for better healing than any medicines I've ever administered." Darcy smiles and leaves the room.

"Can you give me a minute?" Serena asks Liam after Darcy leaves. "I just need to compose myself a bit before we go."

"Sure," Liam says, voice cracking.

Serena closes the door and Liam turns to those in the room who all seem to have trouble putting themselves into motion.

"Well, you heard Zeke. Cops are gone. Let's go home. Connor—grab that blanket. We might have to all hunker down in the back of the truck just so we don't get pulled over again."

"Right," Connor says. He steps toward the bed, but his eyes are still locked on the bathroom door.

Liam claps his hands, twice. "Snap out of it, everyone. We can probably make it back before anyone else is up at camp. Nobody will realize we even left—hopefully."

The room reluctantly whirls into motion with the logistics of sorting out whose shoes and jackets are whose, and who gets the leftover snacks—everyone having apparently gained their appetites back.

Liam casually kicks the wrapper of the granola bar he and Serena shared last night under the counter. The kids look downright famished.

The door to the bathroom inches open, and Serena peeks out just as she did from behind the shower curtain.

"Are you dressed this time?" Liam asks, joking.

"Yes, it's just..." she peeks out further. "I'm sorry for doing that—I didn't realize how much attention it would attract."

"It's fine," Liam assures her. "I think it helped everyone. You okay? You look kind of...pale."

"I don't know," Serena opens the door the rest of the way, moving slower than she usually does. "Not enough sleep, maybe." She pauses, surveying the room. Everyone is busy gathering their things and getting ready. "What?" Serena asks the one person staring at her.

"Nothin'," says Liam. "It's just I was thinkin' about how your song calls to us."

"Yeah, it does that. You, other Undine, the ocean... I guess."

Liam hands her his jacket. "When we were meetin' in the forest before, you called for me, right?"

"Yes," she answers, slipping shaky arms through the sleeves.

"And it was just me that showed up, like none of the other wolves heard it."

"So?"

"I'm wonderin' if you can call to just one." He shrugs, moving to the motel room door and holding it open for her. "Might be useful at some point."

Chapter Twenty-Six

It is still dark as the group rolls into camp. Those in the back of the truck hide under a motel blanket. It is so worn they can see the moon through the faded fibers. The almost complete circle is an ominous warning. It promises one more night of peace, then the full moon will be upon them, along with Alaric's deadline.

Liam pulls the blanket down as they park right in front of Colin and Darcy's double-wide trailer. All three boys have fallen asleep again, and Liam helps carry them inside while Serena and Cecil wait in the back of the truck.

"It's good to see your neighborhood up close," Serena tells Liam once he returns to the truck.

The camp is quiet and still, and her voice carries through the rows of shabby trailer homes.

Liam folds his arms over the edge of truck bed and nods. "Home sweet home."

"It's…nice."

Liam can tell the words are forced. "Homesick?" he asks.

"Maybe a little."

"You know you are free to go back anytime. I'll walk you halfway." He smiles.

She laughs. "Do you remember what happened the last time you tried to walk me home?"

Liam rubs a hand across his throat at the memory of the trident tips pressed hard against him. Her friend Ervin and two other guards had almost run him through. "Nothin' I couldn't handle—as long as big sis was there…"

That makes her laugh again.

Connor gets out of the cab and hands Liam the keys. "See you at the alley in a couple hours?" Liam asks. He pauses, watching Connor run a hand over his face, then changes his mind. "Just go get some sleep. Call when you are up."

They say their goodbyes, leaving just Liam, Cecil, and Serena together.

"We should get out of here before people start waking up and smelling mermaid," Liam says. "I'll drop you and Cecil off. Wanna ride up front?"

"I prefer to remain under the moon, if that's okay."

"Well I'm not okay with it," Cecil rolls to his knees, and crawls toward the tailgate on shaky hands. "I'd take air conditionin', the radio, and a cold beer over the open sky any day."

Liam holds out a hand to help Cecil down. "You know she ain't got air conditionin'—and the radio's broke."

Cecil pauses, looking at Liam with a hopeful eyebrow arch.

"Fine, hold on a second," Liam rolls his eyes, then disappears back into Darcy's trailer. He re-emerges, a bottle of beer in hand.

Cecil chuckles and the pair get in the cab.

Liam hands over the beer. "Here, you earned it."

"Oh, hell—I didn't do nothin' but sleep in an armchair all night." Nonetheless, Cecil pops open the beer and throws his head back—his Adam's apple moving up and down as he finishes at least half the bottle. He shifts in his seat, looking at Liam. "What was your plan anyway? Run away? Leave the rest of your brothers with Alaric?"

"Hey, I intend to give them a choice. If they want to stay with Alaric, so be it. Let them squirm in misery under his thumb if they want to."

"Still don't change the fact they're your brothers," Cecil says.

Liam glances at the old man, then turns the key. The truck sputters to life. "I am the youngest of the clan—why would they follow me?"

Cecil tips his bottle, pointing it briefly toward Liam. "You may be the youngest, but you were born to lead. It's in your blood. I suspect Alaric knew that almost right away. He feels threatened by you." Cecil sighs, the noise pushed out in one big puff through his nose. "Why do you allow him to take your blood anyway?"

Scratching the back of his neck, Liam thinks carefully about how to answer. He has asked himself the same question many times. "If I refuse my blood, he'll either try to take it by force or he'll turn to the others who have shown the most control over their wolf—like those boys. Alaric will find a way to get what he wants, no matter what."

Cecil snorts.

"I'm biding my time, old man. I'm not going to make any big moves until I'm sure the outcome will be in my favor."

"That's funny," says Cecil. "Because while you bide your time, your sister is running out of hers."

Liam glances over his shoulder at the blankets in the back of the truck. "I know."

"So, you've got mermaids who are coming ashore—and they will, whether they want to or not. Then you've got wolves who want them dead—and oh, by the way, neither species can leave the area."

"So?" Liam knows all this. He presses down on the pedal, urging the truck to go faster.

"You've got Serena standing in the middle of all of it—and then there is you, the only one that can escort her safely away."

A long silence stretches between the two men. When Liam pulls the truck off the road, Cecil finally speaks. "So who do you save? Serena—or everyone else?"

Liam glides to a stop next to Cecil's house, and turns off the engine. "What would you do, old man?"

Cecil shrugs. "I think trying to mediate between the two species may be a lost cause. But it really doesn't matter."

"Why?" asks Liam.

"Because." Cecil finishes the rest of his bottle. "I think you've already made your choice."

* * *

"Serena." Liam taps on the side of the truck once they are in front of Cecil's home and parked. He frowns when the lump under the blanket doesn't move. Lowering the tailgate, Liam pulls at the cover. It slides down from over her head and shoulders. She is asleep—fast asleep.

"Do you think she's okay?" Liam whispers as Cecil ambles past. "She looks kind of sick."

Cecil grunts. "If you ask me she's looked sick ever since she got here. Could be her radioactive hair or her Smurf-stained scales. Just carry her in, will ya? She seems to like sleeping in the bathtub."

Liam looks at Serena for a long time, his eyebrows furrowed. By the time Cecil has gone inside, propping the door open after him, Liam takes the rest of the blanket off of her. He hoists himself into the truck, and squats next to her prone body. None of her scales show underneath the t-shirt she wears. Liam peers closer at her skin. It is dry and flaking. The healthy glow Liam always swore illuminated her is no longer there.

He slides his hands under and almost reels back over the edge of the truck when he lifts her up; she is a lot lighter than he expected. It's as if she has hollow bones.

Serena stirs, but her eyes don't flutter open as Liam expects. Instead, she curls into his chest and arms, making his job all that much easier. He walks inside. Cecil has already used the bathroom and is busy making his breakfast.

Boots squishing over lumpy carpet breaks the silence of the dark hallway, and Liam nudges the bathroom door open with his foot. When he lays Serena down, she still doesn't open her eyes, and Liam's frown deepens.

"Goodnight, Serena." He says, bending down to plant a kiss on her forehead.

Liam returns to the kitchen and finds Cecil at the stove.

"Think she'll be hungry when she wakes up?" he asks, tearing into a package of bacon. "I haven't had someone to cook for in a long time."

Liam shakes his head. "She's a vegetarian."

"A what?" Cecil looks like he can't comprehend the question. "Don't she eat fish?"

Liam smiles. "Nope."

"Well, more for me then. She can have an apple."

"I think she's sick."

"I'll keep an eye on her..." Cecil offers. "I won't be noddin' off anytime soon. What will be more interestin' to see," he points his spatula at Liam, "is if anyone else in the clan felt the pain as you and Serena left—or if her people underwater did."

Liam nods. "Yeah, maybe you can mention it to her when she wakes? I'll be back after nightfall; I think today will be pretty busy."

Chapter Twenty-Seven

It is a long day of dealing with politics in the clan, recruiting more numbers, and trying to cover his tracks with Alaric. By the time Liam has a break to go check on Colin, Darcy, and the boys, the stars are just beginning to reveal themselves. He walks toward the double-wide trailer with quick steps and his head down, hoping to deter anyone else from approaching.

A barely discernable shout echoes out from the forest beyond the trailers. It is so faint, had Liam been inside, he is certain he wouldn't have heard it. He pauses, turning his ear to the sound. It comes again, but not as a shout this time—it is more like several elongated notes. They are panicked, sending chills down Liam's spine. His adrenaline spikes, even more so when he realizes the sound is coming from the direction of Cecil's home.

Turning, Liam runs. Before he reaches the tree line he is on all fours, well into his transformation. His clothes bulge, pushed out by a larger body underneath, finally ripping at the seams. He tears the last of the shirt off his shoulders with his teeth, then leans into his run. The eerie, sonorous tones get louder and more urgent as he runs. His legs won't go fast enough.

Finally, the house comes into view and the door is hanging wide open. Skipping the steps and the small front porch altogether, Liam bounds into the house.

Cecil and Serena both stand, shoulders relaxed and a slight hint of humor on their faces.

The wolf sniffs the air and does a quick round of the house. There is nothing amiss. Walking back into the living room, he transforms just so he can speak.

"What happened?" Liam asks. Chest heaving from the run, Liam stands bare naked in the middle of the living room. "Are you okay?"

Serena picks up a blanket from the couch and throws it to Liam. "I was just practicing."

"Practicing what?" He catches the blanket and it goes limp in his hands. His eyes dart around the room, still looking for a threat.

"Would you cover yourself, man?" Cecil spats. "No one here needs to see that."

Serena stifles a laugh with the back of her wrist.

Glancing down as if he just now realizes his nudity, Liam wraps the blanket around his waist. His breathing has calmed, and he narrows his eyes at Serena.

"I was singing—practicing my call," she explains. "Cecil suggested I try calling for just one person. Apparently I can," she smiles at Liam since he stands there as proof. "And not only that but I can invoke a certain emotion."

"So you used me to…" Liam points his finger at Serena, taking a step forward. He pauses when the blanket slips loose. Tightening the knot, Liam glares at Serena. "I was in the middle of somethin' important."

She glances at the blanket. "Okay."

An old table clock ticks, and outside a pair of birds exchange calls. Liam sighs. "It felt like…like my chest was about to explode. It was like watching a small child drown, and I could save him if only I went a little faster."

"Did anyone else hear?" asks Serena, looking out the window. "Is anyone else coming?"

Liam rubs his nose with this sleeve. "I don't think so—I just took off. They would've caught up to me by now if they were followin' your voice. That—well that is pretty incredible." Liam smiles. It quickly dies from his face. "But don't do it ever again."

Serena nods "Sure. Unless I mean it."

"And thanks for keeping the blanket handy." He tugs on the knot again, just to make sure it will hold. "Now what?"

Serena almost mows Liam over on her way out the door. "I have to try one more thing."

Liam glances at Cecil, who just shrugs, then turns to plop down in his armchair.

"Wait!" Liam calls after Serena. "Can't I at least get dressed first?"

Light on her feet down the steps, Serena takes long, quick strides across the yard to the pier.

"Guess not," he mumbles to himself.

Before she reaches the end of the dock, she is singing. The notes are faint, but it is an uplifting tune. Rich, bass-like undertones accompany high sonorous notes. It is pretty, but it doesn't invoke any kind of panic or temptation for Liam. This song isn't meant for him.

Stopping behind Serena, both stand at the end of the pier. After a minute or so of song, ripples bounce across the water, unnatural in their direction and speed.

"Serena," Liam whispers. The ripples move underneath the pier, then out the other side. "Who are you calling?"

The rest of the night has gone still, save for the turbulent, dark water.

Serena gasps, and Liam looks at her before following her line of sight. Bioluminescent hair, followed by a strong, angular face rises up, crowning the water. Liam recognizes the merman as one of the guards—not the biggest one, but the one that is never too far away from Serena.

The guard's eyes lock onto Serena, and as he floats forward the sharpened tips of a trident surface. The golden pikes fall forward, angled toward Serena.

Liam's breath catches in his throat. "Serena!" he manages to croak out as he moves toward her. The merman throws the trident and it flies through the air lightening quick. Leaping in front of Serena, Liam extends one hand and the stem of the trident slams into his palm.

He swings it out. The weapon is lighter than he expected and Liam overcorrects on the other side. Serena has to duck to avoid being clotheslined by it. But Liam keeps his eye on the merman, who is now almost at the pier.

Making an exerted effort to control his newfound weapon, Liam points the tips down, aiming right between the creature's eyes. The trident is stopped short with a loud clank as it clashes with another trident. Sparks burst out, scattering across the surface of the water.

"What do you think you are doing?" Serena's words are edged with fury.

"That's what I'd like to know." Liam's lip curls up in a snarl.

When Serena moves into his peripheral vision, arms crossed, foot tapping on the wooden slats, Liam realizes she is looking at him, not down at the water.

He glances at her, hesitant to take his eyes off the merman. "Wait, you mean me?"

"Yes, you." She holds out her hand, palm open.

The merman shrinks back into the water until the ocean seeps over his shoulders. Liam relaxes his stance, and slowly lowers the trident.

She makes an impatient motion with her fingers, and holds her hand out further.

"Oh," Liam places the trident in her hand.

"He was delivering my weapon. I left it behind so as not to draw suspicion here."

"I thought he was…" begins Liam.

"What?"

Both hands drop uselessly to his side. "I thought he was trying to hurt you."

The merman hasn't said a word. He is silent in the water, bobbing slightly with the waves and watching them. It's creepy.

"Well…" Liam hikes the blanket up a little further on his waist. "You just be careful with that thing. It is sharp."

Serena crosses her arms. The merman is studying Liam, and Liam thinks he can see a small smile on the creature's face.

"Liam," Serena sighs. "May I introduce you to Kai? He is Second in Command of the Queen's Guard."

"Second?" Liam asks.

The smile disappears from the merman's face, which gives Liam some satisfaction, like he has just scored a point.

"And," continues Serena. "He is my…well my…"

Her hesitance in naming their relationship is even more satisfying.

Another point.

Serena scrunches her forehead in thought, then finally looks at Kai. "He is special to me. And is never, ever to be harmed." Her voice has gone soft, and so have her eyes.

Minus one.

"Kai," she says, walking around Liam and toward the merman. "As you well know, this is Liam of Clan Werich—my twin brother who has just as much of the royal bloodline running through his veins as I do." She arches her eye at the merman. "Understood?"

Kai nods his head and says his first words. "Yes, your majesty."

All at once, Serena's jawline tightens, her eyes blaze, and she slams the butt of her trident against the dock. The merman's words have pissed her off.

And we're back up.

Kai knows it, too. He swims forward to rest his upper arms on the pier. Serena is barefoot, her one damaged toe peeking out from under the wide pant bottoms of her jeans. The water calms, lapping gently against the supports underneath the pier. A strong, calloused hand reaches for her foot. Just a few light brown scales dot the back of his hand.

Liam glances down at his own hand where several short hairs rest. Also light brown in color, they are wiry and tough like the werewolf hide that emerges.

The scaled hand hovers over Serena for a second, then sets down gently, covering her damaged toe.

Liam watches Serena's white knuckles loosen from around her trident. They turn pink as blood returns to them. Her lips part slightly, and she takes a deep breath.

Kai reaches up to her jeans, feeling the rough material between two fingers. "What are you wearing?" The merman scrutinizes Serena's clothes, then glances at Liam. "What is *he* wearing?"

Liam looks down at the blanket wrapped around his waist. His fist tightens over the knot, praying it doesn't fail him at the most inopportune moment. He clears his throat. "I'll just…be over here."

Serena nods, giving him an appreciative smile.

Turning his back on her is difficult, but he only walks the length of the pier until his feet hit solid ground and he turns around again. He watches the pair as they talk. She is on her knees, leaning out over the water. Kai cranes his neck back so his curve matches hers. They fit together perfectly. Liam wonders if they know that.

Chapter Twenty-Eight

Liam keeps glancing over his shoulder to sniff the air for other wolves, but he can't get the smell of salt and wet sand from his nose. The two mermaids together make a powerful scent. He crosses his arms and taps his foot.

Serena giggles.

His spine itches in irritation. The fact that they have yet to even glance in his direction makes him feel like a third wheel.

They are inching closer together, each of them smiling.

But it is when the smile drops from their faces, and their lips begin to part, that Liam goes still.

Crap—are they going to kiss? Yes, yes they are kissing. Gross.

Liam fights back the urge to turn away and gag.

When Kai's hands slide up Serena's arms, grasping her above the elbows, Liam's whole body tenses. Kai tugs and Serena falls into the water above him. There is a big splash, and then silence. No longer fighting back any urges at all, Liam is racing toward the end of the pier.

"Serena!" He skids to a stop right where agitated bubbles are racing up toward the surface. He shifts from foot to foot, debating whether to jump in after her. But even now, he can't get past all the emotions the ocean invokes: fear, rejection, desire.

"Serena!" he yells again, squinting into the depths. He can just barely make out two forms intertwined together. Just as he convinces himself she is okay, another element begins to surround them. It is a swarm of small white specks, pushed back and forth by the currents underneath. Liam drops to his knees, squinting even harder. He sees Serena reach out to catch a few white specks with the palm of her hand. It is the same thing Liam might do with snowfall.

Finally, the two mermaids break apart and rise to the surface. They stay like that for several moments, foreheads touching, murmuring to each other.

Serena turns away and pulls herself up onto the pier, waving away Liam's extended hand. As she stands next to him, smoothing her hair and straightening her sopping wet clothes, he tries not to stare too hard. But her skin is no longer flaking and dry. Most importantly, her glow is back.

"Kai would like to speak with you a moment," she says, picking up her trident. "I'll wait for you inside."

Before Liam can respond, she has turned on her heel and is walking down the pier.

"She looks much better," Liam says to the form he can hear emerging from the water.

A spray of water splatters across wooden planks and a thump hits the pier behind Liam.

"We can't go long outside our element," Kai says, standing up on the wooden planks. "She needs to be allowed to return home at least once a day."

Liam gives a short laugh, turning around to face Kai. "If I could send her back permanently, I would."

"Yes, well—I suppose she is not easily *made* to do anything." The hard lines running along Kai's jaw soften as the pair find something in common. Kai takes a deep breath, looking toward the house. "Speaking of which, we must not linger too long."

"Why?" Liam is turned off by his proper manner of speech. With Serena, it is kind of cute—with Kai it is just annoying.

"Because," says Kai. "I believe she intends to turn herself in to Alaric tonight." Kai glances out toward the full moon, just now cresting the horizon. Serena's birthday and Alaric's ultimatum is tonight.

"She can't," Liam turns, taking a step toward the house.

A heavy hand on his shoulder stops him. Liam turns, bristling at the touch.

"Apologies." Kai retracts his hand. "But she is determined. Pushing her in one direction will only make her push back harder. You must appear to be on her side. Just guide her in the right direction with small nudges. Kind of like a mother octopus nudges water toward her eggs for fresh oxygen."

Liam rubs his temple. *Serena wants to turn herself in to Alaric tonight and we're sitting here talking about octopus mothers?*

"Fine, whatever. But if tonight doesn't go well, maybe you should have your people standin' by."

"It is already done, werewolf." Kai utters the last word in a sneer, which causes Liam to bristle even more.

"You should know, *merman*, that I have people fighting with me for your cause. If you come ashore, they cannot be harmed."

"And how shall we tell them apart?" Kai asks.

Liam snaps his mouth shut, stumped.

"Did they not participate in the King's Massacre?" Kai continues. "Maybe we can only target those we recognize?"

Still at a loss for words, Liam doesn't say anything. In fact, his people fought on the side of the werewolves. They all followed Alaric's orders. Liam looks at Kai sideways. Would they even recognize their individual wolf forms? He thought they all looked the same to the Undine; at least Serena has told him as much. He shakes his head, bringing himself back to the moment. Serena is probably planning her meeting with Alaric right now. "I'll be there and I'll be sure to point them out."

"As you say." Kai nods. He takes a deep breath and lowers his voice. "She told me, you know."

"Told you what?"

"About leaving—that if the pair of you are together, it is possible."

"Oh," says Liam, scratching his side. "She said we should keep it is a secret."

"The secret goes no further than me, I can assure you. But you must promise me something, Liam of Clan Werich."

"What?" Liam asks.

Kai takes a step closer. "That if things get bad, and I suspect they will—possibly even tonight…" He trails off in hesitation. "That you will take her and go."

Liam can see Kai's Adam's apple rising to the top of his throat. He swallows it down and repeats the demand with steel in his voice. "Take her and go—far away from here."

"I will, I promise." Liam says, his voice just as low.

Kai turns away, looking out at the moon. Giving him time to compose himself, Liam stares down at the wooden planks they stand on.

Finally, Kai turns back. "We thank you for your protection."

"No worries." Liam holds up his fist, knuckles forward.

There is an awkward pause while Kai studies it, one eyebrow raised.

"It's like a handshake. You just..." Liam demonstrates a fist bump with his other hand.

Tentatively, Kai extends his own arm, fingers curled into his palm. They touch knuckles, but it isn't a bump. It lingers for several seconds. Each hand is similar in shape and size. The only difference is the light brown scales Kai has on the back of his hand compared to the light brown hair on the back of Liam's.

Part III:

Serena

Chapter Twenty-Nine

"You left without saying goodbye." Kai moves in closer to the pier, tilting his chin up to look at Serena.

She bends until her knees touch hard wood, then rocks back until she sits on her heels. "It wasn't goodbye."

Kai glances at Liam, still standing at the other end of the pier, shrouded in dark shadows. "You don't know that, especially taking current company into consideration."

Serena sighs; she doesn't want to argue, especially not about Liam.

"I've missed you," she says. *Your touch, your eyes, your goofy jokes. I miss feeling...safe.*

With the last thought, Serena knows she could never leave Kai. The aching hole in her chest blooms wide and she almost loses her breath over it. "Kai...I really do..."

He pulls himself up, water sliding off his chest and arms. Wrapping one hand around the back of her neck, their noses graze. "Then come home with me."

The temptation is too much to bear. She just has to lean forward a bit, that's all it would take. Release the earth and embrace the depth—sinking, sinking down with Kai until they reach the kingdom together and spend the rest of their days safe within each other's arms.

She rests one hand on his chest, feeling his heartbeat quicken. It is the rhythm all Undine share, steady and strong like the waves beating against the shore. It is the pulse of her people, and if she doesn't fight for it, it will sputter out and die.

Her hands squeeze around the edge of the wooden planks as she secures herself firmly to the pier.

Kai can feel it; he can see the resolve harden in her eyes. He lets go of her neck, sinking back down into the water. "I knew you'd say as much," he whispers.

She swallows hard. "I'm not sorry. I'm doing the right thing." *Am I trying to convince him, or myself?* "The council?" she asks, her voice cracking. "Their assigned duties are going well?"

"You mean besides mine?" He busies himself with skimming the palm of his hand over the surface of the water, but looks at her out of the corner of his eye.

She frowns. "Bitter much?"

"What?" His frown matches hers.

"Nothing," she mumbles, glancing at Liam, still standing where the pier meets land with a blanket wrapped around his waist.

"No one has devoted much time to their newly assigned duties," Kai says.

"Why not?"

"Because it has come to light that our council is preparing Society to live in The Dry, and that does not sit well with everyone."

"Our council," asks Serena. "Not…just me?"

"It caught them off guard. They mostly went along with it so as not to lose their reputation. They don't want to be viewed as unable to control the queen. Better to make it look as if it was their guidance all along." Kai is smiling again.

"Well—that worked out better, probably even more so if I were there."

"Rayne helped; she's good at dropping hints and spreading rumors while Undine eat in her hall."

"She is well? And Ronan?" Serena squeezes the wood planks even harder thinking of everyone she left behind. "Mariam? You have to check on her. She doesn't get many visitors, and she is so clumsy. What about Cordelia? Is she too big even to traverse the passageway to the archives? Did she finish the book—"

Kai places his hand over Serena's own. "All are well, but all wait your return."

Serena bites her lip, choking back tears that catch her off guard.

Putting a finger to her lips, Kai smooths them out. "A queen does not bite her lip."

A single drop of ocean water glides from his finger to her lip. Nostalgia rushes over Serena, and she closes her eyes. It is the rich, salty taste of rain water flowing over the land and washing the earth's minerals into the seas. Serena savors even the few grains of gritty sand left behind on her lower lip. She can smell Rayne's jellied seaweed on Kai's breath, and if she tries hard enough, she can pretend the steady drumming of water against the pier is high tide, rushing in to fill the Great Hall coming to rejuvenate all of Society.

Serena feels Kai's hands slide up her arms and lock above her elbows. When he pulls her in after him, she does not fight it.

Sliding into the ocean and into his arms. Serena finds his lips with her own. He presses into her, hands at first hovering cautiously near her waist, then wrapping completely around her. Despite their proximity to the shore, it is deep near the pier and Kai and Serena continue to sink, her legs wrapped around his tail.

Serena keeps expecting to hit the bottom, but it never comes. Bubbles rising like effervescence, they give the impression that she and Kai are sinking faster. Tiny pricks fizzling up and down her bare arms pull Serena reluctantly from her embrace. Her eyelashes flutter open and she turns her head. They are surrounded by bright white, pink, and green specks. They rise slowly, pushed back and forth by the current.

Kai is still nuzzling Serena's neck with his nose. She smiles, giving him a playful bump to catch his attention.

Look.

She watches his eyes light up as he glances around.

It is a mass, synchronized spawning of polyps. The coral's eggs rise in a colorful blizzard to mix with sperm of other polyps. Kai and Serena are surrounded by the ocean regenerating itself. She reaches out, tentatively. A few polyps bounce along her open palm, then move on their way, in search of their mate.

Kai nudges a few more toward those she just released. She smiles at him then gestures toward the surface. Heads emerging into The Dry, Kai and Serena inhale their first breath of air together, but they can't stop looking down in wonder at the vibrant spectacle below them.

"The polyps are spawning a few days too early. It usually comes after the full moon."

Kai gives a wry smile. "Guess they miss you, too." But the smile does not touch his eyes. His face, for just a moment, is overcome with grief. "You really are leaving me again, aren't you?"

Serena feels her heart wrench for him. "Yes," she says, voice wavering.

"I'll come with you this time," Kai says, drawing nearer if that is even possible. "It is my job, after all."

Serena feels his tail wrap around her legs in a possessive, protective gesture. She shakes her head. "No, I need your help with a few things in Society."

"What?"

"I might be calling for Isadora. If I do, let her leave her quarters, but follow close behind."

"It shall be done…" he trails off, looking away.

"What?" asks Serena.

"She's done well, you know. She has completed the potion, even while confined to quarters."

"She has?" Serena asks. "How do we know it is right?"

"Hailey did some testing and confirmed it."

"Good," Serena blinks. "That is good."

"Do you still believe her to be a traitor?" asks Kai.

"To be honest, Kai, I don't know. But who else could it be?"

He doesn't respond for several seconds. Finally, he looks at Serena. "Okay. What else do you need?"

The pair murmur with their heads together for a few more moments, chins dipping in and out of the water. Serena can hear Liam's impatient pacing behind her on the pier. Once she finishes passing instructions to Kai, she kisses him one last time, determined to savor the heat of his breath against her lips and the tingling sensation he sends straight to her core when he looks at her with those wild, green eyes.

He releases her waist, and they move apart. Suddenly panicked, Serena reaches out, latching onto his wrist.

"Kai. Don't drift," She says, pleading with her eyes. "I will fix everything. Please just trust me."

"I do, Serena Moon-Shadow. I do."

Stealing away the last bit of confidence Kai can give her, she turns and pulls herself up onto the dock, leaving the safety of his arms and the ocean behind.

Chapter Thirty

"Octopus mothers."

Serena hears Liam mumble the words as he enters Cecil's trailer. She smiles to herself as she stares into the mirror. There is a moment of silence from the living room and she focuses on her reflection. Running a finger down the side of her face, her smile disappears. Skin and scales are healed. No more dryness. The small bout in her waters was enough to wash away the arid dry that seeps into her very bones.

What should be gratitude for the restorative session is drowned out by dread. Straying too far from the ocean will never be possible; whether she is with Liam or not. Her people will always need to be near the beaches, and it is quite possible it will have to be these beaches. She will need to make peace with the werewolves, no matter what the cost.

"Serena?" Liam's voice is steady, though she can hear a slight twinge of panic.

"Do not worry," Serena calls from the bathroom. "I am still here." *For now.*

Sighing, she backs away from the mirror and turns to the door. Time to go; Liam will not take this well. When she steps into the living room with her trident, both Liam and Cecil stand staring at her.

"What?" she asks.

Cecil coughs. "You look different holdin' that trident," he says. "More complete."

"Yeah." Liam nods. "You'll never pass as a human now."

"I will take that as a compliment." Serena smiles. "But right now, I don't need to pass as a human." She takes a deep breath, bracing herself for blowback. "I am going to see Alaric. I am going to make this right—for everyone."

She forces herself to hold Liam's gaze, trying to read his face. It is pure stone. He doesn't flinch or twitch, he doesn't nod or shake his head.

Cecil looks from Liam to Serena, and finally breaks the silence. "Well? Are you going to stop her?"

"No," says Liam.

"You're not?" Cecil and Serena ask together.

Liam crosses his arms, looking as if he is getting ready to defend his decision.

"Why not?" Serena narrows her eyes. "If this is some trick to get me to—"

"It's no trick," Liam interrupts, letting his arms go limp by his side. "As much as I want to whisk you away to I don't know—deserted northern territory, tie you down and keep you safe from the horrors that have become our lives—I know I could never leave my clan behind." His shoulders sag, and a dark shadow passes over his face. "And if I respect you at all, I have to respect the fact that you could never leave your mer—," he pauses, swallowing hard and starting over. "You could never leave your people behind, either."

A rush of emotion runs from Serena's chest and straight into her head. Gratitude, admiration, and relief, all underlined by the strong sense of grief.

"Thank you, Liam," she manages to choke out.

"But there will be no negotiating with Alaric. We are too far past that. There will be a fight, Serena— with probably more losses. Are you ready for that?"

She twists her trident in her hand, watching the tips make a neat circle in the air. *If he has me, he'll have to honor his promise. Everyone else can live in peace.* But she can't bring herself to say the thought out loud.

"You have to understand—-this man doesn't stick to his word. All he cares about is his own pride. And that is something that was damaged the moment his mother abandoned him." Liam steps forward, eyes boring into hers. "And he is determined to make all Undine pay for that."

Serena can almost feel Liam trying to impose his will on her. She parts her lips, ready to push back.

Cecil interrupts the exchange. "So you're not going to take her and leave?"

Liam makes an effort to tear his eyes from Serena. "What?"

"You're not going to run and hide—leave everyone behind?" Cecil asks.

"What? No, I just said. We are going to figure this out together." Liam turns and paces, fingers going to his temples.

"Oh." Cecil hangs his head, staring at the ground. "Well, I suppose the pair of you had better get out of here."

Liam is still pacing. "We'll be out of your hair in a minute, old man."

"No—you'd better go now. Take the back way."

"Why?" asks Serena.

In front of the fireplace, Liam has finally stopped pacing.

"Because," says Cecil. "While you two were out on the pier, I called Alaric."

Serena's mouth drops open.

"And told him the mermaid is here, and about to run."

Chapter Thirty-One

"You…you what?" Liam asks. He leans forward, looking as though he is ready to lunge for Cecil.

"I'm sorry, son. But like I told you in the truck this morning—I could've sworn you made your decision. I thought you were going to take her and run; leave all your brothers behind in Alaric's clutches."

"So you called him here?" Liam takes two long strides toward Cecil.

Serena beats him there, standing in between the two. "It's okay, right? I was going to him anyway."

"No, no—since he is chasing you now, he'll spin it so your sacrifice doesn't count. Besides, he's going to be pissed by the time he gets here."

"Okay," Serena says, shooting a glance at Cecil. "Well, let's go. We'll figure this out."

Cecil takes a step back and holds up his hands. "I thought it would be better to be here with your brothers, under Alaric's thumb, than not be here at all. I couldn't let you go—you are the only one that has shown any promise of leading the pack, and the only one that has ever paid me any gratitude. I didn't want you to abandon the rest of my sons; not like I did. And not like her people did." Cecil gestures to Serena.

"I get it…okay," Liam rubs his temples. "But you don't understand—I won't be here under Alaric's thumb. It will be under his executioner's axe."

Instead of going wide with shock, Cecil's eyes narrow, as if he doesn't believe Liam.

But Serena nods; she knows Alaric well enough.

"And you're right." Liam looks up sadly at Serena. "This morning, after we discovered we could leave together if we stayed together, I had convinced myself to take you and run, even if you resisted. But that all changed after I saw you with…him."

"Kai?" asks Serena.

Liam nods. "After seeing you two together, it's pretty obvious. You'll never leave him."

She shakes her head. "That doesn't matter right now. We need to get go—"

Her sentence is cut off by an ear-piercing howl coming from the woods. It's joined by several others surrounding the house.

The chorus sends chills down Serena's spine. In response, armored scales emerge up and down her arms, legs, and torso.

Almost immediately Liam drops to his knees, wrapping his arms around himself. "Serena—calm down!"

She watches as long, spiky hairs emerge out of the back of Liam's neck. There is a sickening sound, like paper tearing, and Serena realizes it is Liam's skin.

Hunched over on the ground, he pleads with her. "Can you stop it?"

"No Liam." She glances at Cecil, then back down to her brother. "Right now, we're going to need the wolf." She picks up her trident and heads toward the back of the house, just as she hears the front door knob jiggle.

"Just a minute!" Cecil calls out in a shaky voice. "I'm indecent!"

"Aren't we all," mumbles Serena. "Come on, Liam—you can transform while we run."

Past the bathroom and the bedroom, there is a loud banging. The back door practically bends inward as something heavy crashes into it. A hairline fracture creeps down the middle of the cheap, wooden door.

"Okay—bathroom window it is," Serena decides.

She brushes past Liam, who is still on his hands and knees—or just on paws. Serena can't tell which. His clothes hang off him in shreds and his fur scrapes against her scales. Once in the bathroom, she stands on the toilet to look out the window. It is dark, but the area around the house is well-lit by the full moon. There are no wolves in sight…yet. "We'll have to do this fast," she mutters. "Lock that door."

The latch clicks shut and she hears claws scrape against it, on her side of the door. Refusing to look at her brother, Serena concentrates on the window. The glass is already pulled open. Aiming her trident at the screen, she thrusts forward. The screen pops out just as one of the doors to the house bursts inward, but Serena can't tell if it's the front or the back of the house. Maybe it is both. Shards of wood clatter against the floor.

"Now, just calm down. She ain't here no more. Went back home. Said somethin' about—" Cecil's explanations are cut off with a grunt. Something heavy thumps against the floor.

Serena turns back to the window and throws her trident through. She takes two steps back until fur tickles her behind her knees, then she sprints. One jump off the edge of the toilet and a dive, headfirst, through the window. She clears the building and tucks her body for the landing. Rolling once, then twice, she stops by her trident in a crouch.

"Liam!" She whisper-yells to the vacant window. There are only low moans inside.

Come on, come on. Serena's eyes jump from one shadow to the next, expecting them to lunge forward any moment.

There is another crash inside the house. Finally, a mass of fur lurches through the window, straight over Serena's head. She follows it with the tips of her trident. Familiar as she is with Liam, she has no idea if that is the underside of her brother or another.

He lands light on his feet and turns, eyeing her with a growl.

Assuming a fighting stance, her trident at the ready and one foot slightly behind the other, Serena studies the wolf. Light brown hair—and lots of it. They all look the same to her.

He stalks closer, then turns his head to display the crescent moon mark just underneath his eye.

Shoulder blades that were up in her neck relax. "What now?" she asks the animal.

He nods his head toward the forest.

"Lead the way," she says.

Under the protection of the trees, Liam and Serena skirt the clearing around to the front of Cecil's house. They should both be running like mad right now, but neither can seem to leave Cecil behind, despite his betrayal.

Liam slinks around shrubs, avoiding loud, crackling foliage on the ground, and Serena does her best to follow in his footsteps. Stopping behind a fallen tree, they both crouch. With a clear view of the front steps of the house, they watch a pair of men drag Cecil out and down the steps.

"Oh no," says Serena.

She feels something push against the scales on her arm. It is Liam, trying to tell her something.

"What?" whispers Serena.

Liam nudges at her scales again with his muzzle, then sniffs.

"Oh," she frowns. *They can smell me.* Slowly she retracts her armor. *It is just for a few minutes,* she tells herself.

"We searched. They aren't in the house," a man announces as he comes out, several wolves on his heels.

Beside Serena, Liam lets out a low growl.

"Shh," Serena hushes her brother.

Another man walks into the clearing. Long black hair billows over a black cape.

"What do you want us to do with this one, Alaric?" One of the men kicks Cecil just behind the knees, and the old man falls onto all fours. Several of them laugh.

"Ungrateful little bastards!" Cecil coughs out. "I raised you!"

"Wrong, old man." Alaric walks toward him. "I raised them. The only thing you did was accept fish-head babies, encouraging their actions. You are an accomplice to their betrayal. No better than any of them."

Cecil quiets his hacking and wipes his mouth with the back of his hand. "You're right, Alaric. It's my fault."

Alaric stops in front of Cecil. "What?"

From under thick, bushy eyebrows, Cecil looks up at Alaric. His voice is steadier than Serena has heard in a long time. "I should've drowned you the moment I laid eyes on you."

"Shut up," Alaric snarls.

Cecil only raises his voice. "I should have stayed on the pier where you were abandoned by your own mother, just to hold your head under the water until your body went limp."

"This is your last warnin'," says Alaric. He pulls a long, silver knife out of a hip scabbard from one of his men.

"You are an abomination," Cecil spits out. "A mutant, an…unholy freak!"

Alaric raises the knife above him.

"No," Serena whispers.

"Your lineage…" continues Cecil, staring Alaric right in the eye. "Will die with you."

Beside Serena, Liam lets out a whine as Alaric slashes the knife in front of him. Serena covers Liam's snout with her hand, holding him back at the same time. She buries her face in his chest, unwilling to watch Cecil slump to the ground with his last breath.

Shifting on his front paws, Liam shakes the shrubs in front of them.

Standing around a still body, all men in the clearing turn their heads toward Liam and Serena.

"Liam," Serena whispers. "Time to go."

Chapter Thirty-Two

Alaric releases the cape on his back. By the time it floats to the ground, a coarse, black mange covers his entire body. Those that aren't already wolves follow Alaric's lead and transform. They tear through the tree line, claws scraping across the fallen log Serena and Liam hid behind.

Running side by side, Serena and Liam duck under low hanging branches and leap over dense shrubbery. Serena's legs are powerful, taking long strides through the forest, but she has a hard time keeping up with Liam.

He slows to a quick lope. She grimaces when he eyes her; eventually the wolves are going to catch up to them.

Sharp growls pierce the air. Serena looks back as they run. Their pursuers are spread out behind them. Those on the end angle nearer, closing in on them like a clam shell about to snap shut.

Liam gives a short bark, catching Serena's attention and running right alongside her.

"No way," she says. "I'm not riding you."

The growls behind them are louder now, and the formation of wolves all around are squeezing in.

Impatient, Liam snarls.

"Fine." She rolls her eyes. "Just this once." Taking a short leap off a boulder, Serena swings one leg up and out, landing right behind Liam's shoulder blades.

He sinks slightly under her weight, but takes shorter strides and adjusts. Blades of moonbeams slice through the canopy above, providing just enough light for them to navigate the forest.

Serena grasps onto the thick hair behind his neck and leans into him. Running faster now, he pulls ahead of the closing trap. One of the wolves on his right flank lunges, just catching Liam's hind leg. Stumbling, Liam pitches forward and Serena is thrown from his back. They both roll, knocking into each other and then a tree.

Hoisting herself to her knees, then her feet, she stares at her hand. It is a wonder her trident is still there.

Forewarned by a whoosh of air, Serena thrusts her trident out, parrying a paw swiping for her neck. Next, she turns her trident upside down, stabbing her spikes into the ground in front of Liam. Another wolf lunging for him runs into the stem of the trident instead.

Liam on his feet, Liam extends his claws on either side of the trident, digging them into the wolf's shoulders and pulling him forward. Liam lets out a ferocious roar, one that shakes Serena to the bone. Spittle flies from Liam's fangs onto the face of his victim. Pulling hard, Liam slams his victim's head into the trident and the wolf falls unconscious to the ground.

More wolves are already coming, and although Serena wishes Kai or Murphy were by her side, she has to admit that Undine and werewolf make a good team. Light on her feet, Serena uses her trident to both their advantages. Liam exerts brute strength where Serena cannot, pummeling his opponents with twice the power she has.

Serena catches on that Liam refuses to fatally injure them. She follows his lead; she wouldn't want to lose her only partner right now. When there is a break in fighting, Serena and Liam look at each other, both breathing hard. He nods to a low hanging branch above them.

"Okay," says Serena. "Give me a boost."

She steps onto the back of his shoulder blade and he heaves himself up, lifting her up the tree.

They run again. This time Serena flies through the trees while Liam shadows her below.

Just like she did as Werewolf Liaison, Serena leaps from tree branch to tree branch, traversing the forest. Each time she arcs into the sky, she feels the pull of the moon fighting against gravity to keep her in the air. This time it is easier to let go—she needs to keep an eye on Liam.

As she lands on one branch it bows underneath her weight. A rogue wolf leaps at the same time, swiping for her legs. Liam intercepts him, plowing into his midsection. They roll on the ground and Serena spots another wolf closing in. His steps are light, sneaking up on Liam while he is preoccupied with another. Serena throws her trident, pinning his back leg to the ground.

The painful yelp causes Liam to turn. When he realizes what happened, he rears up, then slams the wolf's head into the forest floor. Clamping down on the trident with his jaws, Liam plucks it from the soil, twists, and releases so the weapon sails through the air toward Serena.

She catches it, a smile wide on her face, and they run again—her above and him below. Leap, arc, land—and a flutter of feet. Leap and arc. This time she can see the tops of several trailers. They are closing in on the camp, which hopefully means Liam's reinforcements.

Her muscles and her lungs scream for her to stop, but adrenaline pushes Serena forward. Up ahead, two wolves step into Liam's path. Serena angles to the left and Liam follows below. It happens again; the wolves step into the path but do not attack. They are trying to control where she and Liam go.

We are being corralled. But the thought has come too late. Just as she leaps to the next branch, a net, camouflaged by the canopy above, drops down. Strings tighten, clipping her at her ankles so she falls. On the way down, a branch knocks her trident from her hand. The net continues to tighten until the ends are looped around her, cinched down tight. She hits the ground and all the air is knocked from her lungs.

"Liam," she manages to croak out. Dark shadows dart all around her—she can't seem to focus. They tug and pull at the net she is in. "Liam?" she tries again, but her mouth seems so dry. One large shadow, silhouetted by the moon behind it, blocks out all others. It comes closer to Serena and her vision goes fuzzy at the sides.

"Take little miss blue fish to the warehouse."

Chapter Thirty-Three

"Serena!"

Her name comes to her, but it is far too early to get out of bed. She didn't get nearly enough sleep.

"Serena!"

She tries to say something, but her lips barely move. Only a short babble of syllables comes out.

"Your majesty!"

At the title, Serena's eyes fly open.

"I thought that one would get you." Liam says, coming into view sideways. Serena lifts her head off the ground and it roars with pain. Liam straightens out, and their surroundings come into focus. They sit on a dirt floor, surrounded by a ring of old tires.

"Where are we?" she asks. She tries bringing her hands to her head, but they are tied together and chained to a pole sticking out of the ground.

"The fight ring," answers Liam, whose hands are tied as well. He leans against a pole, shoulders slumped. A large bruise covers one side of his face and he has a bloody lip. Pulling at something around his neck, Liam grimaces.

"What is it?" Serena asks, peering closer. A wide metal choker squeezes so tight, she can see his skin going slightly red around it.

"It's so I can't shift," he says. "If I try, the choker will crush my neck, killin' me."

Serena nods. "A fight ring?" she asks. "Is he going to make us fight each other?"

Liam tries raising his hands in an ignorant gesture, but the chain isn't long enough and they stop short midway up his chest. He sighs.

"I don't know what he is going to do. Anything is possible at this point." He bends down to wipe his forehead with the back of his hands. "Are you okay?" he asks. "You took a pretty hard hit to the head when you fell."

Trying to ignore the pain until now, Serena focuses, taking stock of her body. "Nothing broken, I think. My side hurts when I breathe in, and my head feels like it is split open." She glances at Liam as she pushes herself to a sitting position. "What about you? Your face doesn't look so great."

"Hey, careful what you say about my looks. Twins, remember?"

"Right," Serena smiles but can't bring herself to laugh. Memories of the night until now come flooding back. "Cecil?"

Liam shakes his head. "Gone," he croaks out.

"I'm sorry," she whispers, staring down at the dirt floor.

"Oh, hell. He wasn't long for this world anyway." Face crumpling in a brief moment of grief, Liam turns it into a strangled laugh. He takes a deep breath and rubs his knuckles under his nose. "I'm just glad none of my other people were there."

"Do you think Alaric knows about them?" Serena asks in a hushed voice.

"I don't know." Liam picks up a handful of dirt and lets it fall again, running in between his fingers. "Listen, Serena. If you make it out alive, and I don't—"

"Liam don't," Serena interrupts. "Just don't."

"I just want you to know," he says, ignoring her. "I got you your coolers. Two of them. One red and one blue—they're in my trailer. Happy Birthday."

Serena smiles. "Cold food storage at last, without having to dig holes in her cave. Rayne will love them. But it doesn't matter, anyway."

"Why?" he asks.

"Because one—we are *both* getting out alive, and two—" She shrugs. "I don't even know where your trailer is."

"I know where his trailer is…" a female voice drifts out from a shadowed corner of the warehouse.

"Who's there?" Liam shouts. He and Serena both jump to their feet. Lifting his nose to the air, Liam sniffs. "I know that smell. It's your traitor, Serena."

"Isadora?" Serena squints into the shadows; her black scales certainly would blend in. But the voice isn't right.

"Try again, your majesty," the laugh that follows is unnerving and sends chills down Serena's spine.

"I know that laugh," Serena mumbles to herself. The sound reminds her of Poseidon, and the carving that hangs above her bed. But that can't be right—no other maiden ever enters the queen's quarters.

The form steps out from the shadows and up onto the tire ring. Moonlight streaming through rusted out holes in the ceiling splashes across gaunt, high cheekbones and a pointed nose.

"Arista," Serena gasps. "What—what are you doing?" It wasn't the Poseidon over her bed Serena was remembering, it was the one over the prison. "I helped you. I released you from prison…and not so you could ally with Alaric."

"What's wrong with that?" Arista gives a teasing smile. "You have a werewolf ally."

"That's different," Serena says. "Liam is my twin brother."

"Brother, father, cousin, auntie, blah, blah, blah." Arista flips her hand in the air. "We're all related somehow, aren't we?" She turns and begins treading the circle of tires. Her scales shine light blue—pale in comparison with Serena's darker scales.

"So we both escape from prison. Had they found me they would've thrown me right back in. But you, Serena Moon-Shadow. Not you. Instead, they crown you."

Arista jumps from the tires inside the fight circle, her eyes boring into Serena. "I had to go somewhere. Couldn't stay home, but I couldn't leave either. The werewolves were the only other option." Arista pulls a small, thin knife from a braid in her hair, still walking toward Serena.

Liam lunges forward, growling as he goes, determined to intercept Arista before she gets to Serena. But the chain holding him snaps tight, stopping him just short. Arista jumps back, eyes wide. She takes a breath, then smiles.

"Ferocious, isn't he?" She says, giving a nervous laugh. "Reminds me of when I first revealed myself to Alaric. He did take some convincing. But all I had to do was sit back and watch; any fool could see Liam's alliance to you is absolute. Liam is the key to bringing down the Undine Empire; he was the one to watch." She taps the knife on Liam's nose eliciting another round of growls from him. "Your beige undergarment has a small tear in the back; did you know? Left cheek."

"Arista…" Serena warns.

"Still, it took some doing. In all my spare time I had to make sure the kingdom stayed depleted of hydrocoral."

It is all falling in place for Serena. She nods. "Without it, Isadora has a harder time predicting the future, and seeing you in it."

"Very good."

"Or did you do it because that is what the potion takes?" asks Serena. "You didn't want us to transform anyone into werewolves?

"Now that was an unfortunate side effect," Arista looks over her shoulder and lowers her voice. "One that Alaric need not know."

"Arista, you are destroying your own homeland! There will be nothing for you to ever go back to."

Stepping closer, Arista raises the knife. Moonlight reflects off the blade, flaunting itself across Serena's face. "Soon there will be nothing for any of us to go back to. I've put The Deep far behind me, Serena— and so should you."

Serena's jaw clenches. For how maddening Arista is, she is also right.

"Or don't." Arista releases her forced, high-pitched laugh again. "I think Alaric has other plans for you anyway."

"What is he going to do?" Liam yanks on his chains.

Arista runs her blade under Serena's chin. "Oh, something terrible, I'm sure. Of course, I could save him the trouble…" She leans forward, fingers squeezing the handle of the knife. When she takes another step, her foot springs back up.

"Ow!" she yells, as a pinprick of blood appears on the bottom of her toe. "What is that?" she asks, leaning down. "A tooth?" She stands back up holding a porcelain-white canine. "You," she drops the tooth and points the tip of blade at Serena. "Have all the luck."

"Yeah," Serena holds up her chains. "Case in point."

"Hey, chum!" Two large warehouse doors slide open, and Alaric, followed by five of his crew, walks in. "I thought I told you to come get me when they woke."

Quickly, Arista slides the knife back into the braid of her hair. "I was just passing on my condolences of her majesty's father," she explains, turning away from Serena.

"Yes, well," Alaric steps over the tire ring to enter the circle. He pats his stomach. "His death went toward a good cause."

Now Serena is lunging for Alaric, but her chains snap, stopping her short. "May Dagon strike you down."

Alaric has Serena's trident flung over his shoulder, carrying it like a useless sack of flour. He raises an eyebrow. "Who is Dagon?"

"The avenging devil of the sea," answers Serena, her voice low and even.

Glancing once to his right, then his left, Alaric smiles. "I don't see any seas in here, siren wannabe. You are going to have to do better than that."

Arista breaks the stretching silence with her laugh. Even Alaric looks annoyed by it. "Here." He tosses the trident in her direction.

She catches Dagon, albeit clumsily. It bounces from hand to hand until the stem hits dirt, sending the powdery substance up in a plume of air. "For me?" she asks.

"I reward those that serve me," he says before turning to Liam and lowering his voice. "But to those that betray me…"

"You kill me, and you won't have my blood to pawn off on the rest of the pack," Liam reminds him.

"I'm well aware of your blood benefits," Alaric snarls, as if he resents the fact that he still needs Liam. "Fortunately, it won't take much to keep you alive. You can remain here with a little bit of water, and some food every now and then. And you'll be a convenient punchin' bag for my guys to relieve stress or boredom whenever they wish…"

The five large men standing behind Alaric laugh, their veins practically popping out of their bulging muscles. They wear thin, sleeveless t-shirts and loose fitting shorts. Serena looks at Liam.

He answers her unspoken question. "They are plannin' to shift. Whatever you do, Serena, you have to keep your fear under control."

"Alaric," Serena says. Panic edges her voice causing the word to end in a squeak. She closes her eyes, taking deep breaths until she is calm again. Opening her eyes, she looks at Alaric. "You don't need to do this. I came to fulfill the promise made on the eve of my birth."

Alaric turns to her, fury burning in his eyes. "You turned my youngest son against me."

"He's not your son," Serena shoots back. "He never was, and never will be. And he had turned against you long before I arrived."

Sneering, Alaric turns to one of his men. "Let them in."

"Let who in?" Liam tries edging closer to Serena. "What are you plannin' to do?"

Alaric glances over his shoulder, barely acknowledging Liam's panic. "She will be sacrificed as she wishes, to fulfill the debt."

Serena reels, feeling as if she has been hit by a ton of bricks. *This is what you wanted*, she reminds herself. *This is why you came.* She swallows hard, forcing her voice to work. "And you will allow my people back on the beaches safely?"

His back already turned so he can speak to his minions, Alaric pauses, turning an ear to Serena's question. He doesn't even bother to look at her when he answers. "Your people are no longer your concern."

Chapter Thirty-Four

The warehouse doors open even wider, and the entire structure shudders. Silhouettes begin to fill the opening. They filter in, pausing as they spot Serena and Liam. The energy of these people is entirely different than that of Alaric and his crew. They are cautious, hesitant, and some exhibit a fair amount of dread.

Serena pinpoints Connor and Colin in bowling alley work shirts, and the front of Zeke and Doug's shirts both say 'Doug's Pier', but she doesn't recognize anyone else. When Connor spots Liam and Serena in chains, his whole body tenses.

Liam shakes his head, almost vigorously, letting Connor know to stand down. Connor follows the mob filling in spaces around the tire ring, shooting glances between Alaric and Liam. The four that Serena know spread themselves out around the crowd. Liam turns to Colin.

Darcy? he mouths.

At home, Colin answers back.

"Eighteen years ago, some flippy tails made a promise to us," Alaric begins, and the crowd hushes each other until they fall silent. "After acceptin' the King's only son as one of our own—"

"Why is Liam in chains alongside the mermaid?" someone shouts from the rear of the crowd.

"Shut your mouths!" Alaric snarls. "We'll get to him soon enough."

Disgruntled murmurs roll through the audience. As much as Serena hates to admit it, Alaric's assemblies are held much like her fathers...and nothing at all like hers.

"At the Maiden's Massacre, we allowed the king to keep his daughter until her eighteenth birthday. Upon which time, he had to return her to us, and we would return to him his beaches." Alaric walks the ring like it is a stage. Every head follows him. "But he didn't."

"How could he? You killed him!"

Serena couldn't be sure, but she thought it was Doug's voice. Another chorus of murmurs kicks up, some in agreement—others not so much.

"Nevertheless, Serena failed to turn herself in— we had to go and catch her."

"Netted her like a fish!" someone shouts.

Several cheers rise in response. Others are dead quiet. It is obvious how divided the crowd is. There are too many skeptical faces, unsure of which side to take. The undecided could tip the balance for or against their favor. Making a move might be too risky. Serena remains silent, hoping if given the center spotlight long enough Alaric might just hang himself.

"And with her, we found Liam—our youngest member, and the last addition to our pack."

Cheers and mumbling morph into an eerie silence as all eyes turn to look at Liam. Serena can see him lift his chin and try to swallow, made difficult from the tight metal collar around his neck.

"She coerced him!" someone shouts. "It's one of them siren spells!"

"Nah, he's been with them since day one. Tried to stop us from burnin' their wolfsbane patches," one of Alaric's crew argues.

"What exactly happened remains to be seen," says Alaric. "I'm sure Liam will tell one story—and the fish flap might tell another."

"What about Cecil?" Liam speaks up so his voice carries to the back of the room. "Wonder what truths he might reveal?" He pauses. "Oh, wait. He can't say much of anything at all now, can he?"

"What is he talkin' about?" Connor shouts at Alaric. "What happened to the old man?"

Alaric's eyes give nothing away, but his crew shift on their feet, looking uncomfortable in their own skin. It is telling enough.

"I'll check on the old man myself soon enough." Alaric tries to recover the stage. "But until the investigation is complete, Liam must remain here, restrained—for the safety of the pack."

Serena's shoulders sag. Alaric will swing the investigation whichever way benefits him. He can draw it out as long as he wants, and Liam will remain locked up like a caged dog. She keeps her mouth shut tight, closes her eyes, and lifts her face to the slits of moonlight filtering down from the dilapidated rooftop. Heavy feet drag over the dirt toward her.

"Soak it in, Serena. This moon will be your last," Alaric whispers in her ear. His words slide around her, squeezing her chest until it hurts. "But first, I have a request," Alaric shouts.

Her eyes fling open. *What now?*

He walks away from her, turns, and pauses, as if he is waiting for applause that isn't there to die down. "Call your people."

Serena does not hesitate with her answer. "Absolutely not."

He smiles. "I thought you might say that." He nods to the men on either side of him.

One immediately hunches over, and the other raises his chin high, stretching his neck. Spiky brown hairs emerge from their skin. Their fingernails grow longer and...yellower. Their eyes squeeze shut, and their bones pop as their joints move apart then meld back together.

Clothes tear, and the men are both on all fours. One of them opens his eyes, and Serena wishes he hadn't—they are bright red, and staring right at her.

Serena's heart jumps up into her throat and her legs become shaky. She grasps the pole holding her hostage in order to steady herself.

There is a groan, only this time it comes from Liam. Sweat drips off his skin, it's path made difficult by random, thick hairs that emerge then fall out. His neck slowly gets bigger, pressing against the metal collar he wears. He is resisting the change, but her fear is making it all that much harder for him. "Serena," he moans. "Control it—unless you'd rather face a whole warehouse full of wolves rather than just these two."

She glances at the crowd standing past the tire ring. Some are scratching at their skin, several have already fallen to their knees.

Quickly, Serena closes her eyes. She ignores the sounds around her and begins counting in her head. Breathe in for 1...2...3...4...5 and breathe out for 1...2...3...4...5...6...7. She repeats it a few more times and opens her eyes.

The two fully transformed werewolves slink toward her, their claws scraping across powdery sand. Their fangs, always the last to appear, signal the completion of the transformation, cutting through bared gums and dropping blood on the sand as they walk.

Serena tries looking around the werewolves stalking her. "Alaric, stop! Liam will shift; that collar will kill him!"

Alaric is biting his fingernails. "You can stop it at any time, Serena. Just sing. Call your people."

"If he dies, you won't be able to harvest his blood any longer," she tries again, not caring that desperation fills her voice.

"I have some pups I can experiment with," Alaric shrugs.

Serena's eyes shoot to Colin, who steps forward, already lunging for Alaric. He is held back by Zeke who thankfully remained nearby.

"Tick tock, fish loaf," Alaric warns.

Hot air leaves the wolves' mouths as they approach. Frantic for a distraction that will help curb her anxiety, Serena recalls two foes she has learned to endure—Sarafina and Evandre. Picturing their faces over the wolves, Serena expands her imagination, and slowly but surely, impressions of the Great Hall slide over the scene inside the warehouse. Rusty spots become glittering minerals shining out from the cave walls and the vaulted ceiling. Liam stands in the same spot Nerin would; tall, proud, and ready to defend. The mass before her is no longer a potential pack of snarling wolves. They are her people; the Painted Maidens, and even though they do their fair share of snarling, rather than a threat to Serena they can only be seen as a privilege.

"Well?" Alaric asks. Behind him, everyone has stopped itching, and no one hunches over. They are no longer in danger of transforming. "I have plans to expand, and I can't risk any interference from your people. Call them, now!"

Serena allows Alaric's image to come through. He stands distinctly against her conceived image of the Great Hall; a place she no longer fears.

"No, Alaric."

"Fine." Alaric nods toward her brother. "Liam will make a fine plaything until you do as I ask. Just don't kill him, boys."

Serena watches as the wolves divert their gaze to Liam.

"Serena…" Liam says. His voice wavers, and his eyes are wide as the wolves approach him. "Please don't do anything stupid."

Serena opens her mouth…and begins to sing.

Chapter Thirty-Five

At first it is just a humming, so low you have to strain to hear it. Serena increases her volume but not her pitch. The notes slide out like black silk—they are stealthy shadows creeping out from the warehouse and into the forest, down toward the ocean until they mix with the frothy waves at the peak of midnight.

Dark and mysterious, it is the song of her family.

Alaric's shoulders hang low in their sockets while the rest of his body goes still. Liam's wolf quiets and he no longer has to fight it for control. He is down on one knee, breathing hard, but looking at Serena with raised eyebrows.

"What did you just do?" asks Alaric, licking his lips. The song was not what he expected, and he should know; he is of her blood.

"I called for our family, Alaric," Serena says, looking at him with a smile.

He stares at her, eyes narrowing. "Be ready," Alaric barks at his crew. "She is full of tricks."

The tension in the room grows; it is as loud as the silence. At the back, a few pack members start to leave, but are herded back in by guards posted outside. Alaric paces in the ring under increasingly more glares. The shift in allegiances is beginning, and Alaric knows it.

Serena glances at Arista, who is sprawled out on the tires, running her fingers over the tips of Dagon.

There is a shout from outside. "They're comin'!"

Everybody in the room turns to the door in anticipation.

"Well," the voice hesitates. "One is comin'."

Alaric shoots a glance at Serena and snarls. He stands on top of the ring of tires, waving his arms once. "Stand aside!"

Pack members move, creating a jagged line down the middle of the crowd all the way from Alaric to the door. Serena and Liam both move forward as much as their chains will allow and stand on their tiptoes to watch who comes.

Finally, a lone form stands in the middle of the open doors. It is a dark figure; black scales in a rectangle of light. They are the black scales that match Serena's hair and Alaric's fur. They are the black scales of Isadora.

"Hello, my son." Isadora says, staring at Alaric.

Audible gasps emanate from the crowd as everyone glances between Isadora and Alaric, then back again. The resemblance is obvious. Thin noses and angled cheekbones. Gray eyes that rest in between long, dark lashes.

Serena watches Alaric's shoulders rise with a sharp intake of breath. He holds it in, watching as his mother approaches. Stiffening in an unnatural stance for any werewolf, it is apparent Alaric is caught off guard.

The path parts even wider as she walks, uncertainty lighting the faces of pack members as she passes them. As a mermaid, and the mother of their leader, is she an enemy or an ally?

Serena can't be sure, but many pack members even look jealous. Perhaps it is because Alaric is facing a daydream many of them have been having since they were cubs—a visit from their mother.

Isadora steps over the ring of tires instead of on it, her long legs shining black scales; she is fully armored. Her gaze drifts from Serena to Alaric to Arista, her eyes hardening. Isadora stops in front of Serena and turns, her posture full of resolve. "I request that you release my queen," her voice is soft, but the room is silent. No one wants to miss a word.

Alaric laughs. "Your queen was promised to me eighteen years ago. If I return her, you will never have your beaches back."

A shadow falls across Serena's face. She looks up; several holes in the roof above cease filtering the moonlight down as forms move across them. *Feather light*, Serena remembers Zayla explaining to her caste the differences in weight between Ungainlies and Undine.

Working hard to keep the smile off her face, Serena is filled with new hope. She knew Kai wouldn't be far behind Isadora, and the rest of the guard not far behind him.

Shadows continue to dart above, and Arista lifts her chin to look up. She stands, holding the Dagon by her side.

Uh-oh, Serena thinks.

"Um, there's—"

"Keep your words to yourself, traitor," Isadora snaps at Arista.

Arista's spine goes rigid, and she finally looks like the Undine she was taught to be.

"Seems the ring is full of traitors tonight." Alaric makes a pointed look at Liam.

"But let us not detract from the issue at hand," Isadora says. "Our king sacrificed himself to pay the debt, yet you still demand the life of his daughter."

"Maybe," says Alaric, finally stepping down from the tire ring, "it wasn't a sacrifice—we took him down, fair and square."

Isadora raises an eyebrow. "Are you claiming you parted the waters yourself?"

Behind Alaric, one of his crew members coughs.

"Maybe you have an affinity to the ocean that your own people are not aware of?"

Careful Isadora, Serena thinks. If Alaric feels as though he is trapped, he will lash out.

The shadows above have stopped moving; they are in place.

"There were many witnesses on the beach that night," says Alaric. "Give me time to consult with my pack members, and together we will decide if the debt is repaid."

Isadora turns to look at Serena, who shakes her head no.

"But in the meantime, we will hold on to her majesty for you," says Alaric.

Next, Isadora turns to scrutinize Liam. If Serena had hair on the back of her neck instead of scales, it would've been standing up straight. The way Isadora looks at him tells Serena a plan, one she isn't privy to, has been put in place.

"Very well," says Isadora, turning back to Alaric. "But you shall keep our queen alive and in good health. And we shall take one of your own to ensure no undo harm comes to her."

Alaric laughs. "You…think you are going to take one of mine?"

Isadora nods. "This one will do." She points to Liam by aiming her thumb over her shoulder.

Laughter dies on Alaric's lips. "Absolutely not."

"I don't see the problem. After all, he is obviously a threat to you, chained up as he is." Isadora turns and walks toward Liam. She makes a full circle around him, inspecting him from head to toe. She runs a finger over the needle marks on the inside of his arm and she raises an eyebrow at Alaric. "Unless you need him for…something else."

Silence falls upon the warehouse once again, and Serena prays those above her don't make any noise. One wrong step will give them all away.

Alaric hesitates with his answer. Serena herself has a hard time figuring out which twin is more important to him. Finally, Alaric puts his hand in his pocket, digging out a key. "Fine," he grumbles, stalking past Isadora toward Liam.

Turning Liam roughly by the shoulders, Alaric leans over to undo the lock binding his wrists. Serena and Isadora both watch Alaric replace the key back in his left pocket.

"I suggest you keep the neck collar on." Alaric crosses his arms. "It will prevent him from turning."

"Thank you for the advice." She nods to Alaric before turning to Liam. "Exit through the doors and walk straight into the woods. My people will be there to intercept you." She turns back to Alaric. "No one follows, of course."

"Of course," he says through gritted teeth.

Liam pauses to look at Serena.

"Go, Liam," she says. "And happy birthday to you, too."

The wolves loyal to Liam shift from one foot to another. With a quiet flick of his hand, Liam signals for them to stay.

Serena stretches her neck to watch him walk through the open doors. He pauses, looking over his shoulder at Serena one more time.

Be safe, she can't help but think. But Liam only looks forward and steps toward the woods. His form becomes shrouded in shadows, and soon enough he disappears from sight.

Chapter Thirty-Six

With Liam gone, a sense of relief floods her system. When Kai and the guards appear a fight will ensue, and Serena doubts Liam could possibly keep himself from shifting. Serena takes a deep breath. Liam is gone; she needs to focus on herself now.

"What now, mother?" Alaric sneers.

Yes, what now Isadora? What are you going to do about your psychopathic son?

Isadora moves to stand in front of Serena again. If Serena stretches the chain, and her arms, as far as they go, she might be able to reach out and touch her.

"Did you know, son, that I am the Undine psychic? I see a great many things. I see certain paths that each life may take but there are always several possibilities. I have to weed out what is improbable and pinpoint the likely paths."

"And what do you see now?"

"I haven't seen anything for a very long time, son," says Isadora.

Spread out on the tire ring again, Arista stifles a giggle.

"But," continues Isadora. "Right before you were born, I saw only two paths ahead for the future of my son, both shining through as clear as if they lay before me. It was very odd, never had any life I'd foreseen held so few opportunities."

"Okay, I'll bite. Well, maybe not yet." Alaric laughs at his own joke, but no one else does. Serena wishes she could reach out and smack the grin off his face. He sighs. "What were the paths?"

"One was that you became a great leader of your people, protecting and guiding the sons we delivered to you. You kept them safe from Ungainlies, safe from the Undine's selfish desires, and most importantly safe from themselves."

"And the other?" he asks.

Isadora folds her hands in front of her. "The other is an early grave."

Alaric paces, scratching the back of his neck.

"When you were born, you were so sick you were dying. I thought that after we came up with the formula, and you had successfully completed the transformation, the early grave had been avoided." Isadora glances around the room, then back at Serena. When she turns back to Alaric she is whispering. "But now I don't think that is the case. I think both paths are still spread before you. Which will you choose?"

All eyes turn to Alaric, waiting. Serena is sure he can feel the pressure of them on his back. It is like he is on trial, but the difference between his and Serena's is that he is his own judge and jury.

Alaric is staring at his mother so intently, Serena is sure his next move will be to run into her arms and bury his head in her shoulder. He steps forward, slow and steady. When he stops he is standing directly in front of Isadora; they are the same height.

Serena watches Isadora's arms twitch like they want to reach out to embrace her son. But Isadora holds her ground with shoulders back and spine rigid. She doesn't step back, refusing to show fear in front of her son. Or rather, she refuses to show fear of her son. Instead, she decides to show trust. She retracts her scaled armor, starting at the back of her neck where Serena can see.

"Isadora…" whispers Serena.

Fingers go taut, hand extended by Isadora's thigh. It is her way of telling Serena to hush.

More scales retract. Neck, shoulders, and arms. Next are her midsection and her legs. It is the same thing Serena did with Liam when they first met after the King's Massacre. But Alaric is no Liam. Serena wishes Isadora could see that, even if she is his mother.

When Alaric speaks, everyone behind him leans in to hear. Even Isadora herself leans in slightly. He smiles. "The only grave I see, mother—is your own."

Serena gasps even before she observes the flash of a knife in his hand. Alaric's elbow rears back then forward, straight into Isadora's gut.

Her whole body shudders and her breath leaves her in a forced exhale. Extended claws dig into Isadora's shoulder, holding her in place while his forearm rotates. He twists the knife while it is still in her.

"No!" screams Serena. She lunges forward, expecting Kai and the guards to drop down any moment, taking Alaric's life before Isadora hits the ground. But they don't. Serena's chains go taut, stopping her short once again. "Alaric, please stop!" she begs.

But the damage is done. Alaric releases his mother, pulling out the bloody knife with one final twist. She stumbles backward before dropping to her knees.

Serena drops too, still attempting to reach out. Through blurred vision, Serena can see Isadora extend a shaky hand behind her. Her palm opens, and inside is a shiny key. The very one from Alaric's pocket.

"Take it," Isadora murmurs. "Finish the job."

Alaric snorts. "Patience, mother dearest." He thinks Isadora is talking to him, referring to her own life.

While his back is turned, Serena reaches out quickly, grasping the key. She falls back on her hands, scooting to her pole and wiping tears from her eyes. Once she can see halfway straight, Serena glances around. She doesn't think anyone saw, except maybe Connor. While everyone else stares at Alaric, Connor is looking at Serena.

He nods once.

She nods back, grateful. *That is one of them on my side. Where the hell is Kai?*

The rest are still preoccupied with Alaric and his dying mother in the ring. Expressions vary; looks of horror, heart-breaking disbelief, forlorn awe—none of which are good for Alaric. He doesn't seem to recognize any of it; he still has a smile on his face as he walks back to his mother, knife in hand. "This is for The Betrayed—for all of us."

He swings his knife up, pausing at the apex.

Isadora tilts her head back, exposing her neck. "I love you, son," she whispers.

His hand wavers but Alaric has made his decision. He slashes down. The blade hits its mark, slashing across Isadora's throat. A spray of blood splashes across the sand at her side.

The thump of her body against the ground reverberates through Serena. Instead of allowing it to push her down further, Serena thunders back. She gathers strength, forcing energy into focus. Suddenly,

Kai's plan becomes very clear. She knows what she has to do.

Chapter Thirty-Seven

Hunched over, Serena curls her body around her wrists. She unlocks each clamp and buries the key in the sand beneath her. Still holding tight to the chains she straightens, feigning her captivity.

Alaric faces his people. "That waste of water there," he says, pointing to Isadora's limp body, "Ceased being my mother the day she abandoned me."

No one responds. A few shake their heads.

"You should all be so lucky to have the chance to do that. I can help you. We can hunt them all down, take our vengeance."

One member steps forward.

"Colin," Alaric smiles. "I knew I could count on you. We've got to look after those boys of yours. I can help you do that."

"Alaric…" Colin shakes his head. When he stops, he holds his chin high and crosses his arms. "Hell no."

Tentative cheers ring up behind Colin, but it is not everyone. The mob goes tense because of it. Alaric's men push Colin back then prowl around the ring, ready to intercept anyone who gets violent with their own leader. Toward the rear of the warehouse, a fight breaks out in the crowd.

Frustrated, Alaric motions to his crew, including the two that have transformed into wolves. They each jump atop the ring of tires, and several move in from outside. Together, they growl in a simultaneous, deep rumble that shakes the warehouse. Everyone glances around and quiets, not willing to provoke the biggest members of the pack. The fighting in the back ceases, and Alaric gains control once again.

"We will coax those scales and tails from the sea, even if it has to be one by one," Alaric nudges his mother's limp hand with his boot. "Only one of the mermaids here can do that, but she ain't playin'." Alaric turns to both Arista and Serena.

They both stand, spines rigid and senses alert.

"Let's have a match."

Claps, whoops, and hollers rise up from a couple of the men.

"Are you kidding?" asks Arista. "After everything I've done for you?"

Alaric shrugs. "I figure I'd give you a chance to win the favor of the pack. Just make your queen sing."

"I won't do it," says Arista. "This was never part of our agreement."

Alaric steps toward her, keeping his eyes on the ground. Once they are toe to toe, he leans in. "Were you there, the night I tore into the king?" he asks, voice low.

She glances at Serena before she answers. "I saw…from a distance."

He nods, eyes fixed at a point beyond her shoulder. "Then you wouldn't have smelled the fresh blood smeared over his tattered scales. You can't have heard the tear of soft muscle from bone or seen the way the shredded meat flopped in between my fangs."

Arista swallows hard.

Now Alaric looks her in the eye. "If you don't make your queen sing, I'll give my wolves the order, and you can witness all of that first hand. Except it will be your blood smeared over scales, and your muscle tearing away from bone." Alaric steps back, smiling. "How about it, chum? You would really live up to your nickname."

Arista flinches, running the back of a shaky hand across her forehead.

Serena almost feels sorry for her; almost.

His voice raises. "There will be a victor tonight," he glances at Serena. "Or two more graves." He turns walking away and taking his place on top of the ring of tires. "Fighters, shake hands!" Alaric yells.

Arista remains still, and Serena just looks at him confused.

"Or, do it however you do it," he mumbles.

A bell rings out. Arista frowns, but performs a hesitant curtsey toward her opponent as Serena does the same. It is the same thing Zayla teaches caste mates to do during grappling class.

Immediately, Arista moves into a mock warrior stance. She raises Dagon until the trident is parallel with the ground, sitting on her shoulder. Rearing back, she releases the weapon and it flies toward Serena.

Arista isn't trained with a trident. She has angled it too high and doesn't put nearly enough power behind it. Dagon only makes it halfway in between the pair. Tips bury themselves into the ground, the stem ringing with vibration.

Serena drops her chains and runs toward the trident. Momentarily shocked at Serena's freedom, Arista's eyes go wide.

"Go!" Alaric shouts out at her.

Arista bolts into action, running for the trident too. Serena is faster and has a head start, but Dagon stands closer to Arista. Serena pushes harder, narrowing her gaze on her target. She reaches the trident first, but doesn't grasp the stem.

Realizing she lost the race, Arista digs her heels into the sand, trying to stop. It doesn't work; she slides forward directly into Serena. Reaching around Dagon, Serena grabs Arista's braid. Finding the handle of the knife buried within thick locks, Serena pulls it out. Her other hand grasps for Arista, dragging her close. It looks like a hug, with the trident between them.

"What the—?"Alaric mumbles.

The room has gone silent; everyone stares as the two maidens embrace. With her mouth right by Arista's ear, Serena whispers, "For Isadora."

Arista's eyes go wide as the small knife flashes between them.

Dipping down slightly, Serena's hand reaches around the back of Arista's legs, and the blade digs into soft skin.

Thick, crimson blood pools at their feet, mixing with the sand they stand on. Out of the corner of her eye, Serena can see Alaric look down, trepidation lighting his face. He takes a step forward.

Arista cries out in pain, and falls, her whole body shaking. Legs temporarily disabled, she scoots back from Serena with several vain attempts at standing.

Still crouching, Serena pivots on her feet. One hand shoots out and grabs Dagon as she turns. Manipulating the familiar weight, Serena releases as it spins around the back of her hand, then grasps it in a throwing position as she stands up straight.

Alaric has not had time to move; he remains still—almost stupefied.

Serena rears back then throws, twisting her hips as she releases the trident. It catches Alaric just under the rib cage. The force causes him to stumble back several feet—the men around him giving wide berth. Shuffling on the roof diverts their attention. When they look back at Serena, she is already directly in front of Alaric.

Alaric looks down at the trident, mouth hanging open.

Hands grasping the stem of the weapon, Serena pulls. Spiked barbs on the tips rip through Alaric's skin on their way out of his body. She repositions her hands.

"A king for a king," she says. "The sea will have its revenge." She jabs upward. The middle tip spears Alaric just under the chin.

With all her strength, Serena continues to push up. Alaric rises to his toes just as Undine guards jump down into the room from the roof. They position themselves around Serena, tridents and arrows at the ready.

Blood bubbles out of Alaric's slightly parted mouth, and Serena can see the glint of her golden trident inside it. His eyes roll to the back of his head. Serena steps back, lowering Dagon and Alaric to the ground. There is one last gurgle, and he slumps over, dead.

Serena retracts her trident, bringing it to her side. She finally looks up. There are only five Undine guards; including Kai. Beyond them is a room full of frenzied werewolves; and Serena has just killed their leader.

Chapter Thirty-Eight

Connor steps forward. "Serena—"

He is cut off as two guards threaten him with their tridents. Everybody is too tense.

"Liam," he chokes out.

She nods. "Stand down," she orders the guards. "Did they take him?" she asks Kai without taking her eyes off Connor.

"Yes," he answers. "To Cliff Beach."

"Go," she tells Connor without hesitation. Before he makes it out of the warehouse, Serena turns to the rest of the room. "Those that hold allegiance to Liam; go seek him. Tell the Undine to release him, by order of their queen."

Almost all of the warehouse empties of people; all except Alaric's sworn crew, and a few stragglers. Serena is undecided if that many would stand behind Liam; perhaps they just needed a chance to get out of there.

At least the numbers are a little more even; Serena and her five guards against ten wolves.

Serena forces herself to take deep breaths. The wolves look at one another, trying to figure out who will take the lead.

She uses the opportunity to sidestep closer to Kai. "Sending Isadora in alone, making Alaric release Liam—that was all part of your plan, wasn't it?"

"We weren't counting on Arista…" Kai murmurs, glancing at the maiden crumpled over in the dirt. She has managed to wrap a torn shirt around her knees, stemming the bleeding. Another guard is watching her, so Kai turns to keep square with a pacing wolf in front of him.

"So now what?" Serena hisses through clenched teeth. "Where is Murphy? Where are the rest of the guards?" Serena asks.

"They had to stay back at the beach to protect—"

What wolves are left in Ungainly form drop to all fours. Their shift from skin to fur is faster than any Serena has ever seen. The combination of the full moon, and being pumped full of Liam's blood probably helps.

In response, Serena calls forth every last scale she can. Slicing through her skin, tiny shells of midnight blue cover everything from her toes to her chin.

Already armored, the guards don't have to do the same, but Kai issues a slew of orders. "Cover the hole in the left flank, aim for their soft middles or the neck. Protect the queen. No one attacks Serena and survives. I don't care whose sons they are."

Serena glances sideways at Kai. This has been the problem all along; too much violence and too much fighting. But these are Alaric's men and Serena doubts they could ever be persuaded from avenging his death.

When the first wave of wolves attack, it looks entirely coordinated. Every other one lunges for an Undine guard. Just as they leap, those remaining lunge forward, directly for Serena. They aren't playing any more games. Mostly occupied with their own fight, the guards can't do anything about the second wave.

Serena holds her ground, forcing herself to wait until the very last second. When she can practically feel the hot breath of dog against her face, Serena bends her knees and leaps. She stretches up with one hand, imagining she is in the entrance pool to the archives, aiming to scrape fingernails against the gritty ceiling.

There is a whoosh of air just underneath her toes. At the apex of her jump, Serena rotates Dagon so the tips face down. Throwing her feet up and behind her as she falls, the weapon will land first. It makes contact behind one wolf's neck, slicing through until the crescent moon that holds Dagon's spikes together hits bone.

Serena swings her feet wide, using the pinned trident like a tree branch. Kicking another wolf, Serena throws him back. She lands on her feet, and is almost instantly buried by claws and fur. One of them rips a wide gash in her upper arm but their fangs have a difficult time getting past her scales. Weight upon more weight piles on top of her, all of them squirming, trying to get their own piece. Finally, one is lifted from the pile and Serena breathes clear air. Kai's face appears, quickly followed by his hand. Serena reaches out, grasping because her life depends on it. He pulls her from the pile and into his arms while others defend them.

"We need help," she shakes, trying to hold it together. It is hard not to break down now that she's in the protection of Kai's arms. "Where are the others?"

"They won't be coming to help us, Serena," Kai says, breathing hard. "We need to make it back to them."

Another guard hands Serena her trident.

"Thank you," she says, unlatching herself from Kai to take Dagon.

"Your majesty." He bows, almost getting bowled over by a wolf.

Serena rolls her eyes. Their formality will be the death of them.

"Don't let them go!" Kai shouts.

Several wolves run out of the house. The only pack mate they have left behind quickly succumbs to deadly tridents.

"Will they go after those that took Liam?" Serena asks, panic and exhaustion both lining her voice.

"Maybe," answers Kai. "But the problem is we really didn't send him to Cliff Beach."

"What? Where is he?"

"Come on," Kai says, taking her by the elbow. "There is something you need to see."

Chapter Thirty-Nine

The run to Forest Beach is quick. Serena is propelled by the rhythm of feet pounding against the ground in sync. They settle into a pace, Kai running directly beside Serena, occasionally brushing her elbow with his own. One guard is left behind to escort Arista home.

They clear the tree line without any wolf sightings.

"We'll have to move this along as quickly as we can, before they figure out we sent them in the wrong direction for Liam," Kai says in between heaving breaths.

"Move what along? And where is Liam?" She eyes a group of Undine standing in a circle further down the beach.

As Serena approaches cautiously, Kai whispers by her side, "Liam is safe; he won't be harmed. But this…" He gestures to the group in front of them. It is Murphy and the remaining guards. "It's what I was trying to tell you. They had to stay at the beach to protect Cordelia."

The line of Murphy and the guards break as they step away to reveal an Undine in deep burgundy scales hunched over in the sand. Hailey and Zayla kneel beside her, hands rubbing her back and whispering in her ears. There are a pile of crudely shaped glass panes, each with a strap for a handle. It is their bulletproof shields, and their last defense against Ungainly weapons.

Amidst the group of Undine, Cordelia looks up, a sheen of sweat covering her brow and temples. "Your majes—" her own, strangled scream cuts off her formal greeting as her body spasms with pain.

Serena steps forward, shaking her head, but she is at a loss for words.

Breathing hard, Cordelia recovers from the contraction. She licks her lips and looks up at Serena again. "My child will share a birthday with the queen."

"The contractions are very close together now," says Hailey. She isn't addressing the queen, she is mumbling in Cordelia's ear. "Soon you can begin pushing."

As if to prove her right, Cordelia moans again. "Not yet, not yet." She leans forward, touching her forehead to the sand.

"You four watch the forest," Murphy commands. "Arrows at the ready."

"The wolves won't be far behind us," announces Kai.

In the meantime, Cordelia has mounted to a full on contraction. Hailey and Zayla, the guards, and Serena all ride the wave of pain with her. Shouts of encouragement, hands massaging her back and sides; they all help her to stay on top of the crest instead of sinking beneath it.

Every muscle in Serena's body tenses, and she can feel a sheen of sweat on her own forehead.

Kai puts his hand on her shoulder, and Serena turns into him. They embrace, squeezing each other tighter as they listen to Cordelia's cries.

"I feel so helpless," Serena mumbles into his chest.

He strokes Serena's long, wavy hair, and her bioluminescence subsides. "Poseidon won't give her anything she can't handle," Kai reassures Serena.

"Okay, next contraction," Hailey says. "You must begin to push."

Serena peeks out from Kai's arms. Cordelia is nodding, but tears streak down her cheeks and her whole body shakes. If Poseidon were here, Serena would strangle him on the spot.

"You can do this," Zayla coaches Cordelia. "You are going to be a mother—and then the real work begins."

Cordelia manages to squeak out a laugh.

Shouts from the guards rise up.

"Hail the maiden warrior!"

"To the survival of the Undine race!"

"For Ervin!"

The last shout is from Kai, and it draws only silence. Ervin…Cordelia's mate, the father, Serena's best friend, and a warrior killed during the King's Massacre.

Using Hailey and Zayla for support, Cordelia draws strength from Kai's words, and stands. "For Ervin," she agrees.

She throws her head back, raising her chin to the moon and shrieks as the pain comes back. Her screams echo down the beach, carried across the sea. They are answered by a chorus of howls emerging from the forest. Serena, Kai, and the rest of the guards each grab a shield and turn to face the dark. Shadows creep out, and they have claws and teeth.

The shield will do no good against werewolves, and Serena doubts any will carry a pistol while running on all fours. Serena recognizes those they just fought, some with wounds from the struggle. They snarl and bare fangs. More wolves creep out from the trees until the Undine are surrounded on the beach. Almost everyone that was in the warehouse is here now.

Serena's grip tightens on Dagon as she holds it at the ready, and the defenders behind her follow suit. The ocean, their only retreat, is at their backs, but they can't leave until Cordelia has safely given birth.

More wolves emerge, panting hard from the fight and from the run over. Connor, Doug, Zeke, and Colin, recognizable from torn bits of clothing hanging off their backs; they are all in their work shirts. They too bare their teeth, standing shoulder to shoulder with Alaric's crew.

Serena's breath leaves her body in sharp bursts.

What went wrong? Did they still have allegiance to Alaric?

Her eyes hop from one wolf to another. *Liam would really come in handy right about now.*

"Hold!" she orders her guards. They lean forward, dropping the shields, ready to attack and willing to give their lives for the weak maiden behind them. Her moans and screams, and the hushed encouragement from Hailey and Zayla, only strengthen their resolve.

Finally, Connor steps forward to stand in front of the pack. Once he does, he surveys the Undine before him, all pointing their tridents at his pack mates. There are more moans behind Serena, and Connor lifts his snout, sniffing the air.

Telling herself to trust her twin brother's closest friend, Serena lowers Dagon and steps to the side, revealing Cordelia in the sand behind her.

Connor's ears perk and he paws the sand, giving a short whine.

"What is your decision, Connor of Clan Werich?" asks Serena.

The wolf takes two steps forward. Serena can feel the guards tense beside her. She puts her hand on Kai's arm, staving him off. She is still determined to trust Connor, despite the hundreds of teeth bared at her and her kinsmen.

Connor glances one last time at Serena, then turns to face his clan. He grows taller, raising his chin slightly and staring down the brothers in front of them. A few step forward and turn as well. Doug is the first, followed by Colin and Zeke. Like a slow rolling wave, wolves step forward down the line then turn. There are finally just a few remaining facing the Undine, mainly Alaric's crew.

They growl and do not move. A few sharp barks from Connor, and Alaric's crew reluctantly bend their front legs, pressing their snouts into the sand as they kneel.

Serena waves her hand at the Undine guards until they lower their tridents. The entire clan of werewolves, Connor included, now turn to face Serena and kneel, muzzles on the ground.

"You killed Alaric," Kai whispers by her side. "You are their queen now, too."

"Werewolves don't have queens," says Serena, swallowing hard. "They have an alpha…"

Behind her, out of the middle of the circle of Undine Guards, Serena hears Cordelia cry out. "Something's wrong!"

Serena and the two wolves stop, turning their heads to the circle. The guards shift on their feet, but do not chance a peek behind them.

"Deep breaths, dear. The pain will—"

Another screech from Cordelia cuts Hailey short. The laboring mother sits straight up, grabbing her midsection.

On hands and knees beside Cordelia, Hailey's deft hands push and prod into her midsection. "The calfling is breach," says Hailey.

"Colin," Serena says sharply.

Beside her, his ears perk.

"Get Darcy."

Colin turns with a brusque bark and runs in the direction of the trailer park. The rest of the pack who is clumped together further down the beach watch with peaked interested.

"Cordelia," Hailey is whispering but silence has fallen over the beach. Even the waves dare not come too close. "I have to turn the calfling so it can come through unharmed. This is going to hurt."

"Okay," Cordelia nods. She is in between contractions. "Please, just be quick."

Behind Serena, Connor angles closer. She turns to face him. As one of the larger werewolves, Connor's muzzle almost reaches Serena's shoulders.

He looks pointedly at each of the Undine guards, then back to Serena. Serena gets his meaning. *Each of the Undine is here and safe. Where is ours? Where is Liam?*

"What's wrong?" Kai asks Serena, coming to stand by her side without taking his eyes off Connor.

"They want to know where Liam is."

"Oh…" Kai's head shoots back to Connor, and his mouth snaps shut.

Connor is still, fixing Kai with a hard stare. It is not quite aggressive, just…attentive.

"Well?" asks Serena.

"Well what?" Kai looks back at her.

"Where is he?"

Eyebrows knit together under small lines in his forehead, and his hand squeezes her upper arm. "I told you, Serena. He's safe."

Serena steps back from Kai, planting the stem of her trident in the sand. "So go get him."

Kai clears his throat, but it comes out sounding strangled. By now Serena has turned to square off with Kai, with Connor standing by her side.

He pauses, glancing between her and Connor. "What's happening here?"

"What is happening is I'm asking you to go get Liam and bring him to the beach."

Kai's shoulders sag. "I'm sorry, your majesty. I cannot do it."

Serena isn't sure if she worries more because the lines grow deeper in his forehead or because of his formal tone. "Why not?"

"Because," Kai stands up straight, his eyes drifting back to Connor. "He refuses to come."

Chapter Forty

"Why?" Serena is trying not to shout, and trying not to disturb Cordelia, but the men in her life are making that difficult.

"That," Kai says, shrugging his shoulders, "is between you and him."

A jumble of angry words fly from Serena's mouth, none of which make sense, even to her own ears.

"Serena," Kai hisses. "Maintain your bearing…"

She takes a deep breath, embarrassed to be portraying such a temper in front of her subjects; both old and new. Swallowing her pride, she turns to Connor.

"Liam will be returned to your clan, unharmed. I'm not sure why he would choose now of all times to…not be here."

An extra loud moan from the center of the circle cuts Serena off. "Although…"

Connor flips his tail once, blinks, then returns to the pack standing not too far off.

"And that means…?" prods Kai.

"It means he has accepted my answer—for now. But I'm not sure he is happy about it." She turns to Kai. "And I am definitely not—"

"Serena?" Darcy bursts from the tree line, running toward the group. "Are you okay?"

"Oh, thank Poseidon—Darcy! Yes, I'm fine."

"Colin came and got me; wouldn't let me leave the trailer without my medical kit," Darcy holds up a small bag. "Is someone hurt?"

"Here," Serena escorts her to the circle.

Two guards step aside to the let the women pass, but the wolf that accompanies Darcy stays on her heels.

Tridents block the opening in front of the wolf, slicing together in front of his snout. He yelps, jumping back. Crouching, the hairs on the back of his neck perk as he bares his teeth.

Darcy turns to one of the guards. "May I introduce you to Colin, my husband."

The guards exchange a glance. How could they possibly allow a werewolf direct access to a birthing maiden?

Serena steps in between the guards, pushing their tridents back to their sides. "Colin wishes no harm to the calfling or Cordelia; he only wants to remain by his wife's side."

There is no change in posture, and no movements from their guards.

Serena sighs. "Would you allow your mate unescorted inside a circle of werewolves? On the full moon, no less?"

This elicits a raised eyebrow from one of them, and it is enough for Serena. "Come on then, Colin." She stays between the guards until the wolf has passed through. Once they are both inside the guards close the circle behind them.

"The baby is breach?" Darcy asks after one quick look at Hailey's kneading.

"The calfling is, yes," says, Zayla, falling right back in her Caste Master tone.

Darcy either does not notice, or does not care. She falls to her knees on the other side of Cordelia. "No, no, that is too rough."

Covered in a sheen of sweat, Hailey sits back on her heals. "And I suppose you've done this before?"

"Twice," answers Darcy without looking up. "On myself."

Hailey glances at the werewolf standing alert beside Darcy.

"But it goes much easier with help," Darcy continues. "You press down and to the side from the top, here. Gentle because that is the baby's head."

"Calfling," Hailey mumbles.

Darcy pauses, looking up. "Do you want this baby and the mother to survive this?"

Hailey's lips press together tight, but she gives a curt nod.

"Then I suggest we don't argue about what to call it, and focus on birthing it. Now press here."

Hailey hesitates. Serena has never known Hailey to be stubborn, but then again she has never seen Hailey with an Ungainly.

Cordelia moans again. "Please, Hailey, just make the pain stop…"

This time, Hailey doesn't hesitate. She touches the side of Cordelia's hot, red cheek with her cool palm. "As you say." Both of her hands move to the topside of Cordelia's swollen midsection, and begin pressing down.

Toward the bottom, Darcy is working. They alternate between kneading and twisting, with Hailey mimicking Darcy's moves. Cordelia has gone silent. Serena watches the women work, their hands falling in time with the sound of the waves. A wave comes ashore; knead. A wave recedes; twist.

The small lump under Cordelia's skin shifts.

"There!" cries Darcy. "Now hopefully it won't revert back."

Serena stands as solid as a rock against the tide, but she breathes a sigh of relief.

"What's wrong with her?" Hailey looks at Cordelia. The maiden's eyes are shut and she isn't moving.

Darcy checks the pulse at her neck. "Just asleep—she is exhausted. It won't last for long, though. We need to get this baby—" Darcy cuts herself off, looking at Hailey. "This calfling...out on her next contraction."

Half a smile touches Hailey's lips. She reaches out to lay a hand on top of Darcy's. Both over Cordelia's swollen stomach. "Thank you," Hailey whispers. "For helping."

Cordelia's eyes flutter open.

"It's time to push your other calfling out, Cordelia," Hailey coaxes as her hands break apart from Darcy's, ready to work.

Cordelia shakes her head, but no tears come. She is all out of tears. Glancing up at the werewolf looming and panting over the group, Cordelia doesn't even flinch. "Who is this?"

"This is my husband, Colin," says Darcy, addressing Cordelia for the first time. "He is just here to make sure I'm okay."

Cordelia glances at the circle of Undine guards surrounding her, eyes running over their backs, assessing the situation. Her gaze stops back on Colin. "He's very..." she pauses, perhaps searching for the right word. "Impressive."

Darcy laughs out loud. "Yes, he tends to think so."

Colin pushes his snout into Darcy's shoulder, nudging her.

"Is the pain gone, Cordelia?" asks Hailey.

"Yes," Cordelia says. "I cannot feel anything anymore."

Hailey and Darcy exchange a glance. Each of them know that isn't a good sign.

"If..." begins Cordelia, pausing to squeeze her eyes shut. "If I don't make it and the calfling is male..."

Hailey's hand goes to Cordelia's forehead, smoothing back hair.

"If he is dying, give him the potion." She opens her eyes to look at Darcy and Colin. "I want you to take care of him, please."

Serena moves closer, as does Hailey with the bundled calfling still in her arms, closing a tight inner circle around Cordelia.

"What potion...?" Darcy's question trails off as she watches Zayla remove a small vial of yellow liquid from the dry pouch at her waist and slip it to Hailey.

"But he won't grow up like," Cordelia continues, glancing at Serena. "Well, he will know his people. You are all going to just have to stop killing each other."

"It will be done, Cordelia," Serena says. "I swear it."

"Honey," Darcy is feeling the bottom of her abdomen. "You are contracting."

"Really?" asks Cordelia. "I don't feel it—it's nice." Her head flops to one side and her eyes close.

"You have to push now, Cordelia," urges Hailey.

"I'm just so tired," Cordelia mumbles.

"I know—just one more, one more for your calfling."

Encouragement from Hailey and Darcy build with the incoming wave. Serena watches Cordelia's hands digging into the sand, but it provides no sturdy hold for her. Granules slide from her grasp as water rushes toward the group. Cordelia pushes. There are no grunts of labor, no moans of pain. There are no whimpers and no sobs. It is a silent suffering.

The tide has come in and the water reaches the group, skimming over the sand, surrounding Cordelia. A small calfling glides into the world. The water recedes, bringing with it the blood from the birth.

Colin rips his already torn bowling alley shirt off his back and nudges Darcy. Taking the material out of his fangs, Darcy and Hailey work to wrap the calfling in a tight bundle.

But Serena isn't watching the calfling, she is watching its mother close her eyes for the last time. She watches Cordelia's chest perform one last rise with breath, and Serena watches a friend die.

Amidst Undine guards and werewolf soldiers, Hailey holds the newest calfling in one arm, and the vial of yellow liquid in another. "It's a boy," she announces.

Chapter Forty-One

Serena glances at the tiny bundle, then falls on her knees next to Cordelia's side. "Cordelia…" she murmurs, running fingertips over her limp hand. "Cordelia!" she yells.

Ervin, Sasha Sunbeam, her father, and Isadora. Too many have passed into the afterlife; Serena cannot allow another. Not this one. There is so much work to do.

"Cordelia!" she yells again, shaking the maiden's shoulders. Tears blur her eyes, and with the watery view it is as if Cordelia is already sinking into The Deep to be burned in the ceremonial fires.

"There is a better way," Darcy says. She scoots Serena aside, places her hands on Cordelia's chest, and begins pumping with the heal of her hand. Her eyebrows furrow, and she stops to feel around. "Her lungs—they aren't quite like ours. Where is her sternum?"

Serena wipes at her cheeks. "What is a sternum?"

Darcy gives Serena an exasperated look, but doesn't answer. She starts pumping again. "Come on, Cordelia."

Her limp body jolts each time Darcy presses down.

"Your majesty…" Zayla whispers.

Serena doesn't answer, she is mesmerized by the rhythmic pumping of Darcy's hands.

"Serena!" Zayla hisses this time.

Snapping her eyes up, Serena rubs the rest of the blurry tears from her eyes.

"Cordelia will be with Ervin, by now."

Nodding, Serena lays a hand on Darcy's shoulder. "That is enough, let her rest."

Darcy rocks back on her heals. "I still might be able to..." her voice cracks, and she doesn't finish the sentence.

Around the circle of maidens, the guards turn. They bend to one knee and bow their heads, giving their final respects to the fallen maiden. Behind them, Serena can see that pack of wolves have come closer. They begin to change back to their Ungainly forms. Hair falls from their bodies, and they lift themselves to sturdy feet. With the passing of Cordelia there is no longer fear permeating the air, allowing them take control of their wolves and change back.

One of the first to his feet briefly disappears into the forest and returns with a bundle of capes and blankets. The clan covers themselves and two are passed through the circle of guards; one for Colin, who has already shifted, and one for Cordelia.

Darcy covers the maiden's body from the neck down, taking care to smooth out the wrinkles and folds.

"Leave her," Hailey says, her words brusque. "We've got another problem. This little one isn't doing so well." She bends, laying the small bundle down in the sand.

He is only half the size his sister was. A pasty white chest barely rises, and a quiet whistling noise escapes from his mouth.

"It's like his lungs aren't fully developed," whispers Darcy. She runs the pad of her finger across his tiny palm. It doesn't react. "And his reflexes aren't right, either."

"Serena," says Hailey. "With his mother and father both dead, decisions for care of the calfling falls to the Queen."

"What do you mean?" asks Serena.

"She means," says Zayla. "You must decide whether or not to give him the potion."

"You are going to change him into one of us? After all this?" Colin speaks up. "You've seen how we live, abandoned by our parents. Don't abandon this one, too."

Serena shakes her head. "His parents are already gone..."

"I don't think this is what Liam would want," Colin tries again. There are murmurs from the clan outside of the circle. Some agree, but others aren't so sure.

The guards get to their feet, half of them turning to face the pack. They do not break their circle.

Serena finally meets Colin's gaze. "Right now, I will consider what Cordelia would want above all else. And she has already told us of her wishes."

Darcy lays a gentle hand on Colin's arm, "She asked us to care for him."

Colin's forehead crinkles. "Of course, but... can't we just wait a little longer—see if he improves overnight?"

Darcy shakes her head. "Honey, I'm not sure he would survive the night, much less the next hour."

Serena looks at Hailey, still holding the vial. Finally, Serena closes her eyes and nods. She can hear Hailey pop the cork off the top.

"Lift his head a little," she instructs Darcy.

"Wait!" says Serena, eyes flying open to see the vial at the calfling's lips. "I will name him first— while he is still Undine."

Hailey nods, pulling the vial away.

Serena takes a deep breath and looks down at the calfling, laying a hand on his chest. He wriggles slightly. "I name you for your father, Ervin. Your name has been chosen with love and with strength of heritage. May you do your parents and your people proud. We will be watching over you, Ervin." Serena wraps him back up in the blanket, swaddling him tight, and hands him to Darcy. "He will have your last name. A blend of both worlds."

Colin moves to stand by her side, embracing both his wife and the baby.

"Here," Hailey hands the open vial to Darcy. "It should be you."

Darcy glances up at her husband, eyes glistening with tears for the first time tonight. He nods, and Darcy takes the vial from Hailey.

Kai moves into the circle, wrapping his hands around Serena's shoulders. She leans into him for support. Hailey and Zayla, the circle of guards, and Clan Werich behind them all watch as Darcy tips the vial into the calfling's mouth, and the yellow liquid disappears in between his lips.

Excerpt from 'The Taking, Book Three of The Painted Maidens Trilogy'

Now Available

"The sun is taking its sweet time to retire," observes Serena after dipping her hair back under to keep cool from the harsh rays.

"Let it," says Kai. He wraps one arm around Serena, bringing her closer. "More time for us."

"And if someone sees?" asks Serena. She raises the pitch of her voice and over-annunciates, imitating Nerin. "It wouldn't do for the Queen to be caught flirting with a guard member. What would Society think?" Despite the fact their relationship has been publically known for at least a month, Nerin insists Serena and Kai cannot show affection for one another in front of anyone else.

"Come on," says Kai. "I have an idea." He takes Serena by the hand and swims them both into rougher surf.

"Kai, what are you—" Serena is cut off by the next wave that crashes over both of their heads.

Tossed and turned, colliding into each other and pulled apart just as quickly, they flounder like guppies in the water. Serena straightens herself out, finding the surface and popping above just to be pushed below again by the next wave. Kai rolls by in front of her sticking out his tongue while his tail is tangled in kelp.

Serena laughs as she breaks the kelp apart for him. As soon as he is free, he pulls her up. Picking up speed, the pair glide along the surface, angling in to join another wave. This time, they slide in front of it just as the crest folds forward, wrapping them in a secluded tunnel of brackish blue. Kai continues to jut forward, but turns on his back and dips below the surface. He pulls Serena on top of him so her chest rests on his stomach. She rides the wave just as she has seen the Ungainly surfers do, laying down on their boards.

Kai pushes her hands up and out, then releases them. Spreading her arms like wings, Serena's fingertips skim the watery tunnel on each side. Here in ocean's breakers, between The Deep and The Dry, Serena is finally afforded a little privacy from both worlds and her title as queen.

A wide grin spreads across her face as she looks down at Kai in gratitude. She pulls him up just as the tunnel condenses, then collapses in on itself. They endure the chaotic aftermath, tickling each other as they roll into calmer surf.

Catching their breath as their heads bob above water, pure delight dancing across their faces with the last light of the sun, Serena looks at Kai. "I want to pair with you," she says. The words are out of her mouth as the thought enters her head. Her eyes go wide— she can't believe she said that out loud. She looks at Kai, who looks just as stunned.

"Are you sure?" he asks, giving her a chance to retract her statement.

Serena bites her lip, her eyes falling to the frothy water surrounding them. The time between waves lengthens, as if the ocean herself awaits Serena's answer. Finally, she looks up to Kai. "No more waiting, Kai. I'm ready, and I wish to pair with you—if you'll have me."

His eyes light up and he squeezes her face in between his hands, drawing her lips into his. A breath she doesn't know he was holding escapes as his lips relax open. He tastes of salt. Another wave finally breaks, taking them both by surprise. He wraps his tail around hers as their arms snake around each other.

The wave pushes them under in a tumultuous celebration, and they hold on tight as the world spins around them. Hitting the sandy sea floor, they break apart. Serena's hair has escaped her braid and black tendrils reach out, brushing Kai's cheek.

Right here, right now, there are no worries in the world. There is nothing but Kai and all the fun, the security, and the affection he brings. Serena can't pretend the moment will last forever, but she knows if Kai is by her side she can face anything.

Eighteen-year-old Serena reigns as queen of both the Undine of The Deep and the wolves of The Dry. The alliance between her maidens and the werewolves is shaky when all at once the basic necessities of food and shelter are taken away and both their worlds fall apart. After decades of war, the two societies must work together to face what lies ahead. A promised land is theirs for the taking, but first, they must survive each other.

About the Author

Terra is author of the eco-fantasy novels in the Akasha Series, 'Water', 'Air', 'Fire' and 'Earth', as well as the Painted Maidens Trilogy. Born and raised in Colorado, Terra has since lived in California, Texas, Utah, North Carolina, and Virginia. Terra served a 5½ year enlistment in the Marine Corp, has earned her bachelor's and master's degree and presently runs the language services division of a small business.

Terra currently lives in a suburb of Washington, DC with her husband of sixteen years and three children.

Connect with Terra:

E-mail: terra.harmony11@gmail.com
Facebook: http://facebook.com/terraharmony
Blog: http://HarmonyLit.com
Twitter: https://twitter.com/#!/harmonygirlit

Discover other titles by Terra:

The Akasha Series

Elemental powers in the palm of her hand, and it won't be enough to save her. When Kaitlyn Alder is involuntarily introduced to a life of magic, she becomes part of an organization hell-bent on saving the Earth. Follow the saga as one of the most terrifying men the human race has to offer stands between Kaitlyn and Earth's survival.

Read more great novels from
Patchwork Press
www.patchwork-press.com

Featured Title:
The Lost Locket of Lahari

The six novellas of the *Lost Locket of Lahari* anthology pause a moment in time when the locket finds the ripples of its ancestry. From the Victorian-era to the Roaring Twenties, the 1940s to modern day and beyond, this anthology is a collection of stories as dynamic as the authors themselves.

In a dusty, dilapidated stall tucked away in an alcove of a bustling Bazaar in India, a man with a rickety spine and a spindly beard bends over his work bench, forging a locket with accidental magic. There's power in a wish, and there's nothing he wants more than for his children to return home. The locket was intricately crafted, adorned with one dragonfly for each of his children—and the power to find them.

With the guidance of fate, the locket skips through time and journeys across oceans, traveling from person to person in a constant search for the souls whispered into its vessel. Centuries after the magical old man in the Bazaar became near-forgotten myth and whispered legend, the locket has fallen into the hands of those with echoes of the six dragonflies: the seeker, the empath, the dreamer, the confidant, the adventurer, and the dancer.

In the hands of its new owners, the power of the locket adapts, bending and remaking itself to answer need. While the locket never found the children of Lahari, it found the next best thing… Their spirits.